"When Simmons came back he carried a black metal box of a kind that Craig had been told about, a box for which the only antidote was a potassium cyanide pill. He knew then that what he had survived was only a foretaste. Knew, with absolute certainty, that he would tell them everything they needed to know."

John Craig is employed by Department K, whose operators tend to live useful, violent, short lives. MI6 recruits them with this end in view. Department K handles the jobs that were too dangerous—and too dirty—for anyone else.

John Craig is the best. And he is about to discover the limits of the dangerous and the dirty.

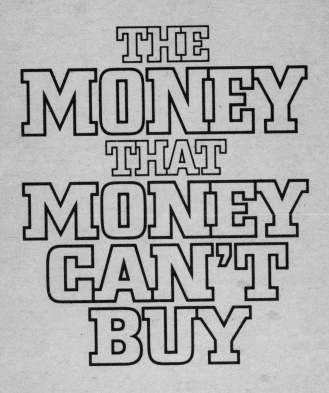

THE MONEY THAT MONEY CAN'T BUY

JAMES MUNRO

CHARTER
NEW YORK

A DIVISION OF CHARTER COMMUNICATIONS INC.
A GROSSET & DUNLAP COMPANY

Published by arrangement with Alfred A. Knopf, Inc.

First Charter Printing March 1981
Published simultaneously in Canada
Manufactured in the United States of America

2 4 6 8 0 9 7 5 3 1

For Mike Legat

1

The three men in the Volkswagen talked mostly about chess, to which they were all devoted. From time to time the conversation veered to ballet and thence to football—one of them had a son who hoped soon to have a trial for his factory team—but mostly they spoke of chess. The landscape did not interest them: lakes, undisciplined woodland, mountains dusted with snow—these were no novelty, and could be ignored; but chess was at once stimulating, familiar, and abstract. It was pleasant to talk of chess when you were on your way to do a job, and pleasant to drive with the windows open after a spell in a deep-sea trawler that had bumped and smashed its way through the North Channel to Whitehaven. The three men were technicians of the highest class: they were used to better transport and accommodation, but grumbling didn't occur to them. Not one wholly trusted the other two, except in the performance of their essential and highly specialized duties.

The driver braked for a "HALT. MAJOR ROAD AHEAD" sign. Like the others, he had never been to England before, but the KGB had taken care of driving on the left for him, as it had taken care of everything else. He knew all about motorways and coffee bars, and which newspaper matched which clothes, and when to order beer and when to stick to Scotch. He and the others had had their hair cut for three months by a barber who had worked in Croydon. The clothes they were wearing had been bought a piece at a time from sports shops in London, Switzerland, Inverness: windcheaters, heavy nailed boots, windproof trousers, knitted hats. Their climbing rope was supple and well-used, their ice ax old and carefully maintained. Their very suntans had been applied with care, layer after layer of sun and wind against pale skin, so that they looked as if the mountains had called them from childhood. Their eyes, it is true, were wary, and blinked little, but climbers also are cautious men.

They turned left at a sign that said "KESWICK— 7 MILES," drove on through the gaunt, pure beauty of the Lake District, and ignored it utterly. At their first glimpse of Derwentwater, their talk was still of knights and bishops, W formations, and *Spectre de la Rose*. Only when they reached the little town they grew silent, until the man beside the driver called out directions from the map he had spent a week in memorizing, and the Volkswagen nosed its way past hotels and sports shops and shops that sold Lakeland jet, woollens and rum butter and postcards and watercolors, into a twisted skein of side streets that the navigator knew as well as the face of his son who might soon play for the factory team, though he had never seen them before. They reached their destination at last, and the driver of a

Volkswagen van which had sprawled across two parking places pulled up and gave them room to park. There was perhaps a certain delicacy in the choice of German transport for such an internationally flavored operation.

The driver and co-driver got out, and the man in the back seat followed them. They stood together, stretched, and lit cigarettes, English cigarettes, king-size tipped. The lighter the driver used was English. He'd been told he could keep it, but they hadn't given him any fuel, and butane was difficult to obtain at home. The driver nodded at a restaurant across the street. The co-driver nodded agreement, but the third man shook his head and moved into the driver's seat. The other two men crossed the street toward the restaurant. It was April in the week before Easter, a cold day, with the threat of snow, and the street was very quiet. The third man pulled the gloves tight over his hands, and felt down the space between the two front seats. The ice ax was there. He pulled the latch of the car door open, laid the ice ax on his lap, and watched the big picture window of the restaurant.

It was a new restaurant, with a décor of plastic designed to look like undressed pinewood. It sold eggs, bacon, hamburgers, sausages, baked beans, and chips in quantities designed to cope with the limitless appetites of walkers and climbers. When the driver and co-driver entered the restaurant and sat at the table nearest the door, it held a party of young men and girls in one corner who had already walked eleven miles that day and were waiting in impatience for their waiter. They could hear him talking in slow, patient English to a woman cook whose Lakeland accent was difficult for him to understand, hear also the sputter of frying fat and the clatter of crockery. They gobbled bread and wondered aloud if they had ordered enough, laughing to hide their embarrassment that they should crave so desperately anything as mundane as food. The two men by the door smoked king-sized tipped cigarettes and waited.

The waiter was Chinese. He was young, tall, long-muscled, and deft at his job. He carried a tray piled with food, and he moved surely and neatly. As he skirted a table, he faced, for perhaps two seconds, the driver and co-driver. The driver spoke one phrase in Cantonese dialect. It had taken him three days to learn to say that phrase exactly right: Cantonese is difficult for any European. The group in the corner didn't hear what he said. Their embarrassment of laughter increased when they saw the object of their desire: rich gold of chips, pale gold of eggs, ham blush-pink, and the bold brown of sausage. But they did notice that the waiter stiffened, and the long, elegant lines of his body hardened with close-packed muscle, that his face showed first astonishment, then despair.

And then the waiter moved. He threw the trayful of food, their beautiful, yearned-for food, at the two men by the door, and next did something even more crazy. He crossed his arms over his face and dived through the window. Glass flew like throwing knives at the group in the corner. One of the girls screamed, and the co-driver shouted "What's going on?" then rushed for the door with the driver. They ran out into the street, the Volkswagen van backed up and they jumped inside. Half a minute went by before one of the hungry ones went out. There was no living thing there: only a youngish Chinese waiter in white mess jacket and black trousers, an ice ax in the back of his head. The hungry one discovered that empty as his stomach was he could still be sick.

* * *

Craig disliked going to Queen Anne's Gate. It meant conferences and paperwork, most of it futile, and rows with a fat, angry man who could never find enough men for the things he had to do. He walked up to the front door and looked at the row of brass plates: Dr. H. B. Cunnington-Low, Lady Brett, Major Fuller, The Right Reverend Hugh Bean. The sort of people you expected to find in Queen Anne's Gate—except that they didn't exist. He pressed the bell marked "Caretaker," and the door opened at once. The man who opened it was short, muscular, and fast-moving, an excommando sergeant who was there because he had killed neatly, precisely and without emotion. Beneath the overalls he carried a Smith and Wesson revolver and a commando knife. From time to time, Craig practiced unarmed combat with him. The caretaker dreaded these sessions.

"Morning, guv," said the caretaker. "His nibs is in."

"How is he?" asked Craig.

"Funny," said the caretaker. "Half the time he's mad, other half he's—well, he acts like something's happened and he can't believe it. Then he gets mad again."

Craig took a tentative step backward. "There's a

chap I promised to see," he said.

"I'm to log you in," said the caretaker, "and you've to stand by."

Craig sighed and went up the stairs to his office. The caretaker scowled. He hated to bring bad news to Craig. Their practice sessions on the dojo mat were bad enough without that.

Craig's office was the flat marked "Lady Brett." It, and his secretary, a grim widow called Mrs. McNab, had once belonged to Philip Grierson. Grierson had been an easy, elegant, amusing man, and Mrs. McNab had loved him, wordlessly and utterly. Grierson and she both had been adjusted to the fact that he might die at any time. Operators of Department K tended to live useful, violent, short lives, and M.I.6 recruited them with this end in view. Department K was the most ruthless branch of the service, the branch that handled the jobs that were too dangerous—or too dirty—for anyone else. The people who worked for it presented no problems for the gerontologist. And Grierson, like the others, had been aware that death was always near, and had been prepared for it. What he hadn't been prepared for was that his nerve would crack, and he would go crazy—utterly, completely, incurably. That too much violence and dirt and secrecy would break loose at last, wrap him in a cocoon of apathy, and that every attempt to break it would be met by tears, that Grierson in fact, without ever being sane enough to know it, might live on to old age, and be a problem for the gerontologist after all. Grierson had been working with Craig when his nerve and reason had left him, and Mrs. McNab knew this. She hated

Craig, and treated him exactly as she had treated Grierson.

She watched Craig slump at his desk and frown at the neatly stacked mound of files that waited for him. She watched the sure strength of his hands, the violence that lurked beneath the elegant suit. *He's left Saville Row,* she thought. *That looks like Sloane Street. Well, well. Let's hope he's not going mod on us.* She looked at the face then: a strong face, with a good nose, the mouth fuller than you would expect, and pale-gray eyes, eyes that told you nothing, eyes the color of cold seas. She could never love this man: he was too strong for her, but she could hate him, for Grierson's sake.

"Mr. Loomis asked me to tell you to stand by, sir," she said. "Would you like coffee?"

"No thank you," said Craig. There would be enough coffee when Loomis received him. He looked at the files. Today it was Morocco. Drugs, homosexuals, banks, smuggling, prostitution, bars. Something for everybody.

Loomis sent for him at ten thirty. He went into the great man's room with its superb stucco ceiling and sash windows, sat or became immersed in a huge overstuffed armchair covered in flowered chintz, and looked at the man who faced him across a Chippendale desk. Loomis was vast: a gross monster of a man with a face the color of an angry sunset, pale manic eyes, red hair dusted with white like snow on a wheat field, and an arrogant nose. In rage he was both spectacular and cunning. He reminded Craig of a charging rhinoceros with a high I.Q.

Loomis said: "Pour coffee," and Craig fought

his way out of the chair to obey. The coffee was as
hot, as dark, as bitter as Loomis himself. He put a
cup down on Loomis's desk, then waited as the fat
man, grunting with effort, produced a crumpled
packet of cigarettes from his pocket and gave one
to Craig as if it were rubies.

"Got them from the minister," said Loomis,
"duty-free."

"Thanks," said Craig. The cigarette was cracked
in the middle.

"Smoke it then," Loomis said. "Ruin your wind.
I don't care." Craig broke the cigarette in two, and
lit the larger end.

"Damn silly thing's happened," said Loomis.
"Up in the Lake District. Somebody's murdered a
Chinaman." Craig choked on the cigarette.

"You don't by any chance think it's funny?"
Loomis asked.

"No, no. A little unusual," said Craig.

"Very," said Loomis. "The only Chinaman for
miles and somebody goes and murders him. Belts
him over the head with an ice ax. One blow. It was
still stuck in him when they found him."

"Any leads?" asked Craig.

"Oh yes. Three fellers drove up in one of those
beetles—a Volkswagen. Two got out, went into the
café where the Chinaman worked, and spoke to him.
The Chinky threw a trayful of food at them and
jumped through the window. The third feller belted
him with the ice ax. At least that's what the Cum-
berland police think. The witnesses aren't all that
reliable."

"They go off in the Volkswagen?"

"No," said Loomis. "A Volkswagen van picked

them up. The police have it now—and the car."

"Fingerprints?"

Loomis shook his head. "They were both absolutely clean," he said.

"One blow could be luck or it could be skill," said Craig. "No fingerprints at all—that means experts." He paused. "You did say an ice ax?"

Loomis grunted.

"Don't they use them for glaciers?" Craig asked.

"They do."

"I used to live seventy miles from the Lakes," said Craig. "I didn't think they had glaciers."

"They don't," said Loomis. "But the three blokes were dressed as climbers. They had all sorts of kit. The ice ax was a mistake really. Except they kept it hidden in the car." He paused for a moment, and Craig saw that he was struggling for words. This surprised Craig. The fat man was usually much too fluent.

Loomis said at last: "If you laugh at what I'm going to say I'll—" He hesitated, then said: "No. It has to be said anyway. A Russian trawler put into Whitehaven the day of the kill. Minor engine trouble. They let a few men ashore. Whitehaven's twenty miles from Keswick. The trawler sailed seventy minutes after the murder."

"Russians?" said Craig, a question in his voice. "Murdering a Chinaman? In Keswick?"

"These men were pros," said Loomis. "Quick, neat job. One blow, no fingerprints, no murderers even. We can't touch them."

"But they were seen," said Craig. "They killed in front of witnesses. The Russian Executive never does that."

"Maybe they wanted us to know," said Loomis.

"Did any of the witnesses suggest they were Russians?"

"Very British, they said they looked. But they would for a job like this."

"And the Chinese?"

"His name's Soong, James Soong. Thirty. Hong Kong passport. I've got their police working on it."

"He came here straight from Hong Kong?"

"If the passport's telling the truth," said Loomis. "He'd worked in Keswick for six months. Big, tough lad, their police say. But kept himself to himself. No friends. No enemies either. Except a bloke with an ice ax."

"But if the Russians really did do this—"

"I know, cock. Right in our own back yard. I don't think I could stand it," said Loomis. His vast body heaved in uncertainty, and the chair beneath him groaned.

"I'm sending you up there," he said. "Take Linton—then it can all be police business if things get normal."

"Normal?"

"As in 'News of the World,'" said Loomis wearily. "Even Chinamen must do some things that make people want to kill them. Let's hope it's that."

"And if it isn't?"

"I'll have those bloody Russians—" Loomis said, and his voice was a battle cry. "I'll have them on toast for breakfast."

2

The Mark X took them North in a smooth surge of power, and Detective Chief Inspector Linton was content to listen as Craig talked and drove. *It was nice doing a job with Craig,* he thought. *Always a good car, and food and drink in proportion. For the survivors.*

Craig said: "Loomis thinks there may be something in it."

"He's got no evidence," said Linton. "No real evidence."

"He's got a hunch," said Craig. "I think it's a good one. If we find he's right he'll hit the roof."

Linton sighed. "There's one thing," he said. "Soong's passport was forged. We had it checked at the forensic lab."

"Does Loomis know?"

"Yes," said Linton. "I telephoned him myself. He was delighted."

They drove on to Keswick, and stayed at the George, an old, staid, leathery, overstuffed hotel like a fat colonel, where the food was excellent and very English, and the central heating nonexistent. Linton approved of it, and Craig noted only that from time to time he slept, or was fed. The job had begun to fascinate him.

Their suite had a small sitting room, and it was here that they talked to the walking party, seeing them one at a time, taking them patiently through the story, over and over again, stolidly enduring the timid complaints of the educated and respectable young when confronted by policemen investigating murder. They learned two things. The first came from Dr. Arthur Hornsey, aged twenty-seven, the elder statesman of the party, now engaged in research in the department of psychology at the University of Lancaster. Hornsey had observed the two men in the restaurant well. Craig showed him a series of photographs—a weird assortment of Russians and Russian-looking types, including dancers, strong men, Orthodox priests, and a genuine prince now working in advertising, and he identified the two men in the restaurant at once. Neither picture was good, and in neither case did the men wear climbing clothes, but Hornsey was sure although Linton pressed him hard.

"I'm absolutely positive," he said. "I've always had a fantastic memory for faces."

"Are they foreign?" Hornsey asked.

"No," said Craig.

Hornsey looked at him. The word was a flat, almost brutal denial of further discussion. To Hornsey, who had been trained for research, such a denial was unacceptable.

"I mean they do look foreign," he said.

Craig said nothing, and Hornsey felt himself blushing. He was a big, muscular young man who had gone out of a restaurant to face a mad Chinese who jumped through windows. His strength and courage were things he had always taken for granted. Yet he blushed at Craig's silence, and the force of will behind it.

"We may need you later as a witness, sir," Linton said.

"Oh yes. Identification Parade. That sort of thing, eh?" Hornsey asked.

"Something like that," said Linton, and Hornsey left. It was only when he got outside that he realized that he knew Linton's rank, and had observed his questioning techniques. (*Linton was well above average*, he thought. *At least beta plus.*) He also realized that all he knew about Craig was his name and beyond that only a sensation, nothing more, of brooding, terrible power. Hornsey had a good mind, and it had been trained well. *It would be best*, he thought, *to keep out of Craig's way.*

The second piece of information came from a girl. Her name was Jane Simmons, aged twenty, Linton noted, educated at Priory Close School for Girls and L'École des Jeunes Filles, Lausanne, Switzerland, a capital investment of at least five thousand pounds. At present she wore a shaggy sweater that surrounded her like a parcel, heavy wool trousers, socks, and nailed boots. No employment. She had tried to paint, but now Daddy gave her an allowance. Daddy was in newspapers and television. Linton trod with infinite caution.

She failed with the photographs—*perhaps as well*, thought Linton, *that she has given up painting* —and her only clear visual memory was of the shape the glass made when the Chinese had jumped through it. Linton prepared to let her go.

Craig asked: "Did either of the two men speak to the waiter?"

She looked at him. Currently she was in love with Frank Sinatra, a golden retriever called Jackson, and Rudolf Nureyev. She added Craig to the list. The little finger of his left hand was stiff, she noticed, as if it had been broken, then set badly. But both his hands were beautiful.

"You'll think this is awfully sill—" she said.

"Try me," said Craig, and her heart turned over. If only she'd thought to have her hair done. But who would have thought that necessary, just to meet two policemen?

"I thought one of them did speak to the waiter," she said at last. "Only it wasn't really speaking. More singing, really. I mean, I didn't hear much, and we were all making such a row—I mean we were absolutely starving. We'd walked miles—but I do remember thinking how silly it was. The singing, I mean. When we were all so hungry. And then —then he died."

Linton thought it was silly too, and wanted to leave it at that, but Craig kept on about it, oblivious to the girl's mistrust of herself, and to her father, who was in newspapers and television, and hence to be doubly avoided by chief inspectors of the Special Branch. Craig sang to her. He sang pop tunes and Rodgers and Hart, gems from Verdi and Russian folk songs, Beethoven and Bach and Bacharach, and to all of them, Jane Simmons said no, and Linton worried. At last he let her go, and Linton asked if he was crazy, but already Craig had the telephone and talked to a fascinated Loomis, who found him an old man in retirement at Grasmere, and they drove there in a powder of snow, and the old man sang into a tape recorder and told them it was nonsense, but nevertheless gave them some astonishing cherry brandy.

That evening Craig sent for Miss Simmons again. This time she had had time to prepare, and wore a neat little number in silk jersey that still looked good even after four days in a rucksack, the pearls Daddy had given her for Christmas—Daddy was old-fashioned; he thought pearls were safe, whereas if one were dark and suntanned, they were in fact very sexy, in a Tahitian sort of way—and a dollop of Je Reviens. Jane knew she looked good, but the pale eyes told her nothing, and she was so disappointed that she even forgot to scowl when she found that Linton was joining them.

Craig bought her one martini at the bar, then they took her in to a dinner of game soup, salmon, roast duckling, and strawberries. With the dinner he allowed her one glass of hock and one of claret. No liqueur, though she absolutely adored Grand Marnier. He might have been her father, Jane thought, then realized that it could in fact be possible. She knew no way of finding out his age. But his sexiness—the passion of his mouth, the cold brutality of his eyes—of that there could be no doubt. She breathed in, and the silk jersey clung becomingly to her, and Craig continued to talk of islands in Greece, and the high cost of villas there, now that everyone knew about them. By the end of the meal she was a little angry, but clear-headed and very much alert, which was exactly what Craig had intended.

After dinner they went back to the private sitting room, and Craig made more coffee, which was heaps better than the stuff they'd had in the dining room. Then he produced the tape recorder and Jane wondered what on earth had got into him. How could he possibly start playing that sort of music with all the lights still on and that grisly Linton sitting there like a duenna or something? Craig ran the tape back to the beginning and switched it on to playback. An old man's voice came through, high and clear. It wasn't singing exactly, but it wasn't talking either; just the same phrase repeated over and over, as if the old man were a priest chanting in some service or something.

After she'd heard the old man's voice twice, Jane said: "I think so," then, after the tenth time, she said: "Yes, that's it all right."

Craig switched off the tape.

"But what does he mean?" said Jane. "What's he chanting about?"

"I'm afraid I can't tell you just yet," said Craig.

"I suppose it's *sub judice,* or whatever you call it."

"Something like that," said Craig.

Not even the daughter of a man in newspapers and television could be told what the tape had said. The voice was that of a retired inspector in the Hong Kong police. The message was neither singing nor chanting, but spoken Cantonese. And what the inspector had repeated, over and over, was: "Comrade Soong, we have come here to kill you."

"I hope I've been able to help you," said Jane.

"Oh yes," said Craig. "Enormously."

Three Russians, he was thinking. *Sent here to kill*

*an agent. The Chinese must be an agent. Loomis will
run amok.*

"I don't know what we'd have done without
you," said Craig. "Have some more coffee."

"Actually I think I'd better get back to the youth
hostel," said Jane. And she added carefully: "Is it
still snowing?"

"I'll give you a lift," said Craig.

In the Mark X she gave him every opportunity
she knew, but he just wouldn't see her. Later, at
home in Surrey, she examined herself in the mirror
one day: thick darkness of hair, eyes, wide and
trusting and brown as a sweet sherry (far too
spanielly of course, but at least you could see the
love in them), and her body firmed by youth, and
with the first hint of ripeness. And all of it offered
on a plate. As if she'd been a roast beef sandwich
or something. Only he wasn't hungry. All she got
was "Thank you very much, Miss Simmons," and
when she asked if he'd need to see her again, "Oh
yes. It's very possible."

And then the tail lights of the Jag, glowing in the
dark. It really wasn't enough.

* * *

Loomis was delighted. His delight lasted for at
least ten minutes, and then he gave way to an ecstasy of rage. The Russians on his patch, knocking off
a Chinky without even saying "God bless you,"
and a Chinky, moreover, about whom he, Loomis,
knew nothing. A Chinky who could have served
baked beans and chips forever, for all Loomis
knew or cared. Except that now he cared passionately. And they had nothing to go on. Nothing at
all. Everything James Soong possessed had been

searched, dismembered, searched again, analyzed, fingerprinted, spectrographed. And it told them nothing. James Soong had lived only in the present. His past, like his future, did not exist.

"You can't stop the Russians from trying to kill people," said Loomis. "I know. I've been through it all before. But this is the first time they've done it and I haven't known why. We've got nothing on this Soong character at all. Neither have any of the other departments. I had to go and *ask*." He shuddered at the memory. "It won't do." He hesitated. "I wonder if he ever went to Morocco?"

Craig remembered the files on his desk the day Soong was reported killed. They had all been about Morocco.

"Anyway, I got somebody working on that," said Loomis. "I got another idea as well. I think it's about time we started chucking our weight about. And I know just where we can chuck it. How would you like to kidnap a Russki for me, son? Be a bit of an interest for you. You knock off a Russki, and they'll have to come and ask for him back. And then," Loomis lay back like a basking whale, "and then we can talk."

* * *

The Comet 4B landed on time at Barajas airport. Everything about it had been predictable: its punctuality, its comfort, the size of its drinks, the dullness of its food, the uncertain glory of its hostesses. Craig walked down the steps and hurried to the waiting bus—the wind from the Sierras was cold. The other passengers, like himself, huddled into their coats, as the bus jolted toward the administration building. There were only twenty of them.

It wasn't enough. Craig preferred the anonymity of a crowd, but this time there wasn't a chance. Loomis was in a hurry, and this was the fullest flight he could get.

That day the two Spanish officials had time to spare. They looked at his passport photograph three times and criticized the photographer, read slowly and earnestly through the details of his *fiche,* and at last let him in to Customs, where a thin, elegant Madrileño ignored him completely as he scrawled on his two suitcases. One man had ignored him; two had looked at him, and his photograph, with care. Craig didn't like the odds. He took a taxi into Madrid, and stopped off at a car-hire place near the Puerto del Sol. They had a Fiat 1800 waiting for him, and once again he waited while Spaniards struggled with his passport—his name this time was Jameson, which they assumed began with a noise like a percussive "H"—then he signed the documents and drove out into the city and to the main highway to the south.

The car seemed good for 120 kilometers an hour, which for a hired car is excellent, and Craig enjoyed the almost empty road, the harshness of the high Sierras as he drove through New Castile. This was a country made for war, hard and pure and arid, its mountains gaunt and white-tipped still, their winter snow matte as a bandage on a wound, so that by comparison the Lake District seemed gentle as the mountains of a dream. He drove on to Toledo and stopped there and got out, as a tourist should, to buy paper knives of Toledo steel, and ate lunch, which was hot, aggressive, and yet eager to please, a very Spanish lunch. Then on again,

through Ciudad Real to Valdepeñas, and there he
spent the night. Valdepeñas was quiet, restful, and
almost devoid of tourist attractions. On the other
hand, a vine grew there which produced an excellent wine. Craig drank it and in limping Spanish
congratulated his waiter, who, being a Spaniard,
took the matter as a personal compliment, and suggested another bottle, then apologized that the
town should have nothing else to offer the for-
eigner. But the gentleman was going on to Granada? Ah, then tomorrow he really would see something worth seeing. The waiter was a Castilian, and
despised Andalusia totally and comprehensively,
but the customer had been nice about the wine. He
thanked the Englishman again, and told him to the
centimo how much his tip should be.

Craig woke next morning early, drove on to
Granada, and hired a guide who gave him enthusiastic and quite often accurate information
about the Generalife, the churches, the old town,
Moorish architecture in general, and the Moorish
contribution to the culture of Spain, then took him
to a souvenir shop, and beamed with a
schoolmaster's pride in a boy who had learned his
lessons while Craig bought purses and marquetry
boxes and mantillas and combs, and the shop-
keeper and the guide said: *"Típico, típico,"* and
when he had bought enough let him go. He
lunched late and well, then set off again in the
warmer air, driving on south, where orange and
lemon groves were coming into blossom, through
village after village where already the preparations
for Easter were approaching the frantic, and petrol
was scarce and not very good, and the mountains

of the Sierra Nevada enfolded it all, an eternity of rock and snow. He bypassed Malaga, and turned west along the coast road, past the little seaside resorts where the foreigners—English, Germans, French, Americans, Swedes—were already arriving with their donations of pesetas to stabilize the Spanish economy, and asking in return only the sun, the opportunity to wear dark glasses, to dress in bright, weirdly cut clothes that they would never, never wear at home. He passed Torremolinos and Fuengirola, and arrived at last at Marbella. There was a bar he had to find, off the Calle Mayor, and he found it at last in a street of whitewashed houses, a bar bright with neon and a jukebox stuffed with the top twenty, and wrought-iron tables with marble tops, and portraits of the Queen and Union Jacks, and Watney's Red Barrel on the counter. Outside, in daylight, one could see an inn sign, with a picture. The bar was called "The Dog and Duck." It was full of Englishmen drinking beer, and Englishwomen drinking gin. Craig went inside, ignored two Spanish barmen, and waited for the attention of a squat, slow-moving, chunky man with pale, thin, nondescript hair and skin still pink from the sun, pale skin that would never darken to more than a fiery, ill-tempered red. When the man turned, Craig recited his formula.

"Forgive me, but you must be George Allen," he said.

The chunky man continued to wash glasses beneath the bar for a second, then said carefully: "I'm George Allen. Yes. Who might you be?"

Craig said: "Norman Jameson—Linda's brother."

Allen said, counting out each word: "Well, well, well." Then added: "How is Linda?"

"Fine," said Craig. "She sends you her love."

"What would you like?" asked Allen.

"Scotch," said Craig. "Teacher's for preference. No ice. Water on the side."

Allen nodded then and brought him his drink. Craig was accepted. Even so, he felt like a fool. Passwords to Craig could never ever sound like conversation, much less replace it. He knew that the men and women around him had heard and forgotten what he had said, but he remembered. He talked for a while about Linda, her husband Frank, and their children—Arthur had failed "O" level French again; Elaine still had a brace on her teeth—went out to dine on *gazpacho, arroz a la Valenciana,* and fruit, then returned to the bar. Allen was waiting for him, and came at once from behind the counter and took him into the living room behind it. The living room was furnished throughout by Liberty's, and on the walls were pictures of George Allen: Allen at school, Allen in the first fifteen, Allen as house prefect. Then more pictures: Allen in the RAF regiment in Aden, Singapore, Hong Kong; Allen as a tea planter, a PRO man, a car salesman; and finally Allen as publican, shaking hands with pop singers, bullfighters, film stars. Craig liked the setup less and less. Allen poured Spanish brandy and Craig asked for ginger ale. When it came, Allen said: "I heard you were on your way. What do you want?"

There was a tycoon's preoccupation in his voice: so much to be done, so little time to do it in. Craig watched as Allen's neat brandy disappeared, and another, larger shot replaced it. He said nothing.

"Look sport," said Allen. "I'm a busy man. I'm running a bar. The bar makes money. I don't live in Wogland because I like it—and this is my high season. Now what do you want? If I can help you I will."

"Your bar makes you thirty pounds a week from April to September," said Craig. "Your boat makes you another twenty—smuggling. That's fifteen hundred a year. We've paid you a couple of thousand for the last three years. You're not doing me any favors, Allen. You're paying off six thousand quid."

Allen picked up his glass and poured down the brandy. His face at once turned a fierce, banked-down red, and he opened his mouth to yell.

"If you start anything," said Craig, "I'll knock you unconscious. And you won't work for us again. Ever."

Allen sat at the table, his hands groping for the brandy bottle. Craig eased it away from the searching fingers, stood up, walked round the table, and hauled Allen to his feet. Allen's body resisted the thrust of the hand in his shirt collar, but he came up anyway.

"I want politeness," said Craig. "And cooperation. And I want them now. We've heard about you, Allen. You're lazy. You want the money. You don't want the work. We don't see it like that. We want you to start earning, old son."

Allen said: "All right. All right. This shirt cost me a hundred and sixty pesetas."

Craig let him go; and Allen smoothed out his shirt collar.

"Just tell me what you want," he said. "If I can help you I will."

Craig's right hand reached for Allen's neck, the V formed by the splayed forefinger and thumb across the throat, the thumb depressing the carotid artery, the forefinger hard on the nerve behind the ear. Pain exploded in Allen's face, but he learned at once how foolish he would be to yell as the pressure of thumb and forefinger increased. Craig spoke to him, his voice unhurried and utterly certain. "You belong to us, Allen. We own you. When we say jump, by Christ you jump. We know all about your smuggling, remember. You try it on and we give you to the Spaniards. On a plate, old boy." The pressure of thumb and forefinger increased, and the pain boiled in Allen's neck, then was suddenly, mercifully gone.

"I'm sorry," Allen began.

"Don't be," said Craig. "You hate me. But I can destroy you. Just accept that."

Reluctantly, hating himself, Allen agreed.

"We're going to pick up a man called Jean-Luc Calvet," said Craig. "You know him."

"Of course I do," said Allen. "He's a French painter. One of these beatnik types. Lives down the road in Estepona."

"You never told us about him," said Craig.

"Nothing to tell," Allen said. "He's just a painter. Sells little sketches of landscapes and fishing boats and that. Does very well too."

"He's a Russian," said Craig. "He also sells little

sketches of Gibraltar, and he's a paymaster for Spanish Communists."

"You're joking," said Allen, and added quickly: "I mean he's a very good painter."

"He's a very good spy, too," said Craig.

3

That night Calvet was giving a party. His little house was crammed with expatriate Swedes, Germans, and Englishmen, including a couple of officers from Gibraltar who were laying down Calvet oils as their ancestors had laid down port. The gin and whisky, smuggled from Gib, were excellent, and the kef, brought from Morocco that day, mixed deftly enough to ensure that it brought nothing but peace, and perhaps a little too much laughter. There were never any fights at Calvet's parties. Craig drove down there at two in the morning, and the party was loud indeed. He left the car in the square, and walked down to the quayside. A group of fishermen were unloading boxes of fish from a caïque-like craft with an enormous and antiquated diesel engine; others were watching from a café, part house, part awning, and with them were a beat-poet, an anti-novelist, a *musique concrète* composer, and their disciples, who drank local brandy and deplored Calvet's party, to which they had not been invited. Craig drank coffee, and listened to their chatter. The party should be through by four.

He finished his coffee, walked out of the village to a headland, sat down and waited. His patience was absolute. He could wait for days, and be as swift and deadly at the end as if he had just arrived at the fight. At last, very faintly, he heard the throb of engines, and saw the riding lights of Allen's cruiser. The engines stopped, and there was the squeak of wood on metal as Allen moved his dinghy to the shore, beached it and scrambled up. His breath reeked of cognac.

"All set," said Allen. "Ready when you are, squire." He lurched into Craig as he moved, and Craig reacted at once to the dense weight of metal on his body. His hand moved, quickly and precisely, and came out with the gun that Allen carried. A Beretta. An Italian automatic, eight-shot, with a light and nervous trigger. The safety catch was off. Craig took the magazine from the butt, put it in his pocket, and gave the gun back to Allen.

"If I want a gun I'll bring a gun," he said.

"Just making sure," Allen said. "He could be tough."

"He is," said Craig. "But we don't want him dead."

He led Allen back to the car, and they drove out of town, then waited in the dark till four, while Allen fidgeted and whined for cognac, and Craig just sat, not smoking, not speaking, waiting until it was time to move. They went back into Estepona and parked near Calvet's house just after four. By twenty past, seven people had left, by half past the record player had ceased.

Craig drove up to the house, got out, and looked at the windows. They were small and steel-framed.

The door was three heavy slabs of olive wood, with a hand-forged lock that he could open with a hairpin, but he had heard the thick slam of metal bolts as the last guests left. He pounded on the door with his fist. The noise boomed and echoed in the empty street. At last he heard footsteps, and his muscles tensed for action.

A girl's voice asked: "Who is there?" and Craig continued to pound on the door. "What is it?" the girl asked again, and Craig shouted in half-incoherent Spanish about guests at the party, an accident on the Marbella road, and a man dying, perhaps dead, and my God why did they have to drive when they had drunk so much?

There was a gasp, the bolts shot back, and Craig lunged at the door as it opened. The girl's weight gave under his, he reached out and his hands were merciful and swift. She collapsed with little more than a sigh. He picked her up and climbed the stairs, up to where one light glistened softly, and, to the left of it, an opened door. His footsteps were firm and loud as he moved, and at the third stair from the top he called out: "I say, is anyone there?" There was no answer, he reached the top, and turned. The room at the top of the stairs was a bedroom. In it was a young man in denim pants, a faded blue work shirt and combat boots. The young man was lean and rangy, clean-shaven, his hands and clothes grimy with paint. In one of them was a Star Model A automatic that pointed where Craig's shirt should have been visible, had he not been carrying the girl. The fact of the girl disconcerted the young man. He had been about to make love to her. Craig walked into the room.

"Oh I say," he said. "Look here."

The young man took two cautious steps backwards, beyond the reach of Craig's hands.

"This young woman's ill," said Craig. "For God's sake, come and help me man. You don't need that thing."

"Put her on the floor," said Calvet.

"On the floor?"

The automatic tilted, aimed at a point between Craig's eyes. Slowly, carefully, Craig put the girl down on the floor, bending his head as he did so. She was a slight girl, too thin for his taste but easy enough to carry. Her hair was fine and golden, and her eyes would be blue, or gray, he thought, and waited for Calvet's move.

The young man was fast. He covered the distance to Craig in two silent strides, and the gun-barrel swung. Craig rolled to one side, the gun's sight clipped the skin of his forehead and Craig, balanced on one arm, reached out the other to grab Calvet's wrist, using the force of the descending blow to pull him further downward, twisting the fingers of the wrist open as he pulled until the automatic spilled from them. Calvet countered with a blow at his neck, a chop that would have killed him, but he lay back as it came, and took it, gasping, on the close-packed muscles of his shoulder, the lancing pain loosening his wrist hold. Calvet wriggled free, and aimed a kick at Craig's head, but Craig was already spinning away toward the automatic and the kick went wide. Immediately Calvet hurled himself at Craig, the one chance he had to stop him reaching the gun, and Craig moved with the kind of reflex action that comes only from day

after day at the dojo mat, days that grow into
months and years. The toe of his shoe landed in the
young man's belly as his hands grasped the sail-
cloth on his shoulders. His leg straightened, his
hands heaved, and Calvet hit the wall, smashed
from it and was still straightening, looking for his
enemy, when the edge of Craig's hand struck at a
point just below his nose. He fell then, a slack heap
of flesh in paint-stained clothes. Craig got up,
winced when he put weight on the shoulder Calvet
had hit, and walked over to him, felt his wrist. It
was steady enough. He hadn't hit too hard. He
tried the girl's wrist then; it was fast and fluttering.
Espionage was hardest on innocent bystanders.

He listened for Allen then; but there was no
sound. Craig swore, softly but adequately, took
some wire from his pocket, and tied up Calvet. His
movements were neat and precise, the knots as sure
as only a fisherman's knots can be. He looked at
the girl again, then picked her up and tied her to
the railings of the bed. She'd wanted to be there
anyway. Then he began to search Calvet's house.
Time was vital, and his movements were swift
enough, but he was thorough. Room by room,
drawer by drawer, case by case, he searched
Calvet's belongings.

First he found money—a drawerful of neat piles
of twenty-dollar bills. He put them aside and went
on searching: under floorboards, behind cupboards, behind walls that sounded hollow but were
only plaster. The radio transmitter he discovered
inside the record player. It was a little beauty, neat,
light, and portable. He disconnected it and took it
back toward the bedroom, then froze. There were

footsteps on the stairs. Craig faced the necessity of
having to hurt a third human being that evening.
The idea neither attracted nor repelled. It was simply a necessity. If he had to do it, he would do it
well. The footsteps moved to the bedroom. Craig
followed, soundless. Allen stood in the doorway,
his eyes moving from the pile of money on the table
to the girl on the bed.

"So many good things," said Craig. "You don't
know where to start, do you?"

Allen whirled. His movements were clumsy,
fuzzy with alcohol. He stared into the flat gray of
Craig's eyes that looked at him without pity, hate,
or even dislike.

"Where were you?" asked Craig.

"I was scared," said Allen. "I'm all right now."

His gaze went back to the money.

"You've found a fortune," he said.

"Yes," said Craig.

"I mean—we could live the rest of our lives on
that," said Allen.

"Yes," said Craig, "we could. There's an R/T
set next door. Take it down to the car. Then wait
for me."

Allen didn't move. He was looking at the girl
now. She was still unconscious, but she'd moved a
little, and the movement had pulled back her skirt
over her knees. Allen went over to her, pulled it
back further, to reveal the black line of her garter
against the pale thigh, the neat V of her panties.

"She's all right," he said. "Bit skinny maybe."

His hand moved again, then Craig grabbed his
wrist, turned him round.

"I was only looking," said Allen.

"Jesus you're nasty," said Craig. "Take the R/T set to the car. Then wait for me."

"All right," said Allen. "What about the money?"

"I'll take that," said Craig. "And Calvet. Move."

Allen moved, and Craig stuffed the money, the gun, and the steel box into a duffle bag, and slung it over one shoulder. He went to the girl then, untied one wrist, hesitated, then pulled her skirt down over her knees. Calvet next, still unconscious. He eased the limp body over his other shoulder, and started for the stairs. As he went, he noted with satisfaction that his hands were quite steady, he wasn't sweating, and his footsteps were still soundless.

He opened the house door one inch and listened. From down the street came the sound of voices. Allen was talking bad Spanish to a *guardia civil.* The *guardia,* talking much better Spanish, was advising Allen to go home. Allen promised to do so, as soon as he could get the car to start, and the *guardia* left him. Craig counted ten, then moved out into the street. Allen had cleared the back seat of the car and Calvet rested on it, at peace. He looked drunk. Craig covered him with Allen's coat, took Allen's bottle and poured brandy over his face and shirt. The car reeked. He walked over to the co-driver's seat then. The R/T set was on it.

Allen said: "Don't worry. I told the *guardia* it was a new car radio I was fitting."

"I hope he's as big a fool as you are," said Craig. "Move over."

Reluctantly Allen obeyed, taking the R/T set on

his lap, then Craig slung the duffle bag into the back beside Calvet.

"That the money?" Allen asked.

Craig switched the ignition on and drove toward the seashore. At the first corner, he flashed his headlights. A *guardia civil* stood in a doorway, watching the car. He didn't look stupid. Craig drove on sedately; he wanted no trouble.

They reached the sea road, and parked the car. Once again Allen picked up the R/T set, and this time he held Craig's case as well, and scrambled down toward the beach. Craig followed, the duffle bag over his shoulder, the still body of Calvet in his arms. The cliff was soft soil and they moved quietly, then suddenly Allen struck a patch of shale, and stumbled. Craig swore under his breath, but they reached sand at last, and Allen's boat, and loaded it up and launched it into the dark, whispering sea. Craig scrambled into the bows and took the oars; Allen in the stern held the tiller. The oars squeaked softly as the boat moved out into the Mediterranean, toward the dark mass of Allen's motorboat, its riding lights clear and brilliant as jewels.

They reached it, tied up, and transferred Calvet, the money, and the R/T set, then Allen's hand moved to the starter switch.

"Wait," said Craig. "Switch off your riding lights."

Allen obeyed, as Craig looked out toward the land, to the thin probe of two headlights, undipped, pushing in to where the Morris was parked. He heard the sound of car doors slammed, and men in uniform moved through the headlight beams, toward the little car. They had guns in their hands.

"We'd better get out of here," said Allen.

"Not yet," Craig whispered. "They can't see us. We'll wait till they go."

"But—"

"Keep your voice down," whispered Craig again. "Sound travels at sea."

And at that moment Calvet returned to consciousness and yelled.

Calvet was a Ukrainian. He spoke Ukrainian, Russian, and French—all three as if they were his mother tongue—and his German, English, and Spanish were near perfect, but all he produced then as he struggled from the blackness of Craig's blow into the blackness of the boat's cockpit was a high-pitched yet very masculine scream: a scream compounded of fear and horror of terrible things that had happened to him, to Calvet, and which he could neither control, understand, nor, at that moment—and here was the real terror—even remember. So Calvet screamed, and the scream died almost at once, crushed out beneath Craig's fingers, but it warned the men on the cliff, and a spotlight on their car snapped on almost at once, its long accusing finger probing out to sea, searching for the sleek twin-screwed cruiser that lay too far out for the light to touch.

Again Allen wanted to go, and again Craig made him wait, until at last the car revved up and went, and then the cruiser's motors too could fire, the twin propellers chop the water into foam. Craig took the small, neat wheel in his hands and set course for Gibraltar. As he let in the throttle, he could feel the twin engine's thrust. *Allen must have been sober when he bought this one,* he thought. *She's just about perfect.* He let in more throttle and the speedometer moved to fifteen knots.

"Let's put on the searchlight—see where we're going," Allen said.

"No," said Craig.

"But she'll do five knots better than this if we see where we're going."

"No," said Craig.

The cruiser forged on, and the false dawn came, a pink smudge across the horizon, pink and yet cold. The cruiser moved on, and Craig strained his ears for the sound of other boats. There had to be other boats, and if the land police had done their job they would pick them up soon.

Twice he thought he heard them and throttled back the engine—his hands were still steady, but they were wet, now, and he was breathing more quickly than he had need—but when at last it came, he was in no doubt. It was a low-pitched, drumming note, deep and steady, and when he heard it he could look, and when he looked he could see the two sets of red and green riding lights, tiny and brilliant. Even as he saw them, the other boats' lights switched on, and began to pierce the darkness section by section, their beams crossing then engaging, like the swords of duelists. At once Craig gave his boat more throttle, and she screamed her eagerness to go. The speedometer needle moved, faster, faster, from fifteen to twenty to twenty-two. Slowly then it dragged on to twenty-five, but still Craig could sense behind him the drum note of bigger engines, the thrust of wider propellers. It was ridiculous, of course: no other noise could survive when Allen's cruiser hit full power, and yet Craig knew the pursuing ships were there, so that when their lights snapped on again and stroked the blackness of the sea to a cold, pure, silvery blue, Craig almost sighed his relief—until one searchlight flicked him, and he began to fling the cruiser all over the water to lose those sure, serene lights that probed the blackness of the sea.

And then one brushed the side of the cruiser from the right, lighting up Craig at the wheel, and Allen crouched beside him. Craig swerved again, but the boat on his left found him, hesitated, and then held until the one from the right could bore through the dark once more, and Craig struggled to find a course in the blinding, silver light. A voice over the loud hailer boomed out in Spanish, and Craig tried the throttle again. There were no more revs in the engines. The boats behind nosed up closer—*Jesus, they must be big*—and again the loud hailer voice boomed out, and Allen was gibbering with fear, and Craig too busy to understand a word. He tried to swerve again, and there was a crackle of gunfire, a stream of tracers drifting across the black sky to disappear at last into the black sea, twenty yards from the boat. Craig threw the port engine into neutral, then into reverse, and the cruiser's weight lunged viciously as she swerved to the right across the bows of the pursuer, then Craig swerved again and tried in vain to coax out more revs. The cruiser's speedometer read twenty-seven knots, and there it stuck. There just wasn't any more.

Craig risked another look behind at the searchlights criss-crossing the sea. The false dawn had faded. Daylight was only minutes away, and those minutes were vital.

"Do you carry a gun aboard?" he yelled.

"You bloody fool," Allen screamed back, "that's Spanish navy stuff chasing us."

"Do you have a gun?"

"Just a rifle," Allen said. "A Lee-Enfield."

"Get it," said Craig. Allen made no move.

"Have you ever been in a Spanish prison?" asked Craig.

Allen sighed, and fetched the rifle, then Craig made him take the wheel. He lay down in the stern of the boat, checked the rifle, and waited. The Lee-Enfield was old—ten years at least—but it seemed in good nick, and Craig was used to it. The standard service weapon of the Second World War, it was the first of the long series of rifles, carbines, pistols, revolvers, and automatic weapons that had passed through his hands. He had learned its care and maintenance when he was seventeen years old, and he had not forgotten. Magazine, bolt, safety catch were all working well. The barrel, all the rifle parts were clean, bright, and slightly oiled, the way the manual said they should be. It seemed that Allen loved a weapon as much as he loved his cruiser.

Craig waited, knowing that this time it wouldn't be for long, while the Spanish navy flogged the sea with their searchlights, then came at them again. Craig snuggled down, the rifle steady against his shoulder. The leading pursuer came up from behind, and its searchlights pointed an accusing finger of light. He fired down its beam, and the light went out. Allen swung the cruiser as he had seen

Craig do, across the bows of the other boat. They made it with yards only to spare, but the other searchlight found them, two machine guns chattered, and Allen watched in horror as lumps of varnished decking flew past his head. Craig fired again, but the cruiser veered too much and the light clung on to him, pitiless. He had to hit it with his next shot: his eyes would be blinded soon.

"Hold her steady," he yelled to Allen, and worked the bolt of the Lee-Enfield. The cruiser settled down on the easy sea, and Craig fired again. Again the light went out; again there were no screams—and, he hoped to God, no casualties. An act of war wouldn't exactly fill Loomis with joy: a wounded Spaniard would drive him demented. Craig looked at Allen by the wheel, then took off the Lee-Enfield magazine. The smell of cordite increased, whipped past him by the cruiser's slipstream, as his fingers fumbled the bullets free and dropped them into his pocket. He took the wheel from Allen again, and held course for Gibraltar.

Allen said, "They got bloody close."

"Good radar," said Craig.

"Think they'll find us again?"

Craig said nothing. There was no way of knowing. When he did know he would act. Until then, his whole being was concentrated on coaxing one extra knot—half a knot—out of the cruiser. As dawn came up they were doing twenty-eight and a half knots, and Allen was ashen. The sun grew brighter, kinder, and two miles away they could see their pursuers, hull down. Ahead of them lay Gibraltar. Craig reckoned that they could just about do it.

"Congratulations," he said to Allen. "We just

defeated the armada again."

Allen was looking at what two Vickers machine guns had done to his deck.

"This'll cost a fortune," he said.

"Send us the bill," said Craig.

Allen prowled past him, examining the damage, working his way back to the bows. Craig sighed. He was pathetic. Allen picked up the Lee-Enfield.

"I think you should pay me now," he said. "You've got the money." Craig said nothing. "Or, better still, take me over to Tangier." Craig held his course, and above the engines' whine came the crisp smack of the bolt being worked. "I mean it," said Allen. The boat held course.

"Look," Allen said, "I'm desperate. Those Spanish bastards saw me. I can't go back to Marbella. I need money. You've got it. Damn it, man—all you really want is Calvet."

Craig held his course.

"I'll kill you," said Allen.

Craig said, "The gun isn't loaded." Allen laughed. "Try it." Allen squeezed the trigger.

"You see?" said Craig.

He risked a look at Allen then. He was sidling toward him, holding the Lee-Enfield by stock and barrel, a foolish, inefficient way to turn it into a club.

"You're stupid," said Craig, "but you're not that stupid. You start something now and I'll put you overboard." Allen halted. "That means you'll either drown or the Spanish navy will get you. Put that thing down."

Allen let it fall, and it banged on to the deck.

"Now take the wheel," said Craig, and again Allen obeyed.

Craig went down into the cabin. Calvet lay there, wriggling in a furious burst of energy to reach the ropes that tied his feet.

"It's too late," said Craig.

Calvet froze, and rolled over to look at him. His eyes were brown, melancholy, Slavic, and they were bright with hate.

"You lost," said Craig. "You were bound to lose eventually. Now lie still. I don't want to hurt you again." Calvet stayed rigid. "You want a cigarette?" Calvet gave no sign that he had heard. Craig left him and went back up top, then risked a look round. Once more Calvet was trying to bend his legs and arch his back, to reach the knots that tied his feet. The Russian, Craig thought, had qualities that made him infinitely preferable to Allen, but he didn't like his taste in girls.

Allen was very close to tears when Craig took the wheel from him again. He could see the great streak of concrete now that flowed out to sea, the runway that opened up Gibraltar to the Viscounts and Vikings and the tourists on their way to Tangier and the Costa del Sol. And behind was the boredom of Gibraltar, the correct little bars and gloomy hotels, which the magic words "duty-free" alone rendered habitable. And behind it all was the Rock, symbol of empire and insurance companies, and the wild yet formal gallantry of eighteenth-century sieges. Now all it held was the apes.

Craig eased back the throttle, and the revs diminished. A white naval patrol boat shot toward them, and a voice on the Tannoy yelled: "Mr. Jameson?" Craig nodded vigorously, and the patrol boat shot ahead of them, piloted them past the liner in the bay, the long line of tramp steamers, into the inner harbor of launches, tugs, and motorboats, to a quay between two moles patrolled by marine sentries. The patrol boat swung in, and Craig responded to a leading seaman's signal, stopped the starboard engine, revved up the port, and eased broadside up to the quay, while the leading hand hooked on and another sailor flung ropes to Allen, and they were tied up at last. Craig stopped the engines, and waited. A commander, R.N., and a surgeon commander left the patrol boat and dropped into the cruiser. The commander's eyes flicked from the rifle to the bullet-torn deck.

"You're a bit conspicuous, Mr. Jameson," he said. "Your people promised the admiral that you wouldn't be."

"Sorry about the rifle," said Craig. "We thought we might have a pop at a dolphin. Unfortunately," his eyes flicked to the damage on deck, "it started to fire back." He kicked the Lee-Enfield down the companionway out of sight.

"Where's my patient?" said the doctor.

Craig jerked his thumb toward the cabin.

"He's violent," said Craig, and the commander, R.N., sighed and followed the doctor. Craig took out cigarettes and offered one to Allen. They smoked in silence, then Allen said: "I'm sorry."

Craig drew on his cigarette. If the doctor got a move on they could catch the morning plane, be in London by teatime. He might even have time for a bath, do something about his shoulder where Calvet had hit him. He knew how to hit. That was inevitable. The KGB Executive trained its members with absolute thoroughness.

Allen said: "I was told I'd be paid when we finished the job."

"Oh yeah," said Craig. "You want money."

He took a check out of his pocket. It was already signed. He dated it.

"Five hundred for the job, five hundred for the boat. All right?"

"That's fine," said Allen.

Craig wrote in words and figures. "One thousand pounds," and gave him the check.

Allen took it, folded it in three, and put it carefully in his wallet.

"I suppose I can cash it in Gib?" he said.

"Of course," said Craig.

"That's fine then," said Allen as he stood up and climbed onto the quay. "I think I'll trot along now. Have some breakfast."

"Do that," said Craig.

"Then I thought I'd pop into the bank."

"Good idea."

"You don't mind if I leave you for a bit?"

"You're leaving us forever," said Craig. "We don't need you any more."

4

The navy ambulance nosed its way toward Gibraltar airport with the ponderous yet swift-moving dignity that only Daimler knows how to build. Inside it were Craig, the doctor, and the commander, who had changed into mufti, and Calvet. Calvet was on a stretcher, asleep, and comprehensively bandaged from thorax to head. Both his legs were in splints. The money Craig had taken was inside the bandages.

"I've given him a sedative," said the doctor. "He shouldn't give you any trouble."

"Thanks," said Craig.

"He's quite considerably bruised," said the doctor. "Particularly in the stomach and just below the nose. Forgive me, but what did you hit him with?"

"I just hit him," said Craig.

The commander stared gloomily at the notices scrawled on painted walls: "260 Años de Libertad," and "Gibraltar es Español," one canceling out the other, over and over again. They stopped at a policeman's signal at the corner of Winston Churchill Avenue, and the commander looked at his watch.

"You mustn't miss your plane," he said.

"I won't," said Craig.

The policeman signaled them on.

"I suppose it has to wait for you?"

"No," Craig said. "But there's lots of time and lots of planes."

"The admiral wants you off the Rock," said the commander. "It's my business to see that you go."

"You mean he doesn't like me?"

"Of course he doesn't like you. I don't like you."

"I find that incredible," said Craig.

The doctor snorted.

"You're in a dirty business," said the commander. "I realize it has to be done, but you can't expect me to approve of it. Of course it's different for you—you seem to enjoy it."

Craig thought of the way he had terrorized, used, and finally abandoned Allen; the blow that had struck the girl; the impact of his shoe into Calvet's belly. He said nothing.

"But the navy shouldn't be asked to help you. The whole enterprise is sheer piracy."

"You talk a lot," said Craig. "The trouble is you never say anything much."

The ambulance arrived then, nosed in past a flurry of taxi drivers and porters, and Craig got out to collect tickets for himself and David Lloyd, the battered victim of a motor accident now being flown back to his parents in Merioneth. He bought cigarettes, Scotch, and perfume at the duty-free shop, and went back to the ambulance. The doctor had gotten out and was escorting a mobile stretcher with Calvet in it up to the ticket barrier.

The commander said: "You'd better leave now."

"Can't I say good-bye to the admiral?" asked Craig.

"He doesn't know you exist. None of us do," the commander said. "It makes me very happy."

Craig said: "I'm a bit sad myself. Four hours in Gibraltar—and I only saw one monkey."

"Go away," said the commander. "Just go away."

"Okay," said Craig, and dropped the perfume in the commander's lap. "Think of me when you wear it, won't you?"

The perfume was called "Our Secret."

Craig walked after the doctor, and showed his tickets at the barrier. Passports and Customs had waved him through. He and Calvet were the first to arrive at the turboprop Viking, and Craig waited while the stretcher was eased into the first-class compartment and the doctor went in, checked, and came down again.

"I've had a look at him," the doctor said. "He won't move till you get to London."

"Thanks," said Craig.

"No really, I've enjoyed it," said the doctor. "It makes a change from picking broken glass out of drunken sailors."

Craig gave him the bottle of Scotch and climbed aboard. A trickle of tourists followed, then the Viking revved up at last, taxied out, and roared over the airstrip and out to sea: Africa was on one side, Europe on the other. It was raining on two continents. The plane climbed, the warning lights went out, and Craig unfastened his seat belt. In three and a half hours he'd be in London, and Calvet would be someone else's problem. He smoked, yawned, drank Scotch and ginger ale, then fell asleep.

There was another Daimler waiting in London, with another doctor, and a man whom Craig didn't know. He handed Calvet and the evidence over, and took a taxi to his flat in Regent's Park. He still hadn't had time to have a bath, and his shoulder hurt like hell. He went home to rest.

* * *

Four days later Loomis sent for him. Craig drove to see him in the latest one of the series of black Mark X Jaguars with the 4.2-liter engine he had used ever since he'd been established in Department K. It was a ridiculously large automobile for one man, expensive to drive and impossible to park, but it suited his cover—that of a retired manufacturer of machine tools—and it enabled him whenever necessary to convey four or five other large men to where they were needed, and to do it quickly—at a hundred and thirty miles an hour, if the need arose. He parked in a mews, and walked back to Queen Anne's Gate, the wary caretaker, and Loomis's vile-tempered coffee.

"You did all right," Loomis said grudgingly. "He's coming along nicely."

"You've got him up at the nursing home?"

Loomis nodded.

"It's lovely up there just now," he said. "The daffodils are at their best. He didn't take to it at first, but he's doing fine now."

"What did you use?"

"Oh, different things," said Loomis. "Bit of this, bit of that. There's nothing like variety, cock. Now he's mostly on pentathol. Seems to like it. His name's Oleg Dovzhenko. Born in the Ukraine, 1938—you were giving a few years away. The KGB spotted him at Moscow University—brilliant linguist, good gymnast—and they gave him the usual tests. All that Pavlovian stuff. He worked in France for a while, then he did a bit in South America, then he went to Marbella. We've got it all down."

"Did he find much stuff about Gibraltar?"

"There's not a hell of a lot to find," said Loomis. "But he did his best. He was busier paying people to do things about Franco."

"Any good?"

"Oh yes," said Loomis. "He'd found out quite a bit about how far they'll support America, and he'd done some research on the Fifth Fleet, too. He had a man on the spot when the Yanks lost their H-bomb, and he'd done quite a bit of work on air-fields. He was looking to the future, as well. Very forward-looking feller. Spotting blokes he could work on when Franco goes."

"What about the girl?" asked Craig.

"The young person you tied to the bed? She's a designer of expressionist jewelry. That means sequins in your belly button, sort of thing. She's clean. From what I hear she didn't even see you. You did all right." Loomis looked surprised.

"And Allen?"

"Bloody fool," said Loomis. "He went back to Spain. Had some money hidden in Marbella, so he put on a false beard and pretended he was invisible. The Spanish police picked him up in an hour. I expect he told them all about you. Not that it matters. You don't exist. They'll do him for smuggling and shooting at their navy. Now then"—he dismissed Allen with a wave of a meaty paw, and glowered at Craig—"that stuff you brought us. The R/T's nice, but we got a better one already. The money's better. We're always short of money here. Twenty-five thousand quid in dollars. Pity!"

"What's wrong?" Craig asked.

"They're all forged." He reached into his inside pocket with a fat man's economy of movement, then threw four twenty-dollar bills on to the desk in front of Craig. "See for yourself."

Craig picked them up and looked at them. They were crisp and clean, with the hard feel of good paper, the portrait of President Jackson sharp and well defined. The color was good, the printing excellent.

"Pretty," said Craig.

"Would you take one if it was offered?" Craig nodded, and Loomis nodded back, a one-inch inclination of the head that was regal in its dignity.

"Me too. Trouble is, there's three thousand bills and only four serial numbers between them. I've had them looked at. Chap at Scotland Yard specializes in this sort of thing. He liked them. Got very excited. Nearly wet himself." Loomis paused, then added: "Thin feller," as if in explanation. "Seems they've had one of these passed in London. He's got some of his young men working on it now. I think you'd better go and help them. It'll be a bit of an education for you."

Craig's tutor was Detective Sergeant Millington, a young, eager copper with an unquenchable thirst for promotion. Craig met him in a pub in Chelsea, a dim, chilly little place where even the feeling of decay was, if not elegant, at least expensive. Millington was drinking beer and eating a sausage. He looked weary yet brimming with excitement, the energy fighting the weariness: as it must do when you work a sixty-hour week every week, and the assistants and equipment you need are eternally promised but never arrive. He was hatless and his shoes were not unduly large for his big man's weight, and yet Craig had spotted him at once for a copper. He had the look of a born hunter. Craig went over to him; he sensed the quick appraisal of the other's eyes. It had been the same when he'd gone to see him at Scotland Yard. Millington was afraid of Craig and disliked him because of it.

"I don't like this idea," Millington said. "It's asking for trouble. Anybody can see you're not a copper." He looked at Craig's hand-stitched gray suit, the white Sea Island cotton shirt, and Dior tie. "You're too well dressed for one thing."

"I thought I might look more like a crook," said Craig.

Millington scowled.

"I can't take you with me to interview people when you look like that."

"I don't want to be with you," Craig said. "Just show me who they are and let me work it out for myself."

"I don't think I can do that," Millington said. "After all, I'm responsible for you."

"Oh no," said Craig. "I don't think so."

Millington looked at him again, not trying to hide his dislike.

"Okay," he said, "I'll show them to you. But what good'll that do? They'll see you with me."

"No," said Craig. "They won't. We've got just the thing for that."

What he had was a Bedford van, with one-way black glass panels in the sides and back. A chain of roses was painted round the van, and on each side was the name "BLOSSOMS UNLIMITED" Millington wasn't amused. The interior of the van was furnished like a caravan with a camp bed and chairs; there were three Leica Ikon cameras with telefoto lenses, a 16-millimeter Eclair movie camera, two Ferrograph tape recorders, and a radio as well. Millington lusted after that van. It would have saved him hours of questioning, miles of walking. The driver got in, and the van drove away. They were going to Soho.

The twenty-dollar bill had been passed in a strip club, a small place just off Greek Street with seats for fifty, a tiny stage, and an enormous bar. Currently its name was "Nuderama." The man who had passed the bill had looked and talked like an American. He had used it to buy champagne for the three stars of the show, and it had cost him five pounds for a magnum. He'd given the barman ten shillings, kept thirty shillings in change, and had never gone back, though the stars looked for him daily. So did the barman. Millington thought he might be a man called Tony Driver, an unusually versatile crook who had done time in Great Britain and Canada for such varied offenses as blackmail, larceny, and the con game. Driver dressed well, lived anywhere, and played poker at least four hours a day. Usually he won. On the day before the bill had been passed, Driver had played for six hours and had lost five hundred pounds, Millington had learned. Then, apart from his one visit to Nuderama, he had disappeared for two days, come back with stake money, played poker again, and won. He handed Craig his photograph.

"You haven't tried to have him identified yet?" Craig asked.

"We were going to—until you came along. Now we've been asked to hold back."

"It's good of you to wait."

"It's orders," said Millington.

The van turned off Shaftesbury Avenue, along Old Compton Street and into Greek Street, then parked at a meter. It was three o'clock and Nuderama was preparing to face a new day. Craig took a pair of Zeiss glasses from a rack, gave another pair to Millington, looked at a yellow door framed in electric light bulbs, and around the light bulbs a wooden frame. At the top of the frame was the name "NUDERAMA" in rainbow lettering; the two sides sported pictures of girls. Mostly they were simply naked, except for that look of outraged hauteur—like a duchess whose bottom's being pinched by a servant—that strippers always wear when they pose. One or two wore muffs, or a pair of doves, or what Craig took to be a piece of salmon net. The most enterprising appeared about to administer the Irish whip to a gorilla.

As Craig watched, a man with the very white skin of one who rarely sees daylight went up to the doorway, opened it and went in. Craig took his photograph.

"That's the barman," said Millington.

He was followed by a chunky, bad-tempered woman—the cashier—and another man.

"That's the barker," said Millington. "He stands outside and cons in the customers."

Craig continued to take photographs.

A Bentley Continental whispered up to the curb and a tall, thin man got out. He was gray-haired, elegant, a white carnation in the buttonhole of his dark-blue suit. He limped slightly as he walked up to the doorway, and there was a smeared scar on one side of his face that suggested unsuccessful plastic surgery.

"That's the owner," said Millington. "Julek Brodski. He's a naturalized Pole."

"Any form?" asked Craig.

"No. He was a squadron leader in the Polish air force during the war. Got a D.S.O. Matter of fact, he's supposed to be a count or something. No, Brodski's all right," Millington said. He looked at a photo of a girl whose inability to handle a sunshade was causing her some embarrassment. "As a matter of fact he runs a nice, clean place."

"That the lot?" Craig asked, and Millington nodded. "What time do the girls arrive?"

"Four thirty," said Millington.

"Let's go and look at the place where Driver plays cards," said Craig.

Driver played in the basement of Luigi's, a sad, ineffective little café three blocks from the strip club. On the ground floor there was a soda fountain and seats that looked like the pews of the Methodist chapels Craig remembered from his boyhood. Three tired waitresses, who looked as if they hadn't left the building for weeks, shambled back and forth serving meals whose cheapness did nothing to compensate for their nastiness. Craig sat in the van and took more pictures—of the waitresses, of everybody who seemed at ease in the place, of a fat man who visited the cash register every half hour and rang up "NO CHANGE," then counted the take. The fat man was the proprietor. His name wasn't Luigi; it was Arthur. Fat Arthur. He was very fat indeed, but he didn't look soft. Downstairs was exactly the same, Craig learned, except that there was a little room behind the dining area, and in that room a poker game went on, sometimes for days. It was a quiet game, restricted to friends of Arthur's, dishonest men who kept their dishonesty to themselves. The police weren't interested. Millington suddenly looked restless.

"What's wrong?" Craig asked.

Millington flushed. "I drank too much beer," he said.

"The loo's in that cupboard," said Craig, and pointed.

Millington, half-believing, opened the cupboard door. It was true.

"You think of everything," he said.

"We try," said Craig. "We have to, in our business."

He looked again into the street as Millington voided his bladder.

"Come here," he said, and began taking pictures.

"I can't," said Millington.

Craig took more pictures, and at last Millington came over to him and looked out of the window at a tall young man in a Brooks Brothers gray-flannel suit, knitted silk tie, and button-down collar.

"That's Driver," said Millington.

Craig looked down at Millington's unzipped fly. "You do pick your times, don't you?" he said.

The van drove off at last, and Craig set up the developing tank inside it, curtained it off, and switched on the infrared lights. The photographs came out well enough, even the photographs of photographs of the stars of Nuderama, Karen and Tempest and Maxine. Craig numbered each picture and took notes on the names as Millington talked. For the first time Millington became aware of Craig's fury of concentration, his utter disregard of everything but the job on hand. Millington began to wonder what a man had to do to afford a fifty-guinea suit, a Longines-Wittnauer watch, Guerlain cologne. He looked for the hundredth time at Craig's hands. They were big hands, for Craig himself was big—six feet two and thirteen stones at least, with a heaviness of shoulder that stretched his suit glove-tight across the back—but they were neat hands too, long-fingered, deft in their movements. The knuckles were strange: each was flattened, so that across the back of each hand there was a continuous ridge of bone, and the skin that covered it looked like leather. The edge of each hand was odd too, because it was not rounded but straight and flat, and covered from wrist to fingertip in the same leathery skin. It reminded Millington of the blade of an ax.

The van pulled over to the curb by a tube station, and Craig finished his notes.

"All right," he said. "This is where you leave us."

"What are you going to do now?" Millington asked. "Can you tell me?"

"I'm going back there," said Craig. "Our people see this as a rush job. So I'll rush it." He grinned. "That's where I've got the edge on you. I can go in there and make things happen. You have to wait and pick up the pieces."

"I have to go back there myself," said Millington. "Not after Driver," he added hastily. "We're laying off him till we get clearance from you. But I may see you."

"You won't know me," said Craig.

"Naturally not," Millington stood up, and surprised himself by holding out his hand.

"Good luck," he said.

"You too," said Craig, and shook his hand.

Millington said: "Yes, well—" and scrambled out of the van. A moment later his head reappeared in the doorway.

"You're parked on a yellow line," he said.

5

The room was bare, efficient, and utterly devoid of decoration. On one cream-washed wall a darker patch showed where a picture had once hung. It had been a portrait of Stalin. Chelichev was glad that such extravagant idolatry was no longer necessary. It was idiotic, and it interfered with the clean lines of his room. So did the dark patch, but he refused to have it painted out. It reminded him of days that had not been gone for very long, days that might, if one was not careful, come back. He settled back in his chair; he looked like an ad for superior whisky, a lean, leathery, handsome horseman; a tough and well-preserved fifty who could still play hell with the ladies. His Soviet army general's uniform had been cut and tailored by an expert. It, like everything else in the room, was fanatically clean, as if room and owner had been purged by fire. He looked at the one note on his desk, tore it into four neat squares, murmured into a desk phone, then sat back, at once at ease and watchful, as a cat sits.

The woman who came in was beautiful. Tall and deep-bosomed, green-eyed, with thick, heavy hair so blond as to be almost white. A former *prima ballerina assoluta* of the Bolshoi had taught her to move, a film makeup man had taught her how to make up, a Hungarian couturier had spent weeks showing her how to choose and match clothes, gloves, handbags, shoes. The result was at once beautiful and splendid: a woman of superb proportions and exquisite taste. Chelichev looked pleased.

The woman said: "This is an honor, comrade-general."

The voice was deep, melancholy, beautiful. An actor of the Stanislavsky method had made it so.

Chelichev said: "For me it is a pleasure. A very great pleasure." The woman lowered her head, acknowledging a tribute that could never be commonplace.

"Soong is dead," he continued. "You did remarkably well in Morocco."

"Thank you, comrade-general."

"The information you passed on to Dovzhenko was relayed here. We knew he had gone to Britain of course—it was just good luck that we found him —but the execution, that was remarkably efficient. Except"—he scowled—"that somebody thought it would be amusing to have one of the executives speak to him in Cantonese. We are not here to be amusing. To be amusing is to betray a secret. In this case I think it betrayed who killed Soong to Department K."

"The British intelligence organization?"

"Exactly. Department K is very good. Very original. They never make jokes." He paused. "No. That is not true. The British always make jokes, but it is part of their technique. Their minds work that way. Soong is a good lead for them." He paused again, and the woman knew she was on trial. It was her turn to speak.

"You mean it might lead them to BC?"

"It might. Yes. Their leader, Loomis, is a terrible man. He is also very clever. Everything that happens he turns to his advantage. How would such a man react if he knew that a foreign group was doing all it could to attack the USSR?"

"There have been more incidents?"

"Two cases of sabotage," he said. "One very spectacular. The theft of a certain archives—they were recovered, and the man who stole them killed himself. That was a pity—but to retain the archives was essential. They were about Beria, and very revealing. BC exists all right."

"Of course," the woman said.

"Of course." Chelichev's voice was ironic. "But there are certain people, even in the Presidium, who do not think so. They blame it all on the Americans and the British. If it were true, it would be an act of war. We must stop BC before our masters start demanding reprisals."

He looked at the woman again, noting the fact of her youth and beauty. His look was not one of desire but of pity.

"Another war could destroy us all," he said, "including those of our masters who say it couldn't happen. Just because we take reprisals against those who have done nothing to us. We must find BC and destroy it. Soon."

The woman said: "Dovzhenko had a lead. BC has a bank account in Tangier. I heard about it and brought in Dovzhenko to find out."

"In a bank called Crédit Labonne," said Chelichev. "They have a million pounds in Deutschmarks."

"A million pounds sterling?" He nodded. "What a strange way to put it. Why not just say however many million Deutschmarks it is? Unless—"

"It's about eleven million," said Chelichev. "Unless what?"

"Unless Dovzhenko found out from an Englishman—or an Englishman put the money in the bank," answered the woman.

"I want you to go to Tangier again and find out," said Chelichev.

"Why not send Dovzhenko too? He's good," the woman said.

"Very good. Unfortunately Department K took him from us two days ago. That is why I feel so sure they'll know about BC by now."

"They kidnapped Dovzhenko?" Somehow she stopped herself from adding the stupid "But that's impossible."

"*He* did, not they. A man called Craig, from Department K."

"He must be a remarkable man."

"Very. He could—quite literally—kill you with one finger. We have a file on him. Read it."

"Do you think Loomis will use the BC information to hurt us?"

"No," said Chelichev. "He doesn't want a war any more than I do. I might even get him to help us find out who the BC members are. At a price."

"You think they're based in England?"

"Soong went to England, and we know he was trying to contact the BC."

He looked at his watch and said: "That is all, I think. You will study the situation here for a few more days, then go back to Tangier."

"Yes, comrade-general," she said, and added, because the thought of Dovzhenko being overcome by one man was too incredible, "but may I ask—"

"Quickly," said Chelichev.

"Are you quite sure this man Craig kidnapped Dovzhenko? He didn't defect?"

"Craig took him," said Chelichev. "There can be no doubt. Loomis sent word to me himself."

* * *

Craig took a taxi to Soho. He wore the same gray suit, and over it a vicuña coat he had bought in Rome. He wished he had Grierson's elegance. Grierson wore clothes with a casual distinction that took two hundred years of selective inbreeding to achieve. Beside him, Craig knew he looked a peasant. Grierson looked asleep all the time, yet was as fast as a cat. He had a way of smiling that was lazy too, as if the world was a hell of a good place to be in, if only he could wake up. Grierson was in a psychiatric home now, lying in bed, tying knots in a piece of string, untying them, retying them. All day, every day. If anybody asked Grierson to do anything else, he began to cry. Deliberately Craig blotted Grierson from his mind. He walked past the club, and the cooing enticements of the barker. "Show starting any minute, sir. Eleven lovely ladies inside. Nonstop strip, sir. Show you all they've got—and they've got everything, sir, believe me."

Craig hesitated. "How much is it?" he asked.

"Twenty-five bob, sir. Includes entrance to the

bar. You can watch the show from there, sir. All
mod cons at the Nuderama."

Craig gave the half-embarrassed shrug every
man gives when he decides to enter a strip show.
The movement was perfectly natural. He was half
embarrassed. He paid twenty-five shillings to the
woman behind the cash desk. The woman had had
a henna rinse and wore a black silk dress and
pearls. She also had the figure and muscles of a
sumo wrestler. Craig decided not to pick a fight
with her, and walked down a corridor with wall-to-
wall carpeting. The corridor was two feet wide.
From time to time, it seemed, the sumo wrestler
sprayed it with My Sin. At least there was an atom-
izer of it beside her, and the place reeked of the
stuff. He felt for the handle of the door leading to
the theater—the lighting was what the man-
agement called discreet—and fumbled his way into
what the eighteenth century would have considered
an adequate drawing room. Now it contained a
stage, a raked auditorium for fifty people who
didn't mind each other's company, and a runway
down the middle of the auditorium. Behind the
auditorium was a raised bar that looked straight
into the theater. Stage, auditorium, and bar alike
were cheap and nasty. The walls were distempered
a vile yellow; the stage curtains, bought as a job lot
before Garrick retired, had once been of red velvet
but were now the kind of pink that clashed viciously with the yellow walls; the seats had long since
lost their springs, and the bar seemed mostly
matchwood. The only thing that surprised Craig
was how clean it all was.

There were perhaps twenty men sitting in the

auditorium. Piped music whispered love to them, but they were all on their own, and all sat either staring straight ahead or looking at their programs, which cost five shillings to buy, six-pence to print, and contained photographs of Karen, Tempest, and Maxine on every page. Their sense of embarrassment was overwhelming: Craig took shelter in the bar. The customers at the bar were in groups. They drank light ale and rubbed their hands and behaved like men who were in for a treat. Each of them seemed to be selling something to the others in his group. Craig eased through them, and went up to the barman, who had "HARRY" embroidered on the left breast of his dinner jacket and a gold loop earring in his right ear.

"Scotch and dry ginger," said Craig.

"Yes, sir," said the barman, and reached for an anonymous bottle of Scotch and a large Schweppes Dry Ginger. He took six shillings from Craig, and went back to opening light ales. Craig sipped the Scotch. It was watered. He drank it and ordered another, straight. The barman reached for the anonymous bottle again, and set a glass in front of Craig. When the measure on the bottle had dropped into the glass, Craig grabbed his wrist. The barman tried to pull away, and found he couldn't.

"I like you," said Craig softly. "You're cute." He sipped his whisky and pushed it back to the barman. "Change this for me, Harry," he said. "I only drink water when I'm thirsty."

The barman said: "I don't understand, sir." The hand on his wrist tightened and he almost yelled out. But he couldn't yell out, not with all the cus-

tomers watching. They thought the man who held
his wrist was teasing him—everybody knew he was
gay: it was worth a lot of tips in a strip club—and
if he started screaming Mr. Brodski would go
berserk. Harry whimpered, and Craig leaned
across to him.

"You're too pretty to be dishonest," Craig whispered. "Pour me a proper drink."

"Yes, sir," said Harry, "I'm very sorry, sir."

"You should be," said Craig. "I might have hurt
you, Harry."

The barman poured him a Teacher's. Again
Craig sipped, but this time he smiled. Harry shuddered and looked down at his wrist. The marks of
Craig's fingers lay across it like red bars. Harry
took the other glass away, and sold it three minutes
later to a man in the costume-jewelry game from
Edgebaston. He didn't notice a thing. Craig waited
till the barman came past him, then said: "Why
don't you buy me a drink, Harry? You can afford
it." This time he hadn't lowered his voice, and the
group on either side of him watched in awe as
Harry poured a double for Craig, dug into his
pocket, and put twelve shillings into the till. Every
habitue of Nuderama knew that Harry never, never bought anybody a drink.

Then the bar lights dimmed, the lights in the
auditorium went out, and a drummer, a pianist,
and a guitar player scrambled into a space the size
of a coffin for the lady sumo wrestler. The piped
music faded and died, the pianist struck an E, and
the guitar player tightened his strings with the air
of a man who has worked in strip clubs long
enough to know that the audience seldom listens to

the music. Some of the men at the bar left then, to try for seats near the runway. The rest took their drinks to the edge of the auditorium, and watched in silence, and with care. After all, twenty-five shillings is a lot of money. The drummer struck a roll, the curtains jerkily parted, and the show was on.

It was memorable solely in that it was utterly devoid of talent. None of the girls involved, not even Karen, Tempest, or Maxine, made the slightest effort to sing, mime, or dance. Their movements were the movements of women, not of dancers. They were tired, bored, and utterly without grace. As entertainment the show failed to achieve the standard of a Girl Guide Gang Show on the first day of rehearsal. But what Girl Guide ever finishes a number naked on a runway, with the nearest cash customer a foot away? And that was the way Karen, Tempest, and Maxine finished every number, while often as not the eight supporting lovelies did the same behind them. Karen was brunette, Tempest was a blonde, and Maxine was a redhead, so there was something for everybody. They were young enough, and prettily fleshed, and the clothes they removed were pretty too. Long gloves, fur stoles, bras and panties of lace and nylon: they were all designed to excite. Their postures too, should have been exciting: the crook of a leg to emphasize the curve of calf and thigh and buttock, the shoulders thrown back to emphasize the sheer fall of a breast, the tightness of the undercurve, the slow recline on a pink divan. *If only,* Craig thought, *they weren't so bored.* But they were bored, and made no move to hide it as they stood under the spotlights and filled the world with nipples and navels, bellies and buttocks and breasts, and thought of nothing but how cold it was if you copped the draught from stage right.

The show finished in an hour and a quarter exactly, and the piped music crashed into the dream world of "Harem Nights" and "The Lady Takes a Bath" with a brass band Sousa medley that scattered the customers faster than a burst from a machine gun. Craig sat on alone, and drank Scotch.

"The show's over," said Harry. "If you want to stay on it'll cost you another twenty-five bob."

"When's the next show?" Craig asked.

"Half an hour," said Harry, and added, "sir."

"I was wondering if those three young ladies would take a drink with me," Craig said.

"They'd take a barrel with you," said Harry, "so long as you're paying."

"Go and ask them," said Craig. Harry went to the bar, and walked toward the stage. "And Harry—" the barman turned around. "Do it nicely," said Craig.

Harry must have done it nicely, because the three girls came back in no time at all. All three had changed into loose-fitting dressing gowns that from time to time slid disconcertingly over the nude flesh beneath, and all three had mink coats slung over their shoulders as casually as fighting troops wearing field equipment. They came up, smiled at Craig, and sat beside him, white legs flashing as they moved. Tempest had belted her gown tightly beneath her bosom: the twin points of her breasts pointed at him like guns. Craig ordered champagne.

"A bottle?" asked Harry.

"For four? Make it a magnum," said Craig.

Maxine said: "I think he's sweet. Don't you?"

"He's lovely," said Karen, and wriggled into her chair. The movement was a comprehensive one that kept her in motion from shoulders to rump. Craig began to sweat.

Tempest said: "I bet he's ever so strong." Her hand ran up his arm to his biceps, squeezed the hard muscle. "O-o-o he is," she said.

"What's your name, honey?" asked Maxine.

"John Reynolds," said Craig.

"And what do you do?" asked Tempest.

"Oh—business," said Craig, and the girls left it at that. And anyway the champagne came, and there wasn't much time, so they drank it in half-pint mugs. Craig stuck to Scotch, and then they had to go.

"Last show's at twelve," said Tempest. "I'm free after that."

"Me, too," said Maxine.

"And me," said Karen.

They stood up then, and rearranged their minks. It was a better show than the one Craig had paid for. He sat back and enjoyed their exit, the slow tick-tock of their buttocks as their long legs moved, then called for his bill as new customers drifted in. Harry brought it at once, and Craig added it carefully. Harry had got it right.

Craig reached for his wallet, pulled out a five-pound note and put it back again, then took out a twenty-dollar bill.

"Change that for me," he said.

Harry looked at it with the horror he normally reserved for spiders, draught beer, and the amorous advances of women.

"It's a twenty-dollar bill," said Craig. "Don't tell me you don't take American money. That's not what I heard."

"What did you hear, sir?" asked Harry.

"You'll take anything," said Craig. "Including rubles."

"Just a moment, sir," said Harry.

He left the bar, taking the note with him, and was back almost at once.

"Mr. Brodski would like a word with you," he said. "His office is just next to the auditorium."

"Who's Brodski?" asked Craig. "The feller who makes your whisky?"

Harry looked shocked.

"He's the proprietor, sir," he said.

"I don't want to see him," said Craig. "Give me my bill back. I'll pay in pounds."

"Mr. Brodski's got it," said Harry.

Craig leaned over the bar, and the new customers listened avidly. Craig looked a little drunk, but he also looked very dangerous.

"I'm going off you, Harry," he said. "You shouldn't give my money away. Now I'm going to see Brodski—and if he isn't nice to me I'm going to come back here and thread you through your earring."

He walked out of the bar and into the auditorium. He knew that every man in the place was watching him, and that was what he wanted: the threat of a scene, a violent scene, in a place where even the tiniest tantrum was bad for business. He reached the door, and hesitated for a moment. Something was wrong. There was somebody in the audience he had seen before. But there was no time to look back now. He walked on into the corridor. Mr. Brodski was waiting for him, his office door open. And Mr. Brodski also looked as if the last thing he wanted was a scene.

"Please come in, Mr.—"

"Reynolds," said Craig. "John Reynolds."

"How do you do? It's nice of you to spare me some of your time."

Brodski's voice was soft, low-pitched, with very little accent. He held the door open invitingly, and stood to one side. Craig went up to him, and his arm came round the Pole's shoulders.

"That's all right, old friend," he said. "I feel like a chat anyway."

His arm pushed suddenly, and Brodski lurched forward. They went into the room together.

Inside the room the fat woman stood. What Craig had thought to be a black dress turned out to be a smock. Beneath it she wore the most enormous pair of trousers Craig had ever seen. She was standing feet apart, her hands by her sides.

"I see you've called in your financial adviser," said Craig. It was quite incredible and all that, but the woman was standing like a fighter. He released Brodski, and stood just out of range of her short, thick arms. At once Brodski walked over behind his desk and picked up the twenty-dollar bill.

"I can't accept this," he said.

"Why not? It's a good one," said Craig.

"Is it?" Brodski asked. "I am not a naïve person, Mr. Reynolds. Look here, for instance, and here."

It was very nicely done. Brodski held up the bill, and pointed to it, then held it out to Craig. If he had reached for it, the woman would have got him. Instead, he merely looked, and for a split second only. In that split second she aimed a blow at his face, an old-fashioned roundhouse swing that was meant for his chin. He ducked, and a fist like a ball of rock cracked into his shoulder where Calvet had hit him. Craig gasped, then flung himself sideways to avoid a kick from a steel-tipped shoe. She moved into him then, and he backed off. He was giving away weight and she had bigger shoulders, but she was a woman.

"Now look, lady," he began. He had never felt more foolish.

She aimed another blow, and he warded it off with the edge of his hand on her forearm. At once she grabbed his wrist and threw him—a perfect hip throw that was supposed to send him crashing into the wall. But Craig had learned how to fall from Hakagawa, a black-belt seventh dan. He floated to the ground like a leaf, and waited for the kick to the groin that was bound to follow. When it came, he pushed up on his forearms, hooked her foot between his and threw his weight to one side. She went down like the *Titanic*. Craig got up, brushed dust from his coat, and waited. The woman came up slowly, gasping, then shuffled forward once more.

"Please, love," said Craig, trying to keep the hysteria out of his voice. "Please, love, don't make me do it."

She feinted with a left, then her right moved across his ribs in a blur of pain. Craig gasped, and she drew back her left again. As she did so, he aimed for her solar plexus in a three-finger strike.

The blow sank into her vast stomach, and her eyes went glassy. Her squat, massive weight was still evenly planted on her steel-shod feet, but there wasn't any more fight in her. Craig pushed her into a chair and she sat there unblinking. When he turned around, Brodski had produced a revolver from the drawer in his desk. It was a Webley 455, the type used by army officers in World War II. It was wildly inaccurate but it could blow holes in brick walls. Brodski handled it with a confidence that made Craig more wary than ever. He straightened up behind the chair.

"Oh no," he said. "Not the gun bit."

"I know how to use it," said Brodski.

"I can see that," said Craig. "On the other hand, are you prepared to?"

"Yes," said Brodski.

"For a twenty-dollar bill?"

The woman in the chair moaned.

"You hurt her," Brodski said.

"She didn't leave me much choice," said Craig. "And you shouldn't employ a lady bouncer."

"Jennifer's very good," said Brodski.

"Who?"

"You find the name incongruous? I did also, at one time. I thought Butch perhaps, or Spike, or even Rocky. But she insists on Jennifer. Men go out more easily when it is a woman who throws them. Particularly this woman." He nodded at Jennifer, now blowing like a beached porpoise.

"Put the gun down. We can talk," said Craig.

"Can we? I'm not nearly as strong as Jennifer. And look what you did to her—with three fingers."

"She shouldn't eat so much starch," said Craig.

"Give me my money back."

"No," said Brodski. "When Jennifer has recovered you must learn a lesson, Reynolds. People
don't come into my place and pass forged money."

Jennifer groaned again, and began to rub her
stomach; her hard, stubby fingers for once solic-
itous and tender.

"She will hold you," said Brodski, "and I will
beat you. With this." He waved the Webley, very
slightly.

"That bill isn't snide," said Craig.

"You are the second one. Did Driver send you?"
Brodski asked.

"I don't know any Driver. That's good money,"
said Craig.

Brodski stood up.

"Ready, Jennifer?" he asked.

Craig said quickly: "You better be, love. Because I'm not taking a gun-whipping. Not even to
oblige a lady." Jennifer groaned for the third time
and sat where she was. "Maybe you'd better shoot
me," said Craig.

Brodski said something emphatic in what Craig
took to be Polish, and sat looking puzzled. He
didn't seem the sort of man who looked puzzled
often. He resented it. At last he put the revolver
back into the drawer.

"I run a quiet place," he said. "None of the girls
on the batter, no hustling drinks, no reefers, no
brasses, nothing." In his soft, slightly accented
voice the vocabulary of Soho was as strange as Jennifer. "Just women with no clothes on."

"The show's lousy," said Craig.

"Oh, I agree," said Brodski. "But you are the

one customer in ten thousand who notices this. And I take 62 £ 10s.od. five times a day, six days a week. The amount of profit I show is almost embarrassing. What do I need with crime? The keynote of my place is discretion, Mr. Reynolds. A discreet promise of bliss, without the tiresome athletics of fulfillment. And then Driver came in. He ordered champagne for Karen, Tempest, and Maxine. He himself drank whisky. He paid his bill with a forged American note. A week later you come in. You order champagne for Karen, Tempest, and Maxine. You drink whisky. You pay with a forged American note."

"Have it tested," said Craig, "or give it back." Brodski ignored him.

"I would have taken the loss," he said. "But a policeman was here when it happened. You would be surprised, Mr. Reynolds, how often policemen find it necessary to check up on the morality of my little entertainments."

"What you want to avoid is theater critics," said Craig.

"I had to go to New Scotland Yard," said Brodski. "I had to fail to identify Driver. And now you come along and start it all again."

"Who is this Driver?" Craig asked.

Brodski sighed. "A man not unlike yourself who plays cards at Luigi's."

"You mean he can lick Jennifer?"

"I mean he dresses well, as you do, but without the distinction you do. And I suspect his honesty, as I do yours."

"Will he be at Luigi's now?"

"Why?" Brodski asked.

"I'd like to meet him," said Craig. "I mean it's an enormous coincidence—"

"He will be at Luigi's," Brodski said. "Please go away now, Mr. Reynolds."

"All right," said Craig. "I enjoyed the chat. Mind if I give you some advice?"

"Even with a Webley in my hand, I doubt if I could stop you," said Brodski.

"You ought to put your heavy on a diet."

Jennifer burst into tears.

Craig left then, and walked down the corridor and past the barker.

"Enjoy the show, sir?" he asked.

"I've never seen anything like it in my life," said Craig, and meant every word.

He walked down toward Greek Street and a burly young man who was waiting at the corner.

"Hallo, Mr. Craig," said Arthur Hornsey. "I was hoping I'd run into you again. Lucky I spotted you at the show."

Craig said: *"Nein, danke,"* and kept on walking. He had no time to waste on enthusiastic young men who enjoyed walking trips. It was time to call on another Arthur: Fat Arthur.

6

He went into the café and down the stairs. The
downstairs tables were all unoccupied, the one
aged waitress behind the counter knitted a sock
with concentrated venom, as if it were a victim.
Craig thought of Madame Defarge and opened the
door to the private room. The old crone made no
attempt to stop him. The room was empty. In the
middle of it was a table, scarred with cigarette
burns, stained with a chain mail of overfilled
glasses; above it a trio of 150-watt lamps threw
light on to it. It was hot in the room, and it smelled
of whisky and cigarettes and excited men. But now
it was empty. There were cards on the table; two
poker hands—a royal flush and a full house, aces
and eights. Beside them were fifty pounds in notes
and silver.

The room was windowless, and very still. The
blaring Soho noise—wide boys in search of money,
mugs too late aware of its loss—had faded to a
hungry whimper. Craig moved to a cupboard in
front of him. It was shut with a swivel bolt from
outside, but he moved warily, his fingers feather-
soft as he turned the swivel, then dived to one side

as the door swung open. Inside the cupboard, hanging neatly by his collar from a coat hook, was Driver. He had the dazed, innocent look of an insurance clerk playing Find the Lady. Even without the switchblade protruding from his heart it was apparent that he was dead. Craig reached inside his pocket, and Driver swung dully from the coat hook, his heels rapped softly on the back of the cupboard as Craig removed his wallet. There were ten ten-pound notes in it, but no twenty-dollar bills. Craig reached forward to return the wallet, and the heels drummed again as a voice behind him spoke.

"That Driver," said the voice. "He never could stand losing money. I suppose that's why you killed him. Or did he find out you were cheating?"

Craig turned, very slowly, his hands by his sides. In the doorway were Fat Arthur and, behind him, for the doorway was narrow, two other poker players. In his right hand Arthur carried a piece of lead pipe bound with insulating tape. Craig couldn't see the hands of the others.

"It's up to us to make a citizens' arrest," Arthur said. "What you've done is a felony. We're bound by law to take you in." He smiled, and the smile was a blend of joy and wonder, as if he'd backed three long-shot winners, then found a gold watch. "You only get one chance like that," said Fat Arthur, and slapped his palm with the lead pipe.

"I didn't kill him," said Craig.

"After we get through with you you won't care what you did," Fat Arthur said. "We ain't women and there's three of us—and we're going to hurt you, boy. Hurt you bad."

As he spoke, he sidled into the room. All his experience told him that Craig should cower now, but Craig stood his ground. Fat Arthur tapped his palm again with the pipe, and it made a noise like bone breaking, then he stepped forward again as his two followers filled the doorway. And it was at that moment that Craig jumped him, erupting into him with a kick that swung all the way from his thigh so that the edge of his shoe sank into the fat man's belly, slamming him back into the two men in the doorway, and still Craig came in at him, to grab one meaty forearm and swing him round. The whole weight of Craig's body went into it, but even so it was like throwing a horse as Arthur spun round the pivot of Craig's body, then screamed as Craig threw his weight the other way, and the fat man's arm broke, the lead pipe fell, and Craig let him drop. He moved toward the other two, and one lashed at Craig with a razor that split his vicuña coat from shoulder to forearm, then spun into the other man as Craig's elbow smashed into his throat. And the other man, off-balance, looked at the murder in Craig's eyes, and dropped the cosh he was carrying. There was a sound from the stairs, and Craig spun the cosh man round, holding him before him as a shield as Hornsey stepped carefully down the stairs. He looked at the razor man writhing on the floor, both hands clasped to his throat, and at Fat Arthur flat on his back in the doorway, looking like a mountain range.

"Is everything all right?" asked Hornsey, and behind him appeared the official feet and the elderly raincoat of Detective Sergeant Millington.

"Everything," said Craig, "is fine."

"We heard a noise," reported Hornsey. "This chap and I were upstairs; then there was a sound rather like a building collapsing—"

"That would be Fat Arthur," said Craig.

"Then everybody left, except this chap and myself. You're all right?"

He and Millington walked toward Craig, and the man Craig held accepted Millington's handcuffs with relief.

"They were trying to frame me," Craig said. "There's a dead man in there."

Millington looked, and went at once to the telephone.

"They've cut your coat," said Hornsey. "What a terrible thing."

Craig looked down at the long, straight cut, then at the razor man, now kneeling on the floor. He pulled the razor man to his feet; the man yelled at what the agony of movement did to his throat, but no sound came.

"Get your voice back," said Craig. "I want you to tell me things." He turned to the man who had held the cosh. "I want you all to tell me things," he said, then added to Hornsey: "I liked this coat."

"It's awfully you," Hornsey said.

Millington put down the phone. "Murder squad's on its way." he said. "I'm sorry. I had to."

Craig nodded. "Our chaps will want a look, too," he said.

"That's fixed," said Millington.

"I'll be off then," said Craig. He looked at his split sleeve. "I'd better buy a raincoat I suppose."

He left then, and a face appeared above the

counter. It was an old and evil face, with hair like moldy straw topped with a waitress's lacy cap. "I haven't seen one like him since they topped Big Harry Preston back in 1927," the waitress said. "I never thought I would. Gorgeous, isn't he, Mr. Millington?"

"You're a witness," Millington said.

"Of course I am. I want to be," said the waitress, and she rose from behind the counter looking very happy indeed. "You know what, Mr. Millington?" she said, and the happiness became tinged with awe. "That feller made Fat Arthur scream."

* * *

"We're going to Paris," said Loomis, and shot straight over a red light. A taxi driver yelled, and Loomis accelerated so as to be in time for the next one.

"Why?" asked Craig, and wished for the thousandth time that Loomis would let him drive. Loomis's car was the most beaten-up Rolls Royce that Craig had ever seen, and no one else was ever allowed to drive it.

"The Russians want Calvet back," said Loomis. "They've invited us to Paris to talk it over."

He went round the Hammersmith roundabout in top gear, his brakes screaming like four Fat Arthurs.

"Are they going to get him?" asked Craig.

"Depends," said Loomis, and settled the Rolls in the outside lane of the highway, where it whispered along at an unvaried 69.5 mph. Behind it the Astin Martins, Mercedeses, Ferraris, and Jaguars lined up in frantic procession. Loomis ignored them all.

"You cut up a bit rough this afternoon," he said. "Belting a woman."

"You wouldn't have lasted three rounds with her," said Craig.

"Wouldn't want to," replied Loomis. "Then you had to go and start a massacre in a café."

"I was supposed to be massacred," Craig said. "They had coshes and razors and lumps of lead pipe."

"You broke Fat Arthur's arm. How big was he?"

"About your size," said Craig.

Loomis looked at him, carefully and long, and the Rolls went on all by itself.

"You're getting cheeky," he said. "Don't get cheeky."

"I like to know what's going on," said Craig.

But Loomis knew that Craig functioned best on an unrelieved diet of frustration.

"Tell me what you found out," Loomis said.

They had, of course, no knowledge of anything when Craig first questioned them in the interrogation room at Bow Street. The game had broken up at five that morning, Driver had been a big winner, and they'd all gone home. None of them had seen Driver again. Then somebody had tipped Fat Arthur off that Craig had murdered Driver and was with the body. The call, Arthur insisted, had been anonymous. He had collected the other two and he, the most improbable Sir Galahad of all, charged to the rescue. Or at any rate tried. Craig had then beaten him unconscious, and that had been all. His alibi—a small, loud, drunken shrew who had despised him enough to marry him—was unshakable. So were those of his allies. The crone who had gone downstairs minutes before Craig knew nothing except that there was one man left unhung.

Craig had persisted, and had learned many things. Brodski owned most of the café, and Arthur was afraid of him; Brodski had disliked Driver intensely but had not banned him from the game; there was no address at which Brodski could be reached when his club shut down. Craig had also been intrigued by the fact that Fat Arthur knew he had fought a woman and had attacked him before he had seen Driver's body. The urge to avenge a friend must have been overwhelming. Fat Arthur and his friends denied, over and over, that Brodski had made the phone call. Craig knew they lied. He left them while Millington was intoning the litany of assault with a deadly weapon, and went back to the strip club.

Brodski had gone, and nobody, least of all Jennifer, knew where to reach him. The telephone number he had left was that of an answering service, and the answering service regretted that they could never, never divulge that kind of thing on the phone. Craig telephoned Millington and told him to check on that angle, then bought more champagne for Karen, Tempest, and Maxine. When Harry served them his hands were shaking so badly that he couldn't get the cork out of the bottle. Craig did it for him.

"O-o-o you are nervous tonight, sweetie," said Tempest.

"You've heard, haven't you, luscious?" said Maxine, and Harry bolted back to the bar.

"Heard what?" asked Craig.

"The way you beat up Fat Arthur," said Maxine. "It's all over the parish."

"What d'you do it for?" Tempest asked.

"He puts saccharin in his coffee," said Craig.

"They say you killed Tony Driver, too," said Karen. She didn't seem worried by this, merely interested.

"I found him dead," said Craig. "I was looking for a poker game."

Karen put an arm round his shoulders, and looked into his eyes. Her fingers massaged the back of Craig's neck, and her eyes were large and limpid. She had drunk a lot of champagne.

"You're not a copper, darling, are you?" she asked. "I couldn't bear it if you were a copper."

Craig said: "I'm a collector."

"What do you collect?" Tempest asked.

"Money," said Craig.

"Oh how super," said Maxine.

He had told them then that he had come to collect some from Brodski, and they loved him more than ever, because they were wary of Brodski, who, they were sure, was as normal as a man could be, and yet never, never failed to show them, with extreme courtesy, how little he needed them. Unfortunately, they knew nothing more about him except that he paid them well and made no demands. Driver had at least made an effort. He'd invited them to a party at his flat. But he'd been broke, so they hadn't gone. But Karen had written his address down somewhere—on her bra, she thought. She looked, and Harry yawned, and Craig sweated, and there it was. He'd had a hard time getting away.

All Driver had carried, apart from his wallet, was a key, and Craig took that to a little street in Belgravia. The key opened the door, and Craig went inside at once, cat-footed warily, but all the small, neat rooms held was emptiness and silence. The house was small and unobtrusive, built in single tiers like a layer cake, bedroom on dining room on kitchen, bath and loo on living room. And all anonymous and noncommittal, rented by the month from a retired major in the Blues, according to the rent book. The house showed little evidence of Driver's ever having been there, apart from his clothes. The clothes interested Craig: they were all bought at Simpson's in Piccadilly, and none of them looked old; in fact, they looked as if they had all been bought at the same time. Craig searched on. Two empty suitcases, an empty grip, an empty Pan Am flightbag. He looked beneath the bed, in the trap beneath the washbasin, the toilet tank, the bath tank. Nothing. Driver was no more than seven suits, five pairs of slacks, six pairs of shoes, and some expensive cashmere. And then he found it, beneath the bottom shelf of the wardrobe—a fiberglass briefcase with the most effective locks Craig had ever seen. He smashed them open at last with a wrought-iron lampstand. Inside the case were a Walther P38 with a three-inch barrel, a thousand pounds in one-pound notes, four twenty-dollar bills that matched the one Loomis had given him, and five decks of playing cards with the seals unbroken. Craig broke them. Every pack of cards was marked.

He emptied the briefcase, then attacked it again with the lampstand, bringing it down with all his strength on the case's lid and container. They

cracked eventually, and Craig probed into the
cracks with a carving knife, his hands careful and
precise. The container yielded nothing except four
clips of bullets for the Walther. Craig pocketed
them, and the weapon: a Walther was always a reliable gun. The lid held an I.O.U. from Fat Arthur
to Driver for one thousand pounds, a Swiss
passport in the name of Dumont, and a German
passport made out to Donner. Both the passport
photographs were of Driver. Craig thought he
must like the letter D.

* * *

"Driver's suitcase was made in Germany," said
Loomis, and for some reason he slowed down to
run parallel with a hearse that was moving at twenty miles an hour. Anguished squeals of brakes behind him proclaimed that other drivers too were
showing their last respects.

"So were his handkerchiefs," said Loomis, and
removed his hat, a battered unconquerable bowler.
"Know what?" He looked at Craig, and accelerated craftily. The Rolls reached a speed of 69.5
mph again, and the Ferrari behind almost stalled.

"The playing cards were made in Germany,
too," Loomis said. "You could win at anything
with those cards. Naughty." He drove on, then
added: "We never found Brodski. He's done a
bunk." More driving, while he scowled at the Ferrari, now visible again in his rear-view mirror.

"Think he killed Driver?" Loomis asked.

"Brodski? For a dud twenty-dollar bill?"

"It could be just for that," said Loomis.

"Brodski chased Driver for one bad debt—
chased him and killed him?"

"Not quite," Loomis said. "The way I see it, Driver was chasing Brodski—only he got too close."

"You think Driver had something on Brodski? And the twenty-dollar bill was a way of letting him know?"

"Didn't you say he'd lost money just before he went to Brodski's club, and two days later he paid up?"

"That's right," said Craig. "So Driver double-crossed his bosses."

"Ah," said Loomis. "I wonder if his bosses were Krauts?"

"It's possible," said Craig.

"It is indeed," said Loomis dreamily. "It's even possible he belongs to the West German Defense of Constitution."

"Driver was an agent?"

"Not a very good one," said Loomis. "He died."

Craig had met operators from the Defense of Constitution before. They did counterintelligence work, and did it well. Hard, arrogant, efficient as Deutschmarks, all four hundred of them. Mostly they stayed in West Germany and hunted foreign spies, particularly Russians. Sometimes they went further afield. Driver had gone too far.

"Where do they come in?" asked Craig. "Those Defense of Constitution boys don't like to get too far from home. They play too rough."

"They got one sacred symbol, you see," Loomis said. "Like a cow to a Brahmin, like Mecca to an Arab, that's the Deutschmark to a West German."

"Money," said Craig. "This case is all money. Dollars and Deutschmarks."

"At least they've chosen the good stuff," said Loomis.

They parked in the VIP car area, and boarded their Comet with minutes to spare. Loomis had insisted on traveling first class, and finished the champagne lunch to the last crumb and the last drop. His passport declared him to be a business executive. He talked all the way of golf, electrical appliances, and the total absence of good tea in Paris. Craig, also a business executive, confined himself to agreement. He knew that he was junior to Loomis. They landed at Orly Airport to find a warm spring day and a pale-blue Citröen. The English driver came over to them, shook hands with them, and took them at once to the car. Inside it, on the back seat, were two parcels: one squat, square and heavy, the other flexible and shapeless. The driver immediately pulled away and got onto the highway to Paris, and Loomis fretted about how the rest of the world drives on the wrong side of the road. Craig put the two parcels into his raincoat pockets; soon they stopped at a café. Craig went at once to the toilet, locked the door of his stall, and removed his raincoat and jacket, then quickly untied his parcels. The flexible one was a holster of black leather, the hard one a Smith and Wesson Chief's Special with a two-inch barrel—the right gun for the job, not all that accurate over too great a distance but a stopper. If you got hit with that you didn't get up. Craig put his jacket and coat back on, stuck the wrapping paper in the gun's box and then the box in his pocket, flushed the toilet, and went out, cutting short the clamors of the woman at the door with a half-franc borrowed from the driver. He drank the coffee Loomis ordered for him, and they drove on into springtime Paris, with the chestnut trees and the Eiffel Tower, and the Arc de Triomphe, the Invalides, and the biggest traffic jams in Europe. But at last they reached the Madeleine, walked around the corner to the Thomas Cook offices, and bought two tickets to Versailles.

They went there in a bus, a big Facel Vega with a sunshine roof and its full complement of tourists. Loomis chose a seat in the middle and put Craig next to the window, then peered past him dutifully as the guide called out the place names all had paid so much to see. At last, when even the television center had been passed and there was nothing more to look at, Loomis spoke softly to Craig.

"He asked for Versailles," Loomis said. "Bloody culture snob. Could have had a nice bit of lunch at the Tour d'Argent. God knows he can afford it."

"Who?" asked Craig.

"Chelichev," said Loomis.

Chelichev was head of the Executive Division of the KGB—the Committee for State Security. Before Beria's death he had headed the GRU, which is Army Intelligence, but after that colossal shakeup he had been transferred, and now he was the only military man in a nonmilitary organization. He held the rank of lieutenant-general. "He rarely leaves Russia." Craig said so.

"He goes when he has to," said Loomis. "Like me. We got something he wants, so he comes to France."

"Not England?"

"He doesn't want it that bad," said Loomis.

"Anyway, he's probably got a deal on with the Frenchies as well."

"What about?" Craig asked.

"Morocco," said Loomis. He would say no more.

They drove on to Versailles, and listened while the guide reeled off facts and figures, lagging behind as the group trudged through stateroom after stateroom; they wondered what it must have been like before the mob smashed its way in and took the gold away. By the time they reached the Hall of Mirrors, they were alone, and Chelichev was waiting for them.

He was a tall man with silvery hair and blue eyes, dressed in light, elegant tweeds like a Frenchman's idea of an officer in the guards. The briefcase he carried was like the extension of his hand. His face was leathery, handsome, and very masculine. To the inexpert, he might have been a male model who specialized in whisky ads; to Craig, he was an expert who specialized in death. With him he had one man, tall, thick-muscled, with cautious eyes and hands conspicuously displayed in front of him, as Craig's were. Craig knew all about that man as soon as he saw him. He was looking at himself.

The moves that followed were as formal as a ballet. The two pairs of men advanced from opposite ends of the great room, and after ten paces Craig and the thick-muscled man turned and walked to the windows in the embrasures that overlooked the canal, turned again and, each unseen by the other, watched their principals meet, fall in side by side and patrol the room, Loomis with his tall, square bowler rammed down hard on his head, Chelichev swinging his briefcase. Chelichev seemed to do most of the talking. From time to time Loomis spoke. Usually it was a monosyllable, and he seemed to be enjoying it. The Russian's face was impassive, but his arguments never stopped. At last Loomis seemed to agree, and Chelichev's arguments ceased. The two men walked back to the center of the room, then each crossed to the embrasure where his man was waiting. Loomis's face glistened with sweat, but he kept his hat on.

Their tour group came back, and they went out again, back to Paris, invulnerably embedded in humanity. The Citröen waited for them in the Place de la Madeleine, and drove them back to Orly Airport. At the last moment, Craig took out the Smith and Wesson, unstrapped the holster, and left them both in the box and wrapping they came in.

"Tidy," said Loomis.

Craig had no idea who bodyguarded them at the airport or on the plane. They were the best Loomis had and hence invisible. Once more they talked of golf, electrical appliances, and the total absence of good coffee in London, until they were through Customs, out of the Europa building, and inside Loomis's car.

Craig said: "That briefcase Chelichev carried. He's got you on tape."

"Ah," said Loomis, and carefully removed his hat, wiped his sweating forehead. Inside the hat's high dome was a tape recorder.

"Made it myself," said Loomis. "Bit of a hobby."

One enormous finger stabbed into the hat with a

forceful accuracy that was entirely Loomis, and Craig tried not to think of Freud, as a tiny motor whirred, and first Chelichev's voice spoke; then Loomis'. Both men talked in German.

"His idea," Loomis said. "Seemed to think it was funny. Matter of fact it was."

His driving on the way back to Queen Anne's Gate was atrocious.

* * *

The two men studied transcripts of the taped conversation, and the text of Chelichev's speech was at first a raging anger. The typewritten words burned on the page. And yet, Craig remembered, Chelichev himself had given no sign of anger; had never looked other than reasonably, gently persuasive while he blasted Loomis with one threat after another, demanding Calvet back, and Loomis, equally gentle, had said no. Chelichev had shifted then, as their images had blurred from one mirror to another, Craig remembered. If they couldn't have Calvet back, they wanted him dead, and again Loomis said no. Loomis was being impossibly difficult, Chelichev had said, but never mind. He'd go further. Department K didn't have to do it. All Loomis need do was set Calvet up and Chelichev would arrange the death himself, and Loomis had asked why.

Chelichev had sworn then for thirty seconds, and in a foreign language, and Loomis had interrupted him. First he explained the old English custom of tit for tat—of Jean-Luc Calvet for James Soong. No one was allowed to come into his parish and knock people off. Not even a man he respected as much as General Chelichev. And to Craig's amazement the Russian had apologized. Chelichev said he realized how unprofessional it was, but he had no choice. And besides, even if Loomis didn't realize it, he, Chelichev, had been doing Loomis a favor.

"He enjoyed that bit," said Loomis. "That's all he bloody did enjoy."

Craig read on. Loomis now knew why Soong had been murdered, though the reasons for this had been omitted from Craig's transcript. The reasons had come from Calvet, that much was clear, and even clearer was Chelichev's unsatisfied desire to know what had made Calvet talk. There followed a lengthy interval of bargaining over an unspecified job Chelichev wanted done, and what Loomis was to get in return; then both men assured each other that nothing must be done to alarm the Germans or the French, and there Craig's transcript ended.

"You're being cryptic again," said Craig.

"Can't help it," said Loomis. "I've got orders, too."

"Do they allow you to tell me what all this bargaining's about?"

"The Chinese are building rockets," said Loomis. "The Russkies know where they're going to be sited. If we do them this little favor they'll tell us. Useful that."

"This little favor," said Craig. "You did say 'we'?"

"More 'you,' really," said Loomis. "I'm too fat —and too important."

"Mind telling me what it is?"

"Of course," said Loomis. "You're going to help them rob a bank." He would say no more.

7

When they went to visit Calvet, Craig insisted that he drive, and this time Loomis agreed. There were things it was necessary to know about Craig, things that no amount of questioning would reveal, things that never reached the cold pale eyes. Craig was beyond everything a physical man; the key to his state of mind lay in the way he handled his body. His embarrassment at having to hit Jennifer, for example: that was good. But on the debit side—the great car whispered its way along the North Circular Road, then exploded into power as it reached the A.1—on that side things were not as they should be, not at all as they should be. George Allen, for instance. Craig had been right to handle him as he did, but need he have used quite so much gusto? And in the matter of Fat Arthur, too, there had been more than a little overenthusiasm. It was not nice, Loomis conceded, to be threatened by fat men with lead pipes and thin men with coshes and razors. But then Craig was the best karate man in Europe, perhaps the best in the world outside Japan. His black belt Loomis knew all about, but what dan he held was a secret. Even Hakagawa, the

Japanese judoka who had taught him in London,
would only say that Craig was better than he was—
and he was a third dan in karate. For Craig, each
hand, each foot, was a deadly weapon. He could,
quite literally, kill with one finger. What use was
lead pipe against that? And he had broken Fat
Arthur's arm, quickly and surely, as one snaps a
dry stick, for no other reason than that he disliked
him. Loomis contemplated the fact that, like
Frankenstein, he had created a monster. In Japan
there were a handful of men who could kill Craig.
Someday, maybe soon, one of them might have
to.

The Mark X sliced past the family saloons as
speedometer and tachometer needles revolved. A
sign that said "ROUNDABOUT. REDUCE SPEED
NOW" went by in a blur. Loomis lay back in the
front seat, squat as a frog, and at the last possible
second Craig eased on the brake and the big car
squealed its outraged protest, circling the roundabout, while a man in a saloon, with his wife beside
him and three kids in the back, stood on his brakes,
inches from the Jaguar, swore once, then turned
green. Craig's foot swiveled back to the ac-
celerator. He said nothing, and Loomis thought
how useful his monster was, and wondered when
the monstrosity would outweigh the usefulness.

"You're not supposed to kill me, son," said
Loomis.

"I never do," said Craig, "or anybody else. Unless you tell me."

He left the A.1 then, and idled through
Hertfordshire, pastel bright in the spring sunshine,
through winding, leafy lanes as sentimental as

calendar pictures, until he reached the nursing home.

It had once been a country house of modest dimensions, and its conversion had been thorough and discreet. The lodge gate was a sheet of steel, the lodge itself of solid stone, with tiny windows. The men inside it were armed, and safe from anything smaller than a tank. The house walls were of smooth stone, without footholds and ten feet high. Electrified wire and barbed wire topped the walls: the angle irons that held them in position each contained the photoelectric cells of an alarm system. From a shed near the house came the hum of a generator: the nursing home had its own power supply. Among the elegant parterres of the flowerbeds were plastic mines. The place was what it was supposed to be—impregnable.

Loomis showed himself at the window, the gate swung open, and Craig drove in. As he did so, he knew he was held in a crossfire, knew too that a pack of dogs watched him, ready to attack if he got out of the car before he reached the portico of the house. By the time they'd reached the house, the doors were open. They could see no people in the hall, but they were there all right. And the dogs. The doors shut behind them.

"Wetherly's been looking after Calvet," said Loomis. "Done a lovely job. Matt Chinn's here too."

Wetherly was a psychiatrist who belonged, body and soul, to Department K. His security classification was as high as Loomis's. It had to be: from time to time he examined everyone in the department, from Loomis down. But Sir Matthew Chinn

was different; he was a civilian psychiatric specialist of such eminence that the rich had to pay his
weight in diamonds to obtain a visit.

"He's been having a look at Grierson," said
Loomis. "After we've finished I want him to look
at you."

He marched toward a door labeled "Group Psy-
chotherapy." As he did so Craig's hand gripped his
arm, and for all his weight Loomis had to turn to
him.

"I'm not going crazy," said Craig. "I just like my
job." Then he hesitated, looked almost puzzled.
"Maybe that's crazy," he said.

* * *

Calvet was waiting with Wetherly. The brooding
Slav look Craig remembered had gone, and now he
was full of life, with a hypermanic's impatience
when nothing was happening. As they watched, he
arranged a table and four chairs, laid out scribbling
pads and pencils, then turned to Wetherly with a
contented sigh.

"We're all ready, I think," he said.

Wetherly, a bland, Pickwickian cherub, beamed
at him, and Calvet sat down.

"You've met Craig before," said Wetherly.
Calvet nodded, not looking at Craig.

"What's he on?" asked Craig.

Calvet scowled, and rapped on the table with his
pencil.

"I'm not deaf," he said.

"Now, now," said Wetherly. "Craig can't help
the way he is. None of us can."

"That's true," Calvet said. The pencil continued
to tap.

"Jean-Luc's on pentathol from time to time," Wetherly said. "He likes it."

"It makes me tell the truth," said Calvet. "That's what I like."

"By the way, he's always Calvet now. Jean-Luc Calvet. Jean-Luc to his friends. There isn't any Dovzhenko."

"Dovzhenko's dead," said Calvet, and the pencil tapped on in the same broken rhythm.

"Morse code," said Wetherly. "Listen."

The pencil said "F-R-E-E" over and over.

"That's how I feel all the time," said Calvet, then his glance moved to Craig, and he snapped the pencil in two, stood up, and walked over to him. Craig moved slightly, his feet apart, weight evenly balanced, hands open by his sides. It was the beginning of the karate ritual. He should bow then, and utter the apologetic words that were also a warning: "I come to you with empty hands." He did neither.

"You killed Dovzhenko," Jean-Luc said.

Loomis growled: "Look, son," and Wetherly touched his arm. He was smiling.

"I'm very glad you did," said Calvet. "You set Calvet free." He slapped Craig on the shoulder and turned to the table.

"Come on," he said. "We've got work to do."

They sat round the table: four men who might be meditating the possibility of a little slam in spades.

"He knows about James Soong," said Loomis. It was like hauling the keystone out of a dam. Jean-Luc foamed words, and the others listened, as Craig took notes.

Soong had once belonged to Chinese Internal

Security, starting with the Tiger Beaters, the men and women who specialized in the detection of deviationists and bourgeois. From there he had been transferred, because of his exceptional promise, to the group called Wrong Thoughts Corrected, a counterintelligence unit that specialized in the surveillance of Russia. He had been one of the last students there before the split, and had arranged the death of S. I. Lemkov, Russia's leading expert on Chinese affairs. From Russia he had gone to Tunisia, then to Morocco, where he had become aware of Russian efforts to find him. (The KGB's Executive Division had put Soong's death, preferably after interrogation, as a matter of top priority. It had been an agent of Calvet-Dovzhenko's who had found him in Tangier.) He disappeared from Morocco, and another KGB man, doing what amounted to a regulation checkup of Calder Hall, had spotted him in Keswick. The need for interrogation had passed by then; the Executive Division had therefore killed him.

"The Russians do not like their opposition to get away with murder," said Calvet. "Personally I find this unrealistic."

"What was Soong doing in Keswick?" Loomis asked.

"Waiting," said Calvet, then frowned. "I was coming to that. Just listen and I'll explain everything. There is no need to interrupt."

Loomis muttered and was still, like a volcano not ready to erupt, and Calvet talked on, oblivious.

Wrong Thoughts Corrected had recently made a deal with another anti-Russian group, this time working from Europe. Its headquarters was in

London, but they had thriving agencies in Paris, West Berlin, and Warsaw. This group was known as BC, which stood for Bourgeois-Capitalist. The KGB as yet had no knowledge of its chief members, but they did know three things: one, that it had access to a great deal of information that made Russia look foolish or hateful to the outside world; two, that it had interfered, by murder or sabotage, in projects that Russia valued highly as influencing foreign opinion; and three, that it banked in Tangier.

Craig said: "Two questions."

Calvet turned red at once, and began to yell about paying attention.

"I killed Dovzhenko for you," said Craig. "The least you can do is listen."

Calvet said: "Of course. I'm sorry," and smiled. When he smiled he looked innocent and young.

"What sort of projects did they sabotage?" asked Craig.

"Space shots," said Calvet. "Two Russian men have died in space. They think the BC had a hand in it."

Loomis sighed, a vast rumble of anger and dismay.

"Why bank in Morocco?" asked Craig. "It's hard to get the money out."

"Not for them," answered Calvet. "They have friends in Morocco. Powerful friends."

He went on talking. The bank was the Crédit Labonne in Tangier. There was something about British newspapers, but he didn't know what. The trouble was that the KGB had only captured one BC operator, and he'd had a weak heart. He'd died before they could find out the names they needed. The Russians were always in too great a hurry, their methods lacked refinement.

"They don't understand," Calvet said. "To be really thorough, one must be gentle."

He smiled at Wetherly, the young, innocent smile, and Wetherly beamed back. Suddenly the smile faded, and Calvet began to talk in Russian. Then the words too faded, and he burst into tears. Wetherly bustled to him like a tubby ward sister, and Calvet clung to him and sobbed.

"Out," said Wetherly. "You've got the lot."

In the room labeled "Matron" Loomis and Craig sat and waited for Sir Matthew Chinn. Loomis looked at Craig, big, wary, and patient as ever, but oblivious to anything that didn't threaten him. When Calvet looked nasty, Craig was ready; when he wept, Craig ignored him.

"Crédit Labonne. That's a bad one. I used to have an account there," said Craig.

"I know," said Loomis.

"Who's going to help me?"

"Later," said Loomis. "You've got to see Matt Chinn now, and I want to think about newspapers."

"Calvet said he didn't know—"

"Then I'll have to think. I hate thinking," said Loomis. "Makes me hungry."

Sir Matthew Chinn was a small Napoleonic man with a head that projected from his shoulders like an acquisitive bird's—a herring gull, say, or a jackdaw. He looked like a man who couldn't remember when he had last been wrong. Craig spent three hours with him, and at the end of it they went to the room where Grierson lay, eyes looking straight ahead, fingers busy with his piece of string. Chinn studied him intently, as if he were a fascinating but quite hopeless problem in chess, then Craig looked at him too, politely, because Chinn expected it. Grierson gave no sign that he knew they were there.

"He's quite helpless," Sir Matthew said. "Can't even control his bowels sometimes."

Craig said nothing.

Sir Matthew permitted himself a small flash of temper.

"Sooner stink than remember, I suppose," he said.

Craig said: "I'd better be off."

"Just a minute," said Sir Matthew. "I want you to tell me what happened just before he got like that."

"You know."

"I want you to tell me."

"We had to kill a man," said Craig. "He had a bodyguard—we had to kill them as well. To get at him. It wasn't easy. I needed a gun that would scare them. I got a twenty-gauge riot gun. That's a shotgun with a sawed-off barrel. The Yanks use riot guns, but not twenty-gauge ones."

"Why not?"

"You have to get close," said Craig. "When you do—if I fired one at you now it would just about cut you in half." He looked at Grierson, still fumbling his string, and said: "I made a mistake in giving him that."

"You did?"

"He wasn't up to it," said Craig. "He killed two

blokes with it, and wounded another—he lost his arm. But then Grierson went funny. I should have used that riot gun myself."

8

"Killing's just a job to him," said Sir Matthew. "Like digging ditches."

Loomis lay back in his chintz-covered chair, watching an early bee bump among a vase of roses.

"Where d'you leave him?" he asked.

"He's waiting in the car."

"He nearly crashed today," said Loomis.

"I know. He told me. Your nervousness amused him. He likes risks."

"I don't," said Loomis, "but I have to take them."

"With him?"

"You tell me."

"For the moment he's a reasonable risk," Sir Matthew said. "He's not a psychopathic murderer in the usual sense."

"Cut out the codology," said Loomis.

"He won't kill unless there's risk to himself," said Sir Matthew.

"Even now?"

Sir Matthew nodded. "At one time he had a love-hate for that kind of killing—it disgusted him, but it exhilarated him, too."

"Like sex to a vicar," said Loomis.

"The established clergy have their own problems," Sir Matthew said. "Most of them are too poor to afford me. Craig is no longer aware of this love-hate when he kills."

"Why not?"

"He's killed too often," Sir Matthew said.

"I made him."

"I didn't say that."

"You didn't have to. Look, I need Craig, d'you see?"

"I do indeed."

"Is it safe to use him?"

"For a while, yes, if you must," said Sir Matthew. "He's good at it, you know, and he's still got it under control."

"And one day he won't?"

"That's very possible. He's no longer aware of his love-hatred for killing, but it's stronger than ever. One day he won't wait for you to find his targets."

"How long?"

"He'd better see me in three months," said Sir Matthew, and stalked to the door, then he turned around. Loomis was surprised to see that his face expressed emotion. The emotion was malice.

"I should make a note of it, Loomis," said Sir Matthew. "One fact is overwhelmingly clear. Once Craig rejects your authority, his first target is obvious."

"Who?" Loomis asked.

"You," said Chinn.

*　*　*

Mrs. McNab brought in more newspapers, and Craig groaned aloud. The room held a couple of thousand already.

"These are the last," said Mrs. McNab. Craig grunted. "Any orders, sir?"

"Keep reading," said Craig.

If Mrs. McNab had not been a lady, she would have groaned too.

They were looking for news items on Russia: copy that knocked the country. Vanishing Sputniks, failure of five-year plans, plane crashes, the defeat of Moscow Dynamo, reputed sex changes in Russian women athletes. Anything that made Russia look bad. There was plenty of it. Craig and Mrs. McNab read of riots in Azerbaijan, attempted kidnapping of defecting diplomats in Sydney, denunciations of poets in Leningrad, towns that changed their names as one after the other of the giant idols—Trotsky, Kamenev, Stalin, Khrushchev—crashed. Carefully they noted the date and the edition of each paper that ran each story. Russian claims to have invented everything from the telephone to the airplane; political theorizing that ruined a wheat crop; drunks and the jet set and the man who made a fortune bootlegging the records of Louis Armstrong, until long before the end it seemed to Craig that only two kinds of people existed: the Russians, who did stupid things, and the rest of the world, who watched. Craig gathered up a pile of foolscap and went to the door.

"You needn't wait," he told Mrs. McNab. "It's almost teatime anyway."

"Very good, sir," said Mrs. McNab.

The time was 8:30. She hated him more than ever.

Loomis seemed to have devoured even more papers in even less time. The room was littered with them. He'd simply hurled them away when he'd finished with them, to make room for more. He sat now before an enormous plate on which was a roast chicken stuffed with truffles. The remains of a sole mornay had been pushed aside, a wedge of Stilton lay waiting. With it he drank a Château Lafite.

"I told you," he grunted. "Thinking makes me hungry. Want a drink?"

"Please," said Craig.

"Find a glass then," said Loomis.

Craig found a teacup, and Loomis shuddered.

"See a pattern?" he asked.

Craig sipped, and nodded, then looked at his sheaf of foolscap.

"*Daily News*, Glasgow *Evening Messenger*, Yorkshire *Mercury*, *Woman's Ways*, and *In*," he read.

"*Woman's Ways? In?*" asked Loomis.

"All the newspapers belong to Salvation Press," Craig said. "They do *Woman's Ways*, and *In* as well."

"*In?*"

"It's a groovy trend setter," Craig said expressionlessly. "The mag that shows you tomorrow's world today. It doesn't like Russia either. Nor does *Woman's Ways*."

"You're not just a pretty face are you?" said Loomis. "That's the way I worked it out as well. Salvation Press is always first with the Russian stuff. Ahead of the *Mail* and *Express* even. And it prints stuff the others don't even bother with."

"That's right," said Craig, and drained his teacup.

"They got a tip-off," said Loomis. "They must have. There's too much coincidence, d'you see? I think that's what Calvet was on about."

"Yes," said Craig. "Nice wine, this."

Loomis grunted and pushed the bottle infinitesimally toward Craig, who filled his cup.

"There's something else," he said. Loomis grunted again. "Salvation Press is run by a bloke called Simmons," said Craig. "C. G. Simmons. He owns Midland Television, too."

"That so?" said Loomis, and chuckled.

"He's got a daughter," Craig said. "Jane. She was with the walking party who saw Soong die."

"Bit o' luck, that," Loomis said. "Linton reckons she was sweet on you."

"You have plans for me?"

"You need a bit of a breather," said Loomis. "Country air. Wholesome food." He speared a mouthful of chicken and truffles. "Surrey. That's the place."

"Where Simmons lives?"

"Ahh," said Loomis. "Go down there and chat her up a bit. See if you can meet her pa."

"What's my cover?" Craig asked. "She knows I'm on to the Soong business."

"Foreign Office," said Loomis. "Far East Department. They had you up there in case Red China got irritated. I'll let you have the papers tomorrow." He chuckled. "Oh son," he said, "I've waited for years to see you in a bowler hat."

"I thought I was going to rob a bank," said Craig.

"That comes later," said Loomis. "When you get help."

"I'd rather pick my own," Craig said, but Loomis shook his head.

"That's out," he said. "Pity. But it'll keep anyway. This Simmons person—pretty, is she?"

"Very."

"Twenty," Loomis said. "And rich. Very rich. Only child, too. Her father dotes on her. And she's daft enough to dote on you. Use that."

"All right," said Craig.

"I give you a free hand," Loomis said. "Do what you like, tell her what you like—only find out where her father gets his Russian news from. And, son, she's young, she'll be looking for glamour. You'd better make yourself—" he sought, found, triumphantly produced the word—"dishy."

* * *

Simmons fiddled deftly with the toy theater, and the curtains parted. It was a lush and Edwardian theater, all red plush and heavy gilt. It reminded Brodski of the millionaires' whorehouse his uncle had described visiting in Moscow in 1911. Brodski's uncle had been a man who had enjoyed life to the very last. That had been in Cracow in 1946, as far as Brodski had been able to discover. An Uzbek infantryman had got him with a bayonet ... Simmons began to arrange cutout figures on the stage: tiny nude models of women, with remarkable fidelity to detail.

Brodski asked: "Is this my new floor show?"

"Good God no," said Simmons. "It's far too good for Nuderama. This is for a party at my place."

He maneuvered the chorus line into place: eight

girls in picture hats. They wore nothing except boots.

"Extraordinary how much more naked they look with their hats on," he said.

Brodski sighed.

"I do not like your parties," he said.

"I do," said Simmons. "They're works of art. A chance for me to be creative. Besides, BC needs a party." Brodski still looked sullen. "Look," said Simmons, "we've done very well so far. You've had the contacts and I've had the money. The security's been just about perfect, because you've stayed here and run the club and the contacts have come to you. They come here and they get paid C.O.D.—every time. We're reliable. We pay big money for big jobs." He looked round Brodski's office. "And a strip club's been the perfect cover, so far. But we're moving on to something bigger still."

Brodski said: "I'm delighted to hear it."

"That's why Jane had to contact Soong," said Simmons. "We're going to mess up a moon shot, Brodski."

He arranged another figure in Edwardian costume in front of the chorus line.

"She should sing one of those inane music-hall songs while she strips," said Simmons.

Brodski said: "A moon shot? How?"

"Soong had a contact for us. I can get it from elsewhere. That part's all right. But it'll cost money. Big money." He pulled delicately on strings attached to the figure; her costume came off. "A million," he said. "I haven't got a million. That's why I need the party."

"You have no money?"

"None. I have newspapers and magazines and a television company. But I don't have money. Not now. BC got the lot."

"You have been very generous—"

"I've done what I have to do. Russia must be hurt. We know that. So far I've spent a million and a half on that very purpose. And you have risked your life many times. We've both given what we had. But for this job we need more." He stared at the tiny stage, and let the curtains fall. "We need Airlie," he said. "He has a million to spare, and he wants to marry Jane. He is also an idealist—he wants to fight the Russians. Good. He's also young and hot-blooded. He likes women. Even better. We can appeal to him on two levels, Brodski. Idealism and blackmail."

"I do not like to blackmail a gentleman," said Brodski.

"Nor I, but it must be done. There's no other way," said Simmons.

"There's Medani. He has money."

"No," said Simmons. "Medani's father has money. In Morocco. He can't get it out. Anyway, we need Medani in Morocco, to fight the Russians there. He's a good Mohammedan—and a nobleman. His father's a very powerful man. If the time comes he could start a holy war."

Brodski said: "We have money in Morocco, too."

Simmons stared at him for a moment, then began to laugh.

"So we have," he said. "But are we really justified in spending it?"

Brodski began to talk about ethics, and Simmons grew bored. He let his mind drift away back to the old days, in Yugoslavia, up in the mountains. Tito's men had been doctrinaire and tiresome, but he'd met a group that had worked with Mihajlović. Guerrillas who fought because fighting was what men were for, fighting and drinking and women. For three months his life had been a wide-screen epic. But in the end he'd been recalled and his men had been betrayed. Not to the Germans, to the Russians. The men, and the woman Simmons adored. When Simmons got back he learned that even heroes could die, and die horribly. The woman had died most horribly of all. Since that time sex had been something to be exploited in others, nothing more. Love was something else again—love was what a man had for his daughter. It was just as well, he thought, that his wife had fallen off that damn horse.

Brodski stopped talking and Simmons said quickly: "Aren't you forgetting what the Russians did to you? Tell me about your brother."

Slowly, reluctantly at first, Brodski told him, then as the story went on the words came faster. Torture, agony, betrayal, death—for Brodski's brother, his wife, his father, his uncle. On and on went the story, and always it was the Russians who were responsible. The Russians. The Russians. The Russians. Simmons began to relax. Brodski was going to be all right. He had learned to hate almost as well as Simmons himself. And anyway, it was time to get him out of the country.

* * *

Craig pondered the need for dishiness; unquestionably it existed. Girls like Jane Simmons had everything. To achieve novelty with them was an impossibility. Next morning he asked Mrs. McNab about it, but Mrs. McNab was still angry. She would talk only of Grierson and how irresistible he was because he was a gentleman. Craig could never be a gentleman and knew it. But he could buy a dark suit, a Royal Navy tie, a black briefcase, an umbrella, and—from Scott's—a bowler hat. He had never owned an umbrella or bowler hat before. The thought amused him. He'd owned part of a tramp-shipping line, a V8 Bristol, a vast assortment of firearms, a house in Northumberland, a small Greek island, even a slave. But not a bowler. The one he bought delighted him: it had a low crown and a narrow brim, and made him, he thought, elegant but respectable. Mrs. McNab thought it made him look like a bookmaker. Loomis said it was exactly right.

"They take all kinds of fellas in the Foreign Office nowadays," he said. "Here're your papers." He handed Craig the special passport, the pass, the visitor's card, the necessary files that some genius had spent the night preparing. Craig worked through them slowly, carefully, and Loomis glowed approval and lit a vile cigar.

"You'll have to use your own name," he said. "Doesn't matter if Simmons rings up about you. We'll have the call rerouted here." He leaned back, looked at Craig, six feet four from the soles of his Lobb shoes to the crown of his bowler.

"You went into the Foreign Office from the navy," he said. "You weren't at public school. You're classless. A New Man."

"That's right," said Craig.

"But you're still in the F.O.," said Loomis. "Don't hit anybody." Craig grinned. "You figured out how you're going to be dishy?"

"I always am," said Craig.

Already he'd gone over in his mind his two previous meetings with Jane Simmons, and the answer was obvious. Jane Simmons was attracted to him because she was afraid of him. She'd sensed the power in him, and the danger, and they had frightened her. She'd never been frightened before. That was all the novelty he had, but it might be enough.

He drove his Mark X back to Regent's Park, locked it in the garage, then took his suitcase, briefcase, and umbrella and got on a bus, then took the tube. He got off the tube at Piccadilly, then darted back on again at the last possible moment. He was almost certain that no one was following him, but if they were, that trick nearly always worked, even if the man following had been trained by Department K. For Loomis sometimes had his own people followed; Loomis had at all times to be sure, and Craig, while he could see no harm in this, felt almost shy of Loomis's hearing about his latest possession. It lived in a little mews garage in Knightsbridge, a glistening, scarlet success symbol that had nothing at all to do with rolled umbrellas and bowler hats: a twelve-cylinder, 4.5-liter Lamborghini Miura, with a top speed of 180 miles an hour, ample room for two and no room at all for three. Five thousand pounds of his own money, and the only thing left for which he could feel any affection. The Lamborghini was as efficient as he was, its lines, like his own, dictated by the end for which it was created. But it was also a splendid thing to own. Expensive, illogical, flamboyant, and splendid. It made him happy. He got in, tossed the bowler hat behind him, and turned the key. The engine exploded into life, then modulated at once into the most superb of all mechanical sounds, the whisper of perfectly controlled power. Craig eased her out into the mews, locked the garage, then set off for Surrey. The best part. Where even the temperature of the rain is thermostatically controlled.

Simmons had quite a lot of space in *Who's Who*. Educated at Rugby and Magdalene College, Cambridge, only son of Reverend Percy and Mrs. Dora Simmons. Married Lady Jane Manners (deceased), oldest daughter of the Earl of Worthing. Clubs: White's, Athenaeum; hobbies listed as various. Age forty-five. Christian names Christopher Galahad. *Who's Who* didn't say that he owned a national daily, a national Sunday, seventeen provincial newspapers, three magazines, a television station, and a small but growing paperback publishing firm. But he did. It didn't say that during the war he had fought in the Balkans with various unorthodox units and won a D.S.O. But he had. It didn't say that he was worth seven million pounds. But he was. Craig opened out the Miura as he reached the Surrey road and wondered what a millionaire seven times over meant when he said his hobbies were various. Doubtless he would find out.

He'd heard already how he had made his money. That had started with his father. The Rev. Percy Simmons had been an unabashed hell-fire Baptist during the earlier part of his life. His visions of hell, described graphically and at length, had drawn enormous crowds three times every Sunday. That was in the 1880's, when hell still smelled of sulfur and northern congregations knew how to groan. A jobbing printer had approached the young, brazen-tongued reverend with the idea of printing his sermons, and a great career was born. The minister found he had another talent, another duty, besides that of preparing devout and quivering Yorkshiremen for the imminence of hell. He could publish—and prepare—the whole world, or at least that part of it which could read the English language. He started with *The Bible Weekly*, then a Christian daily, *The Good News*, then *The Christian Woman's Companion*, which was to evolve, gradually but remorselessly, into *Woman's Way*, weekly net average six million. There was a period when the Reverend Simmons founded three publications a year, and a lot of them crashed, but the ones that stuck did very good business indeed.

When World War I came, Simmons combined religion with patriotism, and his readers in the trenches found that his vision of hell was by no means exaggerated. After that war, the Christianity slowly but surely diminished but the patriotism stuck. Simmons gloried in his Englishness, and persuaded a lot of other people to glory in it too. It was what God had set him to do, and it paid a six per cent dividend. In 1921 at the age of sixty, he'd made a million and discovered he had no one to share it with, so he married a lady missionary who bore him Christopher Galahad (the latter name was her idea; she read a lot of Tennyson) and died when the child was three. Christopher had been sent to public school and Cambridge, though his old man had prayed at him for a solid hour every day of every vacation. He'd been destined to help his father when he was twenty-one, but the war stopped that. After five terms at Cambridge, at the age of nineteen, he became a cadet at Sandhurst. By 1942, on his twenty-first birthday, he was on a mission to Tito in Yugoslavia. When the war ended he was twenty-five, with the substantive rank of major. He never went back to the university, though they gave him an honorary doctorate after he built them a new college; instead, he went to help his father, then eighty-four, who was running the firm on an unrelieved diet of Union Jacks and brimstone. The old man dropped dead quite suddenly in the late summer of 1945—Loomis said it was because Labour won the election.

Christopher Galahad took over at once as chairman of the company, and within a year was managing director too. He had all of his father's canniness and drive, and a shrewdness for handling nicely calculated odds that slithering about the Balkans two jumps ahead of the Gestapo had honed to a very fine edge indeed. He was Britain's leading expert on the technique of making money out of the printed and spoken word. In 1946 he married the daughter of a sporting peer, and she promptly bore him a daughter, then died on the hunting field when the child was six months old. He never went near a place of worship.

9

Craig fumbled his way among the houses of the fairly rich—"two minutes from station, superior view"—to the stone-walled estates of the very rich indeed. Here the road spiraled gently around the curves of the downs, and copses and spinneys of firs were a black drama of lances against a blue pastel sky. Here the grass was short and plentiful, apt for the hooves of superior horses, and villages hid their lack of wealth discreetly, between folds of the smooth, expensive hills. The Lamborghini became more and more the right car to be driving; a Bentley would have been cowardly.

He found the place at last. About four miles of flintstone wall, pierced by lodge gates with a pretty eighteenth-century cottage at the side. He slowed as he turned into the gates, but the lodgekeeper took one look at the car and waved him on, through a mile of elm trees to a house designed during Queen Anne's reign by a pupil of Christopher Wren; a plain, neat rectangle of a house, flanked by identical wings, its brick faded to an enduring rose, its portico unpretentious, its chimney stacks slim and austere—a house entirely beautiful because of the perfection of its proportions. He drove on to a graveled area, flanked by barbered lawn, and heard the whoosh of stones beneath his racing tires. Five other cars stood on the graveled area: two Rolls Royces, a Mercedes 800, a Ferrari, and a little Alfa-Romeo; there was plenty of room for the Lamborghini.

Craig retrieved his bowler, settled it at the right angle, then took up his briefcase and umbrella. It was time to pay his respects to Mammon. As he slammed the Lamborghini's door the whole scene seemed to freeze; himself with a ten-guinea bowler standing beside a five-thousand-pound automobile, with a quarter of a million pound's real estate as background. It looked like a whisky ad in a Sunday supplement. And then he remembered the night when he and his father had been out in the coble and the mackerel had run with the crazy death wish of which only mackerel are capable, so that the boat was heaped with the graceful shapes of fish, urgent even in death, that the moonlight had turned to a pale-winking silver, and his father's voice had said: "There's a fortune here, Jackie lad. A fortune." And he'd been able to do no more than nod, he was so bone-weary, but when they reached the little Tyneside port, every fish had had to be gutted and boxed and packed in ice. Then his father had had to carry him home on his shoulders, and he felt so marvelous—tired as he was—it was like riding between the stars. His father's share of the fortune had been four pounds thirteen and ninepence—and mackerel for a week.

The memory came sharp and clear, and Craig dismissed it, erasing it from his mind like a sponge erases the writing from a blackboard. That kind of thing took your mind from the job in hand; it made you vulnerable. He walked across the gravel toward the broad, shallow flight of steps that led to the house, and already a man was there, waiting for him. Craig felt a swift flash of disgust with himself; if he hadn't been standing daydreaming he'd have been ready for this man, instead of being watched by him.

He was a man to be ready for: taller than Craig's six feet, wide-shouldered, barrel-chested, but with an economy of movement that made Craig think of a mountaineer he had known in Crete. There was the same combination of tremendous strength and physical control. This man wore striped gray trousers, a short black coat, a black-and-silver tie. His face was round but without weakness, the cheekbones set rather high, the eyes very dark. A face rather Slav than Teuton, but without the usual free play of Slav emotion. It was the face of a man who would treat cruelty and kindness with equal indifference.

Craig said: "Miss Simmons, please."

The man said: "I will inquire, sir. What name shall I give?"

"John Craig."

He could have said: "Tell her we met in the Lake District. I inquired into the death of the Chinaman." Or even: "I've come to make further enquiries." But his name alone was better—if she remembered.

The butler opened the great half-door behind him and Craig walked into a hall floored in black and white marble, and furnished with the kind of wealth going shabby that only utter certainty of riches can afford. The picture over the mantelpiece needed cleaning, but it was by Van Dyck; the breakfront table had a scar on it, but Sheraton had made it. And the whole place was littered with coats, a fencing mask, two shotguns in a case, and a pile of *Woman's Way*. The wealth here was to be used. Craig sat in an armchair and looked at the shotguns as the butler moved away with the long, tireless stride that can keep going all day. The guns were a matched pair, their barrels chased in silver, but they looked bloody accurate, the balance exactly right. Money could buy you that, and every variation of it, but it couldn't teach you to hit the target. Money bought you butlers too, even this butler, who looked about as much in place here as a leopard would have. *He's in his early thirties,* Craig thought. *The absolute prime for a man like that, a man who'd seen a lot and done a lot more, till he knew there weren't many men he need be afraid of —and yet he moved cautiously just the same.* Craig looked around; the butler was walking toward him across the marble, and a cat would have made no more noise.

"I'm afraid Miss Simmons is unobtainable, sir," said the butler. "She and Mr. Simmons are in the paddock—if you wouldn't mind going out to join them, sir."

"All right," said Craig, and rose.

"Would you like to leave your umbrella, sir?"

"No," said Craig. "Just the briefcase."

He'd grown very fond of his umbrella.

"Very good, sir. This way, sir," the butler said. His face was quite expressionless, but Craig had the uneasy feeling that deep inside, where no one could reach him, the butler was laughing.

He led Craig into another room, with French windows opening on to a lawn and beyond the lawn a rose garden. Beyond the rose garden, he learned, was the paddock. Craig stepped out on to the lawn, and heard the windows click shut behind him. His feet moved soundlessly on the grass, and then he was enfolded in a great tunnel of roses, hundreds, thousands of them wreathed and entwined seven feet in the air, small and heavily scented, while great bush roses sprang from the ground to meet them, their beauty powerful, even arrogant. It was a set for a film by some clever Frenchman, and Craig detested it. It was like the flowers themselves, too slick, too contrived.

At the end of the garden was a brick wall, pierced by a latched door. Craig opened it and stepped into the paddock, shutting the door behind him. The paddock was L-shaped, and Craig found himself in the shorter arm of the L, his view of what lay around the corner obscured by the garden wall. He walked across the foot-high grass, and realized at once that the umbrella had been a mistake. So, for that matter, had the bowler. They didn't belong. No wonder the butler had been laughing where no one could hear him. Then he heard it. A rhythmic, loping sound, horses on heavy grass held to a hand gallop and cutting across that the sharper, more staccato noise of another heavy beast running. Craig looked for cover and there was none, and behind him only an unclimbable wall. Already he knew what he was going to face, and he had no time to prepare. It

shot round the corner of the paddock in a great
swerve of concentrated power, cat-footed for all its
size. A Hereford bull, half a ton on the hoof and
fighting mad, its black hide shining as if it had been
rubbed with oil, its horns ivory bright, questing for
a target. Craig stood very still. The bull slowed to
a walk and sniffed the breeze, the horns slowly
turned to hold him in their splayed-vee shape.
Then to Craig's astonishment a cowboy cantered
around the corner, a cowboy that Remington
might have painted, with plains shirt, ten-gallon
hat, neckerchief, jeans tucked in Mexican boots,
and a Colt .45 in a holster. He was riding a
palomino and swinging a rope. As Craig watched
the rope's loop spun out, seeking the bull's horns.
It missed, and the rope smacked the bull's face.
Without warning, with seemingly no instant between the cautious walk and incredible speed, the
bull put its head down and went for Craig.

To run was to invite being maimed at least; to
stand, unless one had taken lessons from El Cor-
dobés, was to die. Craig compromised by scram-
bling quickly to one side, then lashed out with the
weapon of ultimate respectability, the umbrella, as
the Hereford thundered past, aiming for the eyes,
but the brute hooked with its horns and Craig felt
as if he had been holding an umbrella that had
been struck by a train. His arm seemed to vibrate
in its socket and the umbrella, now V-shaped, spun
in the air like a boomerang, then stuck point down
in the grass as the bull skidded, swerved neatly, and
came in again, and again Craig swerved aside. This
time as it charged he snatched the bowler from his
head, and the man on the palomino, who had been

laughing, suddenly gasped aloud, for at the next charge of the bull Craig ran to meet it, swerved again, and struck with the bowler hat's hard edge. It spun up into the air, then impaled itself in ruin on the bull's right horn. The Hereford bellowed in agony, and the man on the palomino kneed the horse into action, rode up, and threw his rope. He was joined from nowhere by other cowboys, gaudy as butterflies. This time the rope flew accurately, settled round the small wicked horns, and the Hereford, still bellowing, was still. He'd been through it all before.

Craig walked to the angle of the L-shaped paddock, and found himself in what looked to be a film set. Ranch house, hardware store, and smithy, raised boardwalk, hitching rail, the Last Chance Saloon, sheriff's office, livery stable, even a Wells Fargo stage, with four horses poled up and a man riding shotgun. He was in the middle of a TV series, three-dimensional, life-size. Craig began to realize what a multi-millionaire meant when he described his hobbies as various.

He leaned against a hitching rail, and the quarterhorse tethered to it snorted, being in character. He discovered he was shaking. To a man on a horse, his encounter with the Hereford must have had a Keystone Cops quality; for him, on foot, it had held nothing but terror and, as always, terror had generated rage so that inevitably he had chosen to attack rather than submit, opting for astronomic odds rather than no odds at all, and again it had worked, because his speed and skill were as perfect as a human being's can be. But each time might be the last time, and his body shook with the knowledge of it. He began to breathe consciously, deliberately, in and out, timing his rhythm, so that when he heard the clop-clop of hooves on the dusty main street, he was relaxed, easy, and wary as a cat at Cruft's.

The group coming toward him might have been coming to rob the Dodge City bank. The man on the palomino came first, and near him was a slighter figure in a buffalo coat and white Stetson. Behind them more gaudy cowboys, among them a Mexican vaquero, his high-crowned hat slung back to his shoulders, his clothes and saddle glinting with jangling silver. The cowboy in the buffalo coat kneed the pony into a trot and swung up to him. The pony circled daintily, and Craig leaned back on the rail and looked up.

"Why howdy, Miss Jane," he said.

The girl looked down at him and marveled. All her life she had been told of the advantage of looking down on horseback at the peasantry. It was obvious that Craig had never shared her lessons. He looked as relaxed, as easy, as when he had given her dinner in Keswick. His mahogany-colored hair was unruffled; his shoes still shone; his pale eyes told her nothing at all. He filled her with a terror she still found quite delicious.

"I-I hope you're all right," she said.

"I'm fine," said Craig. "How's the bull?"

The man on the palomino came up in time to hear it, and laughed aloud.

"Daddy," said Jane, "this is Mr. Craig."

Simmons swung down from his horse and ground-tied it to the manner born. He strode over to Craig and held out his hand. Craig took it, and sensed the power in the man. Simmons was tall and lean and deadly, and Craig knew it at once.

"Welcome to the Lazy J," said Simmons. "The bull has a black eye but he'll live."

"That's nice," said Craig.

"I think so," Simmons said. "I paid five thousand pounds for him when he was a calf. Come and have a drink."

They walked down the boardwalk to the Last Chance, the batwing doors swung, and once again Craig found himself completely at home in surroundings that had been familiar since he'd first gone to the movies: the long bar, a barman with a Texan longhorn mustache, nude pictures behind the bar, and above them the mirror that reflected a roomful of rickety tables and chairs, a worn piano, and a tiny stage. At one of the tables a dude gambler dealt himself poker hands to keep in practice; at the piano the perfesser banged out a honky-tonk blues that suggested he had finished his musical education in a whorehouse—Mahogany Hall, New Orleans, say, about 1892.

The cowboys followed him; one of them was a lord known as Charlie, who was very much in love with Jane, the rest were rich and restless and young. Craig saw with no surprise at all that one of them was Arthur Hornsey. The vaquero was an Arab. His costume was the gaudiest of the lot, and he wore it with a lack of self-consciousness as complete as Simmons'.

"What'll it be, gents?" asked the barman.

"Whisky," said Craig, and the barman banged a bottle and two shot glasses in front of Simmons and himself. The others asked for beer, and the foaming glasses skidded down the bar to them. The vaquero and Jane drank sarsaparilla.

Simmons poured, and Craig and he touched glasses, then swallowed their drinks at a gulp. Craig noted with relief that it was Scotch, not red-eye. Simmons poured again, and this time saloon etiquette allowed a man to sip.

"I really am sorry about the bull," said Simmons. "That fool of a butler must have misunderstood what I told him. Caesar always goes for men on foot. He should have known that. These foreigners—"

"Ah," said Craig, as if everything had been made clear. "Foreign, is he?"

"Yugoslav. I met his father during the war," said Simmons. "Still—as long as you're all right?"

"I'm fine," said Craig, and turned to Jane. "It was you I came to see."

"Oh?" said Simmons.

"I'm from the Foreign Office," Craig said. "It's about that Chinaman—"

"That'll keep," Simmons said. "I've been waiting for weeks to play cowboys."

"It's urgent," said Craig. "I should get back to London."

"On Friday?" said Simmons. "The F.O.'ll be empty now. You must stay till Monday, my dear chap. I insist. Anyway, it'll give you more time to talk to Jane."

"Please stay," said Jane. "It's the least we can do after—"

Craig looked at the gambler clicking cards as the blues chords pounded their sorrow. This was the dream world the orphanage had shown him at strictly rationed intervals, the world where the cowboy climbed his horse and rode off to where there were no more problems. The world, it was obvious, that Jane loved to live in, and so he had no choice. He must live in it, too.

"It's awfully good of you," said Craig, talking Foreign Office.

"Glad to have you," said Simmons. "I'll lend you some kit."

So Craig too faced the world in a blue gingham shirt and denims, cowboy boots, and a black plains hat with a silver band. Simmons found him a gunbelt, too, a wide strip of leather polished black, with a cutaway holster and a pigging string to tie it to his thigh. Then he found him a gun in the sheriff's office, which was an armory of racked shotguns, Winchesters, and one enormous and terrifying Sharps buffalo rifle. The gun he chose was a rimfire Colt .45, picked, it seemed, at random from a collection that swung by their trigger guards from nails driven into the wall. Craig broke it, spun the magazine, snapped it together, and sighted along its six-inch barrel.

"Are we going to fire these things?" he asked, and Simmons nodded.

"Then I'd rather have that one," said Craig.

He picked out a Smith and Wesson .38, slimmer, more compact than the huge Colt .45, but far more accurate, with all the stopping power that anyone could need; the great-grandfather of the weapon Craig still used, longer in the barrel, heavier in the butt, yet still familiar. Simmons watched him check it, try its sight and weight, then thrust it into the holster.

"My men'll think you're a sissy," he said.

Craig pushed back his hat and stared at him gently.

"I hope not," he said, and his voice was so exactly the voice of the tall Texan who's a stranger in town that again Simmons laughed aloud.

"Come on," he said. "There's a lot to do before dark."

It never occurred to anyone to ask whether he could ride, but Craig took care to choose the oldest cow pony he could find in the remuda, and clung on grimly while the others galloped and swerved, threw and hog-tied bull calves, and roped a frantic longhorn that had cost Simmons a fortune in freightage. Then they rounded off the afternoon by holding up the Wells Fargo stage, killed the man riding shotgun with blank cartridges, then formed a posse (Simmons acting as sheriff) and arrested themselves. And throughout the whole crazy business, the Arab vaquero rode with a deadly skill that riveted Craig's attention: he was the most superb horseman he had ever seen, and Simmons was frantically trying to conceal his jealousy. To be good at what he undertook would never do for Simmons; he had to be superb. In his dealings with his daughter, for example, it wasn't enough that she should love him, she had to adore him. For the same reason he chased after Hamid Medani, time after time, and finished second. To Craig his good-natured laughter was as false as a whore's promise, but it wasn't his business, and he plugged on in the rear and left all the decisions to the horse, who was grateful for it.

At the end of the day, while the light still lasted,

they rode over to a walled area with a safety barrier that was a shooting range. The targets were the classic ones, tin cans, and by the time Craig arrived the others were blasting away, the .45's booming like cannon. Their kick was tremendous, and their impact, when they hit anything, reminded Craig of battering rams, but their lack of accuracy was appalling. Medani didn't hit a can once. Then it was Simmons's turn, and he was very good indeed, hitting the can four times out of five. (No one in his right mind leaves a shell in the chamber the hammer rests on.)

Simmons grinned, slapped Medani on the shoulder, and looked up at Craig.

"You and your sissy gun. Beat that, John," he said.

Craig went up to the barrier and wondered whether he should do as Simmons said. If he failed, Simmons would like him and that might be useful: if he beat him, Simmons might get angry, and an angry man can be very vulnerable indeed. Craig took the Smith and Wesson slowly, carefully from its holster, and the young men tittered, then stopped, ashamed. Rich, restless young men don't titter at those less fortunate then themselves. Craig ignored them, taking his time, settling his balance, the gun barrel pointed like a prosecutor's finger. The Smith and Wesson had a sharper bark than the Colt's smothered boom, and it cracked out five times in a steady rhythm of fire. The first shot cut low into the can, sending it spinning in the air; the other four kept it there, bouncing like a ball from shot to shot. When it fell, there were five holes clean through it. Behind Craig a young man whistled, and Medani touched his arm.

"I think you have done this before," he said.
"Eh Christopher?"

"You surprised me," said Simmons. "The Foreign Office has hidden talents."

"I used to shoot for the navy," said Craig, and it was true in a way. He had shot for the navy—all sorts of people.

Simmons said: "Let's change now. It'll be chow time soon."

Craig, Medani, and the rest of the young men changed in the bunkhouse. Simmons and his daughter went to the ranch house. The bunkhouse had showers and electric razors, and the broadcloth pants, white shirts, and string ties that cowboys wear on their night off. Craig stripped and changed with the others, then sat apart and began to clean the Smith and Wesson. Hornsey came up to him, watched the deft fingers busy with oil and rags.

"Nice to see you again, Mr. Craig," he said.

"Yes, indeed," said Craig. "How's Lancaster University?"

"I'm on leave of absence," Hornsey said. "I'm doing research into abnormal behavior patterns and their impact on conventional morality."

"You picked a good spot for it," said Craig.

"Here?" The idea delighted Hornsey. "I couldn't do it here. Jane invited me." He paused. "You're an awfully good shot."

"Thank you."

"Better than Jane's father." The idea seemed to amaze Hornsey.

"I cheated," said Craig. "I used a better gun."

His hands moved again, deft as a surgeon's, and the gun was assembled and back in its holster. The young lord known as Charlie came over.

"I'm Airlie," he said. "My friends call me Charlie." Craig nodded. "You were right to choose the Smith and Wesson. That Colt's a brute. You shoot a lot?"

"Not any more," said Craig. Not unless he had to.

"Pity," said Charlie. "You're bloody good at it." He looked round the bunkhouse. "Weird setup this place, isn't it?"

"It is," said Craig.

"I mean there's Hornsey, he's a don, and you're from the Foreign Office, and Ino there—he's a banker—and Richard's at the Bar, and Hamid—What the devil do you do, Hamid?"

"I'm a gentleman," Medani said. "I exist. Beautifully."

"Yes, well, and then there's me."

"And what do you do?" asked Craig.

"I'm a lieutenant in the Honourable Artillery Company," Charlie said.

"He's a lord, too," said Hornsey. "Seventh Earl of. Also he's a suitor." Craig looked puzzled. "For the hand of Jane," Hornsey explained. "He's 6 to 4 favorite. Comes of being an earl."

"It's not just that," said Charlie. "I'm rich, too, remember."

Hornsey threw a boot at him, and they wrestled together. Craig thought he was getting old. Medani came up to him, slim, graceful, very arrogant, and Craig thought of the Siamese cats rich women own, how pampered they are, and how pitiless.

"I wouldn't do that," Medani said, and smiled. "That is not existing beautifully."

"You do that best on a horse," said Craig, and Medani smiled like a lost angel. His skin was a very pale gold color, his eyes hazel, and his nose straight. In this he was Berber rather than Arab. Only the thick, glossy black hair suggested Arab blood—that and his pride. Craig decided to take a chance.

"What part of Morocco do you come from?" he asked in Arabic.

"Talouet," Medani said at once. Then he paused. "I see you are clever with people as well as guns, Mr. Craig. How did you know?"

Craig said: "The F.O. sent me on a mission to Morocco once, because I spoke Arabic." This was a lie. Craig's only mission to Morocco had been to work for himself, as a smuggler. He'd done well at it too, before Morocco became united, and respectable. "I met a lot of people who looked like you," he said. "Chiefs and the sons of chiefs."

That at least was true; only the ones he'd met had all been possessed by the same passion, for contemporary firearms in good working order. They'd trade anything for a Schmeisser machine gun or a Remington repeater: dates, olives, horses, girls, boys, even money, when they discovered that Craig would take nothing else. And the firearms were for use: against the French when things went right, against each other when the uneasy alliance between liberation movement and tribes broke down.

"My family used to own Talouet," Medani said. "We still do quite well there."

I bet you do, Craig thought. In the old days, before liberation, Morocco was as feudal as thirteenth-century England, and when a man said he owned a town he meant precisely that. He owned it—buildings, animals, and people.

"You like playing cowboys?" Craig asked.

"Adore it," answered Medani. "It gives me an idea of what it must have been like at home. I was only ten when we were liberated"—he pronounced the word in French, and it pulled his face into a sneer. "But this isn't all that far from it, you know."

Horses and guns, Craig thought. *That's all an Arab from the Rif or the Atlas can think of. When they get enough to make them happy they start a war, and then they're ecstatic.* He remembered seeing a band of El Glaoui's men in Rabat, just before the final crash of independence: Turbanned, white-robed, magnificently mounted, they'd spun and swirled their horses as Medani had done, playing cowboys. In their hands they'd carried incredible muzzle-loading muskets five feet long, inlaid with brass, with silver, even with gold. But these were playthings, used only for ceremonials and showing off. When it came to business they had repeating carbines.

"I wish the old days were back," said Medani, and Craig believed him.

They went out to eat then, to the inevitable barbecue, and Simmons was masterfully efficient among the steaks and chops, but it was other, lesser cowboys who served the potato chips, the salad, and the château-bottled claret. *One could strain after authenticity for just so long,* Craig gathered.

There were limits. Then two more cowboys appeared, and their faces were pale and they had trouble with their Stetsons. One of them held a guitar, the other a fiddle, and the fire blazed up in a shower of sparks behind them. They played hoedown music very well indeed, and the real cowboys took it in turns to dance with Jane, who was now the purty schoolmarm in blue-checked gingham. Simmons danced with her best of all, and grinned when the others applauded. Craig thought it best not to compete, and so did Medani.

"I was educated in Paris," he said, "but I cannot get used to this. It is bad for a man to dance with a woman. Much better to make the woman dance for him."

He began to speak then of the belly dancers of Marrakesh, and this took time. Craig listened with the respect that is every expert's due as Medani talked on, in Arabic, and Craig realized that sex also can make you homesick.

Simmons heard the swift, guttural sounds and came across to them, Jane beside him, flushed and adoring for her wonderful daddy. Medani had remembered an Egyptian he had once seen who seemed able to revolve in three directions at once. Craig hoped Jane didn't speak Arabic.

Simmons said: "So you speak Arabic, too?" He didn't seem very surprised.

"That's how I got into the F.O.," said Craig. "I took a course in the navy." *Well not a course, exactly,* he thought. *Her name had been Kamar; she had danced like Medani's Egyptian.*

"I hope we weren't being rude," Medani said.

"It was a pleasure to me to speak my own language."

"Not at all," said Simmons. "What were you talking about?"

Medani stiffened, then his glance went from Simmons to Jane like two cuts of a sword.

"We spoke of women," he said, "and the way they ought to dance."

Even by firelight Craig could see Simmons fighting to control his temper. When he finally succeeded he was sweating with the effort of it. At last he said: "How amusing for you."

Craig thought Simmons must need Medani very much; otherwise he would have killed him.

The fire burned low, and Simmons turned to whisper to his daughter. The young men stiffened in excitement as Jane smiled good night, then came across to Craig.

"Daddy says it's bedtime, Mr. Craig," she said. "So it's bedtime."

She held out her hand. It was a strong little hand, very sure of itself, but it trembled in his before she turned away and the skirts of her dress whispered over the grass.

Simmons watched her go, then winked at the others.

"Well, boys," he said, "let's take a look at the town."

10

They should have saddled up, Craig thought, and
ridden for miles over rolling grassland, whooping
like maniacs. Instead they walked—the saloon was
only a hundred yards away—but at least they did it
properly; in line, thumbs hooked in their gun belts,
before pushing the bat-wing doors aside.

The saloon glowed with the soft, warm light of
oil lamps, and the perfesser was still playing the
same solid blues. Almost at once two of the young
men were playing cards with the gambler, and the
rest of them were drinking steadily, except for Simmons. He seemed content to watch the others
drink, and walked round with the bottle, topping
up glasses. Medani still drank sarsaparilla, but
Craig let Simmons serve him once, then resisted.
Getting drunk was no part of his plans.

"Ah, come on, Craig," said Simmons. "I'm
Ganymede."

"I thought it was Galahad," said Craig.

"Ganymede was cupbearer to the gods," said
Simmons. "Don't you F.O. types know anything?"

"I know he was queer," said Craig, and Medani
giggled.

Simmons said: "You're right. I'd better stick to Galahad."

"Righter of wrongs," said Craig, "defender of distressed maidens, bulwark of civilization."

"Exactly," said Simmons. He wasn't laughing. "That's what being in the newspaper business is for. Righting wrongs. Defending civilization." He smiled. "That and the money."

"You didn't mention defending distressed maidens," said Charlie.

"How could I?" Simmons asked. "I've distressed a few myself. That reminds me—"

He nodded to the barman, who pressed a buzzer behind the bar. "What good is a saloon without dancing girls?" Simmons asked.

The perfesser moved in three clean chords from "I Thought I Heard Buddy Boldon Shout" to Offenbach, the curtains parted, and Craig was back in Nuderama, with Karen, Tempest, Maxine, eight supporting lovelies and all. But this time they were doing a can-can, and doing it well. Simmons must have been paying them a lot of money, he thought, but at least he got value for it. He glanced quickly at Simmons, as Karen crashed down in a split. On his face was the look of a man who was getting value for money.

After the can-can the show reverted to Nuderama all over again, but there were two differences. The apathy of the Soho show had gone completely. These were women to whom undressing was a prelude to making love, and an invitation aimed straight for the men at the bar. Look at me, each rich, swaying body said. I'm desirable. Admit you want me. And perhaps—who knows—I can be had. The creamy rose-tipped flesh yearned out toward the male with a frankness that could mean only one thing, and the men at the bar knew it. They knew, too, that they were still out West in the old days, because the clothes the girls removed were Edwardian. Craig had never realized before the erotic quality of corsets, frilly panties that reached to the knees, picture hats two feet across. But Simmons—or his choreographer—had. There was a scene in which Tempest, in a yellow muslin gown with a bustle, a straw hat, and parasol, sang "You Are My Honeysuckle," and she and the perfesser between them extricated all the sugared innocence the song contained. As she sang in a small, true, little-girl voice, Karen and Maxine appeared, dressed as French maids, all white starched caps and frilly skirts, and slowly stripped Tempest naked. As the smooth-rounded body appeared her innocence became an ecstasy of shame and as she struggled piteously against the encroaching hands that showed her to the eyes of men her voice still whispered the suggestive lyrics to the avid silence.

"You can't beat the old songs, eh Craig?" asked Simmons.

"Not the way they sing them," said Craig.

"Ah—dear girls aren't they?" Simmons said.

"Dear?"

Simmons laughed. "I like you," he said. "You've got a way of getting straight to the point without being obvious. No—when I said dear, I meant lovable."

"I see," said Craig. "Do you do this kind of thing often?"

"Not often, no," said Simmons. "This type of

show's a hobby of mine, you see. I like to arrange
one now and àgain, just to see how it works with
my young men. It looks as if they're enjoying it."

It did indeed, Craig thought. Eleven girls offered, like bones to dogs, to half a dozen rich
youngsters, one of whom was about to become engaged to his daughter. A man's hobbies couldn't be
much more various than that.

"Women are usually stupid and invariably expensive," said Simmons, "but they're worth it,
don't you think? Their effect on men is so amusing.
Just look."

He nodded at Charlie, who was staring at Maxine. What Maxine was doing reminded Craig of
Tangier all over again.

"It reminds me of my lost youth," said Simmons.

"I thought you spent that in the Balkans."

"Oh, I did," Simmons said. "Killing people for a
good cause. That's always been an interest of mine.
Just as well my mother had me christened
Galahad."

Then the curtain came down and he went off
with his bottle, pouring drinks. Craig set himself to
memorize the names of the men to whom he'd been
introduced. It would be as well to find out who
they were, what they did. It might even explain why
Simmons found it necessary to debauch them. And
it would upset Loomis. Loomis was a prude.

The girls made their entrance into the saloon
then, and Craig stayed well away from Hornsey.
Each girl wore a tight-fitting low-cut gown, black
stockings, and high-heeled shoes. They hadn't had
time to wear much else. Simmons was busy again,

with champagne this time, building an elaborate
fountain of goblets, then pouring the wine so that
it frothed down, spilling over from one glass to the
next, while the girls giggled and the men cheered,
and sweated for what they saw as Simmons took
the three stars of the show and introduced them to
one man after another. They came to Craig at last,
and their eyes were bright with the knowledge of
what they had done to men so much richer and
more powerful than they could ever be.

"Hello," said Tempest.

"Do you know Mr. Craig?" Simmons asked.

"No," said Craig. "I'm sure I'd have remembered seeing you ladies before."

"Didn't you ever visit our club then?" Maxine
asked.

"No," Craig said. "I wish I had. Where is it?"

"Nuderama's closed down for a bit," said
Karen. "We're on holiday. Pity you never saw us."

"Indeed it is," said Craig. Out of the corner of
his eye he could see Charlie coming over, with
Arthur Hornsey. Charlie was drunk.

"Well, anyway, you've seen us now, all of us,"
said Tempest, and took his arm.

"Pity you had to be so far away," said Craig,
and Karen giggled. Maxine said he was naughty,
and Tempest squeezed his arm muscle. Charlie
stood in front of them, his hand on Hornsey's
shoulder.

"That one's mine," he said to Craig.

Simmons said: "Now, Charlie. Don't start anything." He didn't mean it.

Charlie said again: "That's the one I want."

Craig felt the girl's hand tremble on his arm, but

she continued to smile, to hold back her shoulders so that Charlie could see the teasing promise of her breasts.

"I want you," Charlie said.

"You're pretty drunk, Charlie," said Craig.

Charlie let go of Hornsey, and lurched toward him. His coordination was still good.

"I liked you when I was sober, didn't I?" he said, and Craig nodded. "It doesn't make any difference. Ask anybody. They'll tell you. Ask Chris here—" He gestured at Simmons.

"Ask him what?" said Craig.

"What I'm like when I'm drunk."

"He's nasty," said Simmons. "Very nasty. And very strong."

"That's right," Charlie said. "There's plenty of other girls, Craig. Take one."

"The trouble is I like this one, too." He looked at Tempest. "You're not twins, are you, love?"

She was doing her best, but fear crept slyly over her face and she couldn't control it. She was pretty, with a promise of sexual expertise that couldn't fail to excite, but he didn't want to fight for her. She'd known what she was doing when she took Simmons's money, after all. On the other hand, Charlie seemed fairly determined that Craig would have to fight for her, and Simmons was making no move to stop him. Nor was Hornsey. He just stood and waited, like a man waiting for yet another treat in a night full of treats. He'd even turned to pick up his glass when Charlie struck the first blow.

It was a hard, looping right aimed at Craig's jaw. Craig swayed from it, and pushed Tempest from him. She tripped over Maxine and fell, her gown floating back to reveal the round whiteness of her thigh above her stocking. None of the men even looked; they were absorbed in the fight as Charlie leaped in again, feinted with a right, and landed a left to Craig's middle. Craig gasped, and moved back. Someone had taught this boy how to hit. Charlie threw another left, and Craig grabbed the fist, pulled, and swerved into a carefully controlled throw. After all, he didn't want to hurt Charlie. He was drunk. But drunk or not Charlie landed with a beautifully timed break fall, rolled over once, and got to his feet, circling around Craig, then leaped high into the air, legs curled up, parallel with the ground, until one leg straightened viciously, slamming at where Craig's face should have been in a karate kick, and Craig, ducking, felt the impact of a boot heel on his shoulder that sent him slithering back into a couple of the eight supporting lovelies, while pain trickled like acid into his upper arm.

Charlie landed neatly and aimed another blow at Craig, again a karate strike, a punch this time, the arm rigid behind the impact of hard muscle. Craig swirled aside just in time, and thought: *All right. All right, you noble bastard. So you're not drunk and you've learned a few tricks. All right.* Charlie tried another kick and Craig read in his face that it was coming. His body arched, his hands swept up from beneath him, and smacked on the boot's leather, forcing the leg up and over so that Charlie fell, awkwardly this time, no break fall, the body slamming on to the wooden floor. But he came up again almost at once and rushed Craig, taking the fight to him again, except that this time Craig moved in to meet him and Charlie's arms were still trying to put a lock round him when the edge of Craig's hand struck below his chin. The blow traveled six inches, and was clearly audible. This time when Charlie fell he didn't get up.

Craig bent over him and pulled the .45 from its holster, then began punching the shells from the magazine. Simmons came over to him, carrying a glass. This time Craig took it.

"Exactly," said Simmons. "To the victor the spoils. I trust I make myself clear?"

"You do," said Craig.

"After all, there always has to be a fight in the saloon. You played your part very well."

"Thanks," said Craig.

"I didn't know that you practiced karate."

"That was Charlie," said Craig. "I used jujitsu."

"You're very good at it."

"It keeps my weight down. I never thought it would do anything else," said Craig.

"Forgive me," said Simmons, "but will poor Charlie be unconscious for long?"

"He will unless somebody helps him," said Craig, and Simmons waved for the barman.

"Those shells are blank, you know," said Simmons.

"Five of them are. The sixth one was under the hammer," Craig said, and threw it over to Simmons, who caught it neatly.

"When that one came out of your back it would leave a hole the size of a teacup."

"Yes indeed. How very nasty," Simmons said. "Charlie must have overlooked it when we left the firing range. He really is very careless."

"Doubtless he'll learn in time," said Craig.

He went back to the party, that was minding its own business of propositioning women. Tempest sat alone at a table, repairing her damaged makeup.

"I suppose it's thank-you time," she said.

"There's no need," said Craig. "He asked for it. By the end I enjoyed giving it to him." He leaned toward her and spoke softly. "Anyway I should be saying thank you for keeping quiet."

"We like you," she said. "You're not like the other—"

She started to speak again, and Craig shook his head, as Simmons and the barman went by, carrying Charlie.

"You fixed him and I'm glad you did," said Tempest. "He would have hurt me."

"I doubt it," said Craig. "It was me he wanted to hurt." He stood up.

"You're not going?" Tempest said.

"It's late. I want some sleep," said Craig.

"Well, honey, we all do. But you can't leave me. Not now I'm here for you."

"For me specifically? Those were your orders?"

"No. He just said there'd be a fight. I was to go with the winner."

"Go where?"

"The feedstore," said Tempest. "Do you know where it is?"

"Yes," said Craig. "Come on."

They walked out, and Craig heard Simmons murmur "Bless you, my children." When they walked away, the party in the saloon sounded very loud indeed. Tempest shivered.

"He offered us a lot of money," she said. "Rehearsed us himself. Didn't even make a pass. Then he told us we had to sleep with somebody tonight or the deal's off. He must be queer."

"No," said Craig. "Just odd."

"Put your arm around me," Tempest said. "I'm cold."

His arm came round her and they walked down Main Street, the cowboy and the dancehall girl. Beneath the thin stuff of her gown he could feel her body's firmness moving under his fingers. She stopped and turned to him, and her mouth opened and flowered to his, her tongue fluttered, and his arms tightened round her.

"You're a hell of a strong bloke," she gasped, and pushed closer to him. "What are you up to?"

"Who's asking?" said Craig.

"Just me, honey. I'm nosy."

"I'm working for the Foreign Office," said Craig. "A Chinese citizen was murdered a few weeks ago and Simmons's daughter saw it happen. The Chinese People's Republic wants to know why —and I've been sent to ask if she knows. When I got here I had a fight with a bull and Simmons asked me to the party."

"Poor bloody bull," said Tempest. "I bet he lost."

"He didn't win," said Craig.

She kissed him again. "Let's go to the feed store," she said.

"I'd like that," said Craig.

He opened the door, and they went inside. Craig lowered the curtains and flicked his lighter, then showed the woman how to light the oil lamp. As it glowed, warm and soft, she looked around the room. It was furnished with a brash Victorian opulence: all gold-painted wood and scarlet drapes, and Cupids and Venuses in marble, and a huge reproduction of Etty's "Youth at the Prow."

"He certainly likes them to take their clothes off," said Tempest. "Do you suppose he gets his kicks out of watching?"

"I don't suppose anything any more," said Craig. "Two fights in one day, and now you."

She chuckled. "I've given in already," she said, and began to peel off her stockings. Her legs were beautiful, and she looked at them in frank affection.

"Nice, aren't they?" she said, and Craig nodded. "Help me off with this thing."

The gown was held together with hooks and eyes, and Craig fumbled happily, watching it open across her back, which was soft and smooth and gleaming in the lamplight, letting it slide to the floor. She stepped out of it with professional elegance, then turned to face him.

"Still nice?" she asked.

"Marvelous," said Craig.

"Worth a fight, maybe?"

"Two fights," said Craig, "and one of them with a bull."

As he pulled off his boots, she raised one hand to her head, rounding one firm, tender-nippled breast, letting her thick yellow hair fall down to her shoulders.

"I've let my hair down," she said. "That shows how much I like you."

Her fingers moved to his waist, and she unbuckled his belt.

"It's nice to strip somebody else for a change," said Tempest.

She made love with a demanding passion that was strong and beautiful, and without pretense. Her sophistication was a fact he knew all about, and she used it for his pleasure and her own, neither flaunting it nor hiding it, but being to the very fullest extent herself, healthy and beautiful and friendly, even when making love.

At last she said: "You really are strong, aren't you? I can always tell." And she slept neatly curled up against him.

When she woke up it was an hour later, and he was out of bed, his fingers gently exploring the wall as they had explored her. Skillful, careful fingers. She had kissed them, and her mouth had told her how hard and dangerous they could be. The little one on his left hand was broken. His whole body was scarred. They were his scars, and she loved them.

"What the hell are you looking for?" she asked.

"Wires," he said. "This room's got to be bugged."

"O-o- I hate bugs," said Tempest.

"You'll hate these, all right," said Craig.

They took some finding, but they were there. The wire recorder was two flat disks, let into the molding of plaster round the wall. Craig ran the wire back and played it through, and Tempest heard herself being loved. As the sounds came through she blushed an angry red and pulled the sheet up to her chin, and her shame was so deep she never noticed that Craig had possessed her in silence, and his words before their love-making were just words; polite and meaningless. Tempest hadn't time to think of this; her mind was pinned down on her shame. Then he found the video tape recorder. The camera lens was set in one of the splendid brass knobs of the bed, the tape ran down the brass pillar and curled on to the spool of the machine that had its own compartment in the enormous mattress. Sustained pressure on the bed set the camera going, and just in case one preferred love in the dark the machine had its own infrared bulb. Simmons thought of everything.

"Congratulations," said Craig. "Simmons just made you a filmstar."

She wanted to smash it there and then, but Craig wouldn't let her. Instead he took her nail file, and slowly, patiently made a tiny hole in the camera, then set the machine going again. That way Simmons couldn't be sure, and it would be as well to keep Simmons guessing.

"You going to say anything about this?" he asked.

She didn't answer. When he looked toward her he saw only a huddle of bedclothes. He cursed her inside his mind: this wasn't the time to have delicate feelings, but it seemed she had them anyway. What about the honeysuckle and the bee now? he thought. Or maybe that was just money. He went over to her, rubbed her shoulder.

"Hey," he said. "Hey look. This is me, remember? I was a filmstar, too."

His voice was gentle, soft, a friend's voice, and she looked up at last. She was crying.

"Put the light out," she said. "I look awful."

"No," said Craig. "You're beautiful, Tempest.

That's a bloody silly name."

His hand gripped the sheet and he began to pull it down. She clung to it.

"Who's side are you on?" Craig asked. "Yours or his?"

"My real name's Margaret," she said.

"That doesn't suit you either," said Craig.

His hand scooped beneath her neck and round her body, holding her. The woman struggled, and found it was no use. When she lay still at last, he pulled the sheet away and held her in his arms.

"That's better," said Craig, and she nodded. She was as helpless and obedient as a child.

Later she said: "I've been here twice before. He pays awfully well, and the blokes aren't bad. I suppose you think that's horrible?"

"You know what I think," said Craig, and she laughed.

"Only I never knew about the cameras and things," she said. "What's it for?"

"To give him a hold on people."

"Like you?" Craig nodded into her shoulder.

"But darling, why should he?"

The word "darling" almost made him wince. It wasn't a stage word; she meant it.

"People like me have information," he said. "That's useful when you run a newspaper. Tell me about the blokes you met here."

And she told him, not questioning his explanations. To her a rich man just took whatever he wanted, because he had money. That's what he had it for. Craig stroked her soft back, helping her to relax, and go on talking.

"You going to complain about this?" he asked.

"Brodski introduced us to him. He got us all together and made the proposition. Some of the girls said no at first. Then Jennifer came and talked to them alone."

"You know what happened?"

"No," said Tempest. "But they were scared of Jennifer. We all are. They said they'd go. Brodski didn't like it. He's a sweet man, really."

"Did Simmons have a hold on him?"

"He must have done," Tempest said. "You after Brodski too?"

"Yes," said Craig. "His passport's expired."

"I think he's in Morocco," said Tempest.

"Morocco?"

"I heard that Arab talking to Charlie, and he said the only other gentleman he knew was Polish and he lived in Morocco. Then Charlie said he'd do all right there because he'd kept a harem in London too. Then he looked at me. I'm sure he meant Brodski . . . Darling?" That bloody word again. "Is this helping you?"

"Very much," said Craig. "It'll all go in my report. No names. Just 'information received.' "

"You could use my name if you liked," said Tempest. "I don't mind. I'd do anything—"

You bitch. You stupid, stupid bitch. Why do you have to get involved with me?

11

The ranch-house door was open, and Craig knocked and went inside. Simmons and Jane sat at breakfast, he in city clothes, she in a yellow dress. He looked up and smiled as Craig entered. Craig wore the work outfit again, and twiddled his plains hat in front of him as a nervous cowboy should when he goes to meet the boss.

"Ah, Craig, you're up early," he said. "Sleep well?"

"The best sleep I've had in years," said Craig. "Thank you."

"I don't think we'll see the rest of the boys for hours yet," he said. "They got pretty drunk last night. You were wise to turn in early."

"I think so," said Craig.

She'd wept when he'd got up to leave her, made him take her address and telephone number, promise to come to the new show when it opened in a couple of weeks. The new show was interesting. She didn't even know who was financing it. It wouldn't hurt to find out. And so he'd been nice to her. . .

The butler served him eggs, bacon, and coffee.

Craig sat and watched the smooth assurance of his hands, the bland ease with which he stepped back, his job well done.

Craig turned to him.

"What do you say we go and have a walk around the bull?" he asked. "Just you and me."

"I'm very sorry about that, sir," the butler said.

"You should be," said Craig. "I didn't know Yugoslavs were so forgetful."

Simmons's hand moved briefly, and the butler left. The breakfast was delicious; when he'd finished Simmons said: "I've had your briefcase brought over. Perhaps we can go over the business with my daughter now."

"I have just a few questions," Craig said. "No need to keep you really."

"All the same I'd rather stay," said Simmons. "Can't trust you F.O. types."

Jane said: "Oh daddy," like a dutiful daughter, but her eyes were on Craig.

They sat by the window and watched the horses running in the paddock, playing at combat in the rich summer grass. Once more Craig took her over her story and Simmons listened as the answers came, now sure, now hesitant. He blinked as Craig mimicked the noises that the Russian killer had made, the Cantonese sing-song that told Comrade Soong he was going to die, and Jane nodded her agreement.

"What on earth is all this?" he asked. "Why is the F.O. involved?"

"We have reason to believe Soong was a spy," said Craig. "So were the chaps who killed him."

"I suppose that's secret information?"

"Oh, absolutely," said Craig. "As a matter of fact you never heard it. Neither did I."

"You're telling me a spy can come here and literally get away with murder?"

"Anybody can," said Craig, "if they've had the right training." He paused. "Charlie could."

"Charlie?" said Jane.

"He and Craig here had a fight last night," said Simmons. "It was all just cowboys."

"Who won?"

"Craig. It seems his hobby is jujitsu." Jane looked puzzled.

"That's judo with atimi-attacking blows," said Craig. "It's about the only defense against karate there is."

"Charlie used karate?"

"Oh yes. He seemed quite adept," Craig said. "It's just as well I kept up my jujitsu classes. The F.O. runs a very good club, you know."

"Do they teach you how to fight bulls, too?" asked Simmons.

"No," said Craig. "You have to find that out for yourself." He stood up. "You've really been awfully helpful—"

"Not at all," said Simmons. "I hope you catch them."

"Me, too," said Jane. "But you're not going, are you?"

She glowered at Simmons, who suddenly realized that Craig couldn't possibly leave. He had to go to town for a couple of days to see an editor, and Craig must and should stay on to entertain his daughter. He kissed her, said goodbye to Craig, and left. They sat and watched the palomino stud move like mercury across the meadow. Behind him two mares trotted, submissive. The girl looked at Craig. She realized that she had more than her fear of him to combat. With it there came a paralyzing shyness, and this also was new.

"I hope you and Charlie haven't quarreled for good," she said. "I rather like Charlie."

"I should hope so," said Craig, and she blushed, a sullen, unattractive red. She felt about fifteen years old.

"Daddy's sure I'm going to marry him," she said. "I'm not as sure as he is. Did you hurt him?"

"Not much," said Craig. "How's the bull?"

She giggled then, and felt more girlish than ever.

"He's still got a black eye," she said, and tried desperately to be the hostess once more.

"What would you like to do?" she asked.

"What about the others?" asked Craig.

"They never want to do anything after one of Daddy's parties."

"I've got a bull as well," said Craig. "Come and have a look."

They walked through the rose garden and into the house. The butler appeared at once, like a djinn from an uncorked bottle.

"Thank you, Zelko," said Jane. "We won't need you."

He bowed, and left, and Craig turned to her. "Zelko?" he asked.

"That's his first name really," said Jane. "His second name's Gabrilović or something. Far too complicated, Daddy says. So he's Zelko."

"Your father seems very fond of him."

"That boring old war," said Jane. "His father

and Daddy saved each others' lives all the time in
Yugoslavia. Let's look at your bull."

He showed her the Miura, and she was
enchanted. "You'd better make yourself dishy,"
Loomis had said, and the car was all it needed. She
adored everything about it, from the fighting bull
emblem to the comfort of the two vast seats that
nearly filled the car. Craig pressed the starter and
thought: *What quality did I value most when I was
twenty?* And the answer was rebellion, obviously.
At twenty one could not, would not conform. The
engine fired, roared once, then relapsed to its whisper of easy power. Craig decided to break some
laws.

Jane had been in E-types, Maseratis, Ferraris,
had driven and been driven at speed, but this time
the car, like the man, was new to her, and powerful
and frightening. She felt the threat of it as he drove
her back toward London, and the speedometer
flicked to seventy, and the engine purred, half-
asleep. At seventy the car made no effort at all; it
was waiting for the signal that would send it forward with a speed that makes the loping look like
stillness. And so it happened. Craig found the road
he was seeking, when two lanes swelled at last to
four, and his right foot moved smoothly, inex-
orably down. What followed was something she
had never known before—a ride in a high-perform-
ance car handled by a master. The road was quiet,
and the outside lane for the most part empty, so
that the car's speed soared from fifty to seventy to
a hundred and twenty, and the engine still whispered its song, contemptuous that the road would
allow no more as the little saloons flicked by on the

inside lane. Once she heard the sound of a police car and looked back, but the car was a white blur in the distance that dwindled into a dot.

"Don't worry," said Craig. "They were too far away to get the number."

"I'm glad," Jane said. "I hate policemen."

They came to a roundabout and Craig felt his way to the byroads that would take him back to Simmons's house. He was delighted with the Lamborghini. The fastest way to a girl's heart . . .

"Don't let's go home for lunch," said Jane.

So he drove again into the winding lanes, and she rejoiced that she had worn a yellow dress that could at least survive against the Lamborghini's triumphant scarlet. He found a pub that would do, low-shingled, deep-walled, authentic, with polished horse-brasses in the bar and a primly chintzed dining room. He bought her a gin and tonic, and bitter for himself. The barman looked at his workshirt and jeans, and visibly doubted his ability to pay. His amused contempt brushed off Craig like a feather off armor plating, and he offered her a cigarette, then took one himself.

"I like to get away sometimes like this," she said. "You've no idea how dull it can be, just sitting around in a period gem."

"I bet," said Craig, and stared at the barman, who was far too near, until the barman flushed, moved away, and began to polish an already sparkling glass.

"What do you do all day?" asked Craig.

"Well—entertaining for Daddy mostly. When he's at home. Otherwise it's just Charlie or something."

"Don't you go to London?"

"Sometimes," she said. "Daddy isn't awfully keen on it."

"He let you go on that walking tour."

"It was his idea," she said. "He thought I needed the exercise." She paused. "He does let me off the hook sometimes, you know. I'm not a prisoner exactly."

"Go where?"

She thought: *He's so hard he doesn't even recognize his own hardness. It's just a fact, like the way his eyes tell you nothing. Even now. And yet he must be interested, or he wouldn't ask.*

"Oh Ischia and Paris and Cannes and Mykonos," she said. "You know. The places one goes to. Holidays and all that. And he takes me away on business sometimes. I've been to West Berlin and Rabat—and Yugoslavia. We're going to Morocco again next year. Then to the States, if I'm a good girl."

"What does that mean?"

"Being true to Charlie," said Jane.

"Is it worth it?"

"I've never tried it," she said, "so I don't know. And I don't want to start now."

He looked down at her, and for a moment she could see emotion in his eyes, and in the way his mouth relaxed, but it vanished too quickly for her to read it, which was as well. Craig had begun to pity her, but he stopped himself well in time.

"Would you like to eat?" he asked, and she nodded, and moved toward the dining room. Craig looked toward the glass in the barman's hand.

"You go on like that and you'll break it," said

Craig. "You're too rough."

The barman polished the glass more viciously than ever. Its stem snapped.

"I told you," said Craig.

At the dining-room door a headwaiter met them, looked back at his impeccably dressed clientele, then at the two in the doorway once more. The girl was fine, almost too good, he thought. But the man . . . Craig read the look. "It's all right," he said. "I'm an eccentric millionaire."

"Indeed, sir?" said the headwaiter.

"Indeed," said Craig. "That's my car outside."

The headwaiter's eyes flicked once to the window, and the Lamborghini it framed, and he led them to a table, a good one, secure from eavesdroppers and with a view of the garden. His hand flicked away a *"Reserved"* sign as if it were an abomination and menus appeared in front of them like a trick with giant cards.

"You'll have to order all the expensive things now," said Jane, then blushed.

Craig laughed. "It really is my car," he said.

She ordered vegetable soup, roast beef and apple tart, was nervous about claret and settled for Burgundy.

"They're really very good here," she said, "and Daddy only likes French food, except when he's playing cowboys."

"Do you like playing cowboys, too?" he asked.

"Oh yes," she said viciously. "I like everything that Daddy does."

"Do you really?"

"I have to," she said. "If I didn't, he might not

leave me his money when he dies. He won't die for ages, either."

"He looks healthy enough," said Craig.

"You've no idea," said Jane, and another warning was stored in Craig's memory, as he began to talk to her about the places he had been to, and the wars he had seen. There was a violence to her that her father had given her, and she listened eagerly, scarcely noticing the food she had chosen so carefully.

When the coffee came she said: "You're very like Daddy." He was silent. "I meant that as a compliment, really."

"I thought you hated your father," said Craig.

"Just sometimes," she said. "He expects too much. That's where you're different. You never expect anything."

"So I'm never disappointed."

"Will you tell him—what I said?"

"No," said Craig.

"Why not? Because you like me?"

"Because I like you," he said.

"There," said Jane. "It didn't hurt to say it, did it? You know, maybe it's true. Maybe I do like everything Daddy does." Her knee rubbed firmly, insistently, demanded to be trapped between his.

"Those bloody dancing girls," said Jane. "Daddy thinks I don't know," she said. "That's stupid. He should have realized I'd find out."

"He didn't want to realize it," said Craig.

"I'm twenty," said Jane. "A woman. Daddy acts as if I'd been written by Hans Christian Andersen. His *pal*."

Craig stayed silent. Her knee was a restless stim-
ulus reminding him how pretty she was, and how
violent.

"You don't even care, do you?" said Jane, and
smiled. "I want you to make love to me, you
bastard. There. Does that satisfy your great big
masculine ego?"

Craig wondered what Loomis would say. First
Tempest, now Jane. And Loomis so prudish, and
so avid for information.

"It's nice to be asked," said Craig, "but there's
no need to be so rude about it. And stop saying
'bloody.' It spoils your image."

"I'm sorry," said Jane. "But you don't know
what it's like, do you? Being mixed up in something
you can't control, I mean. I bet that's never happened to you."

Craig said: "Why did you choose the café where
Soong worked?" and Jane scowled, disliking the
switch in conversation.

"We didn't," she said. "We just went there. It
looked nice."

Craig said: "Don't lie. It wastes time," and she
scowled again.

"All right, clever. You work it out," she said.

"Your father told you to go," said Craig. "He
wanted you to call on Soong. You had a message
for him."

The scowl vanished; amazement replaced it.

"It's not true," she said.

Craig said: "You're still wasting time."

She looked at his face, desiring more than ever
the deadly strength he masked so carefully.

"All right," she said. "He was going to be one of

Daddy's charities. All I had to do was tell him to ring Daddy at home. Someone had told him about Soong—he was very bright, you know—and Daddy thought he could use him."

"How?"

She shrugged. A very pretty movement.

"Daddy helps all sorts of people. Usually it makes him more money. But—" She looked puzzled again. "How did you know? Daddy doesn't like people to know about his charities. I got that mob to the café so that it looked—you know—just chance. I didn't tell Charlie or Arthur or anybody."

"Information received," said Craig. "Arthur a friend of yours?"

"He has to be. Daddy wants to collect him." The frown came back. "Please can we go now?"

"Where?" asked Craig.

"I know a place," she said. "On the coast. It's mine. Mummy left it to me. We can be back before dinner."

The Lamborghini whispered, and they skimmed to a deserted headland, clambered down rocks to a remote and private beach. No other cars, no boats, no trippers: just one sea gull fishing, screaming his unsuccess, and a beach hut that held nothing but blankets and towels, a bottle of Scotch and two glasses. Craig watched as the girl spread blankets on the sand, poured and gulped down three fingers of Scotch. She was smiling as she undressed, and there was a madness in the smile that reminded him of Simmons. She lay down on the blankets.

"You scare me," she said. "You know that, don't you?"

And later: "If my father were to find out, he'd kill you."

"Why me?" said Craig.

She wept then, and Craig put his arms about her, waiting. If you waited long enough, they always stopped crying.

"All right," she sobbed. "I've done it before. But not like this. This is different."

"How?" said Craig, and forced kindness into his voice.

"The others were younger than you—and not nearly so strong. You're stronger than Daddy."

The thought amazed her even as it delighted.

"I love you," she said.

What you mean is you hate Daddy, Craig thought, *and you've dealt him the ultimate hurt.* It would be as well to leave before Daddy got back.

The scars on his body fascinated her, even the broken finger. For Tempest they had been a source of suffering, since he had suffered, but for Jane they were a source of pride. He allowed her to touch them, caress them, willing his mind to forget the beatings, the knifing, the gunshot that had marked him where her hands explored. Instead he set himself to learn her secrets, and she talked freely, easily, her mind obsessed with the strength and power of the man who had possessed her, until he made love to her again: a box of chocolates for a good little girl. When they had done, he made her swim in the sea, and she gasped at its coldness that seemed to him only a word. He swam far out in an ugly, powerful crawl, letting the water chill away the effects of a love that had seemed neither clean nor dirty, merely necessary at the time. When he got back she was drying herself with a towel, her pretty body somehow pathetic even in its firm and shapely youth. He supposed that once he would have been moved to pity, to protect anyone as young as that. But that had been a long time ago.

They stayed out on the beach until evening, then Craig drove her back to the showpiece of a house and she went away from him at once, to play at flirtation with Charlie, even though her father was away. Craig went to lie down in the bunkhouse, to think what came next. Nuderama had gone, and the eight supporting lovelies; but he knew where to reach them. He had all the general information he needed on Charlie and his friends. And Hornsey. And maybe he knew where Brodski was too. It was time to get back to London, he thought. Sleep a while, shave, bathe, dine with Jane and Charlie— and perhaps learn a little more—then go to London and talk to Loomis. And maybe rob a bank in Morocco.

12

When he woke up he knew that something was wrong. He knew it immediately, as his eyes opened, so that he was already rolling away from the blow aimed at his head, and his hand lashed out above the blow; he felt bone give as Charlie fell. But there were two other men there, very good men indeed. He managed to throw Zelko, sprawl away from Simmons's kick so that it missed his stomach, caught him at the side of the knee. But he was limping after that, limping too much, and they attacked him from left and right together. He hit Zelko again, a sharp stab at the throat that brought the big man to a rigid halt, but he didn't fall, and the blow left him overexposed to Simmons, whose own blow came fast as a duelist's, the edge of the hand laid deftly against the line of his jaw. He fainted.

Zelko said: "A good man. Strong. Quick." His voice was a whisper.

Simmons said: "Almost too good." He bent to feel Craig's pulse, and smiled. "He'll live. For a while anyway."

Zelko rubbed his throat, then kicked Craig in the ribs.

"Not yet," said Simmons. "Look after poor Charlie."

Zelko bent over Charlie and picked him up, handling him as if he were a puppy. A bruise blossomed on Charlie's forehead like an orchid in rain.

"Poor Charlie," Simmons said. "He seems to have no luck at all with Craig, does he?"

Zelko said: "He has a lot to learn."

"He's learning," said Simmons. "Can you bring him around?"

Zelko said: "I think he needs a doctor."

"We'll see," said Simmons. "Put him out."

Zeiko carried Charlie to the feed store, then came back to Craig.

"This one won't need a doctor," he said.

He took piano wire from his pockets, put Craig's hands behind his back, twisted the wire round them. If it is done properly, there is no way in the world to get free from piano wire. Zelko did it properly. Then he began to slap Craig into consciousness.

Craig came round to a rhythmic repetition of pain. When his eyes opened, the slapping stopped, and he looked into Simmons's eyes, which were bright with expectation. Craig knew at once that he was going to be hurt.

"I didn't stay two days after all," he said. "You should have gone while you had the chance. What made you think I would?"

"Jane," said Craig.

"Jane knows so little about me," Simmons said. "Or about you, for that matter. She doesn't even know you're going to die when we've finished.

Your car will crash and burst into flames. No doubt the Foreign Office will miss you—even after I tell them you've had too much to drink. You do belong to the F.O., don't you?"

"Yes," said Craig.

"That's what they told me, when I finally got through. They lied of course." He paused. "They've all gone home now except Charlie, and we think you've given him concussion." Craig stayed silent. "It might be a good idea to yell," Simmons said. "It'll help you to get the pitch of the roof. You'll be doing a lot of yelling soon . . . No? But shouldn't you be indignant, old man? F.O. type attacked and tied up? Surely you should ask what it's all about?"

"What's it all about?" asked Craig.

Simmons stepped back and nodded, and Zelko began the beating.

He was thorough, and carefully trained, and the pain from the very beginning was intense, but it was apparent to Craig, before pain engulfed him, that he neither liked nor loathed what he was doing. It was just a job. To Simmons, it was a pleasure he did nothing to hide. That, and a sweet revenge. Until he fainted for the first time there was no attempt to ask him questions, merely the methodical application of pain to a body that had been schooled to resist pain as well as a human body can. Craig gasped at the blows that attacked his kidneys, his guts, over and over, gasped, then moaned, then cried out, but there was a part of his mind that hung on, so that when the questions came, and the blows that interspersed the questions, he still told the same story. He was from the

Foreign Office, he knew nothing about the men who killed Soong, he knew only that the People's Republic of China had protested.

Then the questions were about Simmons's daughter and what she had said to him about Simmons, and Craig swore, over and over, that she adored Simmons, because if he had denied that fact even for a moment he knew that Simmons would kill him, and Craig wasn't yet ready to die. Then more blows, and questions about Tempest, and what they had done together. Something about a camera. Craig remembered there had been a camera, but the part of his mind still immune to them said No, and he denied it. Simmons asked him again about his daughter, and the things he had done to Tempest—Had he done them to Jane? And Craig said No, No, No, and his voice was a scream as Zelko worked on the finger that had been broken once before till he fainted again.

When he came round he believed that he had won. Zelko was bathing his face, and making no attempt to hit him. Simmons had gone. Then Craig came further back into reality and realized that he was wired at chest and thighs to a heavy wooden chair, and that he was naked. When Simmons came back he carried a black metal box of a kind that Craig had been told about, a box for which the only antidote was a potassium cyanide pill. He knew then that what he had survived was only a foretaste. Knew, with absolute certainty, that he would tell them everything they needed to know.

"You know about this?" said Simmons, and Craig nodded. "The Germans invented it. They used it on Resistance people—the ones who swore they'd die before they'd give anything away. This always broke them. It's going to break you."

The box had two terminals and wire from them that ended in heavy clips. Craig winced as they snapped onto his flesh, then Simmons moved a pointer across a dial and there was nothing in the world but pain. Nothing at all. The sounds that came from his mouth were great, inhuman bellows, his body arched and kicked until the wire cut his skin. Then the dial moved back, and the pain receded to an agony only just bearable.

"Tell me about my daughter," Simmons said. "Tell me what you did to her."

But the last sane part of his mind flickered once more, before it died, and Craig knew that if he told one thing he would tell it all.

"Went for a drive," he groaned. "Had lunch. She told me she adored you."

"That's not what she told me," said Simmons. "I want the truth." Craig was silent.

"If I go on," said Simmons, "I'll make you impotent. I mean to go on."

He moved the dial again, and again Craig screamed, on and on in the agony that was his whole world.

At last Zelko said: "You'll kill him," and Simmons moved the dial back.

"Who sent you?" he asked, but Craig could only babble his agony, and the words he made were meaningless. Zelko smacked him across the face, four smashing slaps, and Craig was silent.

"Was it a man called Loomis?" Simmons asked. "From Department K? What does Loomis know about me? What does he know?"

And Craig could only think: "I can't die. I can't die, so I'm bound to tell."

This time he screamed before the dial moved.

Hornsey looked in at the window, and vomited once. The noise from inside hid the sound of his retchings. It was necessary to go in, and Hornsey doubted that he had the nerve. He looked at the Luger in his hand. Hand and gun were shaking. He closed his mind to everything but the gun, the way he had been taught, and the shaking died. Hornsey ducked beneath the window, reached the door. He knew exactly where Simmons and Zelko stood. He thought that if he missed, they would do the same to him and the thought almost defeated him. It had to be now. He pushed the door open and Zelko's hand went at once to his coat. Hornsey shot him dead. Simmons looked at him, frozen, and Hornsey yelled across Craig's screams: "Turn it off. Turn that bloody thing off."

Simmons didn't move and Hornsey rushed him, the gun barrel flashed, and Simmons fell. Hornsey looked at the dial; the machine was off. But Craig still screamed for almost a minute. When the screams died at last, he wept.

Hornsey untwisted the wire from Craig's chest and tied up Simmons, then was sick again at what he had to handle as he took the clips away from Craig. He looked at the dead Zelko, then turned back to Craig, and spoke to him softly, gently, and Craig said "Hornsey" and began to weep.

Hornsey said, "I'm sorry, Craig. I couldn't get back sooner. I had to let Loomis know."

Craig said "Loomis?" and the relief in his voice

was absolute, because now he could tell everything and still not betray.

* * *

The night bell buzzed on and on, demanding an answer, and the caretaker, tired or not, came awake completely, pulled on overalls on top of his pajamas, slid his feet into heavy-duty shoes. As he walked down the corridor he checked his Smith and Wesson; felt to make sure the knife was in place in the leg of his trousers. The spy-hole showed him an empty porch, but he opened the door warily, even so. There was nothing—the whole street was empty—nothing but an empty car at the curbside, a bright splash of scarlet that looked purple in the lamplight. The caretaker moved over to the car, and his steps were still wary. The passenger's seat was covered by a rug. The caretaker took the rug in his left hand, the Smith and Wesson rock-steady in his right. He pulled the rug away and jumped to one side, then looked down.

"Jesus," he said.

* * *

For once Wetherly forgot to smile. He sat facing Loomis across the great desk, Sir Matthew Chinn on his right, and his face was grave.

"The physical injuries are relatively minor," he said. "Two broken ribs, a dislocated fingerbone, considerable bruising, particularly in the area of the kidneys. That induced a slight incontinence, but we feel it can be cured." He glanced at Chinn, whose head came down in agreement like a pecking bird's. "He also had cuts across his chest and thighs. We think that these were made by the wire that was used to hold him down while they—" he paused.

"Get on with it," said Loomis.

"Exactly," Chinn said. "There is considerable burning of the testicles and penis, and minor burns on the right nipple. Craig was given a series of violent electric shocks."

"The agony must have been appalling," said Wetherly.

"It always is," said Loomis, and Chinn's head flicked toward him; Wetherly coughed as if in warning.

"Is he still a man?" Loomis asked.

"It's too early to say," Wetherly said. "He's a hell of a mess. These men were experts."

"Real experts?" Loomis asked.

"Experts' experts." Wetherly hesitated, then said: "He's not precisely sane yet, Loomis. He may never be sane again."

Loomis glowered at Chinn.

"I thought you told me he was going off anyway," he said.

"Not like this," said Chinn. "This may have altered the whole rhythm of the process. If you'd any idea what they did to him—"

"But I have," said Loomis, then added, "an idea. I want to know how it affects his mind."

"He'll be in pain for some days yet. We have him under strong sedation."

"Is that really necessary?"

"Essential," said Chinn. "We reduced the dosage this morning, and a nurse came to change his dressings. His left hand is bandaged. He almost killed her with his right. If Chinn and I had not been there—"

"He's extraordinarily strong," said Chinn, and shot his cuffs. One was crumpled.

"And fast," said Loomis. "And clever. Not fearless. Not even loonies are that crazy. But he thrives on fear. He needs it."

"He uses it," said Wetherly, "to drive himself. Or he did before this happened."

Loomis sat very still.

"Are you telling me he's finished?" he asked.

Wetherly shrugged. "I can't answer you yet. He's in shock. Deep shock. He's bound to be for several days. If we try to interfere with that he really will be finished."

"All right," Loomis growled.

"All we can go on so far is what comes out of his unconscious mind. He relives what Simmons did to him continuously. And of course he screams—"

"You're sure it's Simmons?"

"Sometimes he's a cowboy figure, a sort of Jesse James—sometimes he's a tycoon, but it's always Simmons. And a man called Zelko. And a girl. Jane. She's in the background somewhere. She betrayed him to Simmons."

"Simmons's daughter," said Loomis. "What a way to protect your daughter's honor—"

"There's a great deal of cowboy fantasy involved," said Wetherly. "Gun fights, stagecoach, saloon. All that. What happened to him may overlap a childhood fantasy."

"I doubt it," Chinn said. "The detail is too clear, and too consistent."

Loomis said impatiently: "You can sort that out

when he's conscious."

"There's one thing we may not be able to sort out," Chinn said. "He weeps, Loomis. Weeps all the time. His pillow is constantly wet with his tears."

"He tried to kill the nurse," Loomis said.

Wetherly said: "He wept even when he was doing that."

Loomis sighed, his pendulous cheeks inflating like balloons.

"It's a bloody nuisance," he said. "I need him. Need him badly."

"No doubt you have a job for him tonight," said Chinn.

"I have a job for him every night," said Loomis. "But I can wait a week."

Chinn looked at him as if he were a problem in chess.

"I didn't think it was possible for me to hate anyone any more," he said. "The nature of my work insulates me from"—his hand gestured—"all that. But I find you singularly repellent, Loomis. That man has suffered unbelievable agonies on your behalf. There is more than a chance that he did not betray you—"

"We're covered if he has," Loomis said.

"—and all you can think of is to subject him to the same risks once more."

Loomis said: "I need him. I need him to destroy Simmons. Because Simmons and his pals are making trouble for us with the Russkies. So far it's just middle-sized trouble—the kind that ends in iron curtains. But it could be big trouble in time. The biggest. The kind that ends in twenty-megaton bombs and Chinese commissars in Wigan. So I want to stop it now. And Craig's the best weapon I've got for it."

"What about this man Hornsey?" asked Chinn.

"What about him?"

"He rescued Craig," said Chinn. "Brought him back here. Craig loves him for it."

"You mean he's a fairy now?"

"I mean he's formed a strong emotional attachment based on gratitude. Emotional involvement has always been difficult for Craig."

"I wish it had been impossible," Loomis said. "What were you going to say about Hornsey?"

"Couldn't he do Craig's job?"

"No," said Loomis.

"But surely—"

"He doesn't work for Department K," said Loomis. "And now you tell me Craig loves him."

* * *

After three days they relaxed the sedation; after five, he could control his bladder again. By that time the marks on his body were fading, the dislocated finger usable, the cracked ribs reduced to a caution against unwary movement. Even the burn marks had begun to heal, and the pain lived most vividly in his nightmares, though these were still frequent and intense. Carefully Wetherly and Chinn began to explore the damage that pain had done to his mind, moving into it with the caution of architects in a house suspected of dry rot.

It took them three days, but at last they were sure, and left Craig enshrouded in sleep, like a silkworm in silk. Then, and only then, would they permit Loomis to look at him. He waddled into the room set aside as a ward with the vast, clumsy menace of a gorilla, then looked down at Craig, peering into his face. For the only time since Loomis had known him, Craig made no reaction to his nearness. He lay perfectly still, his breathing almost silent, the harshness gone from his face so that it seemed as if he were his own younger brother, married and mortgaged and at peace.

"What's he on?" said Loomis, and they told him.

Loomis grunted. "We could march a brass band through here and he wouldn't even dream."

Wetherly nodded. "He needs all the rest we can give him," he said.

"Looks a bloody sight better than he did before Simmons got him," Loomis said, and added with the painstaking thoroughness of one to whom praise is meaningless: "You blokes must have had your work cut out."

Chinn said: "At least he's sane now," Loomis glowered at him. "Sometimes people who have undergone his particular form of maltreatment become hopelessly neurotic. Craig has not."

"Reflexes?" asked Loomis.

"The indications are that they are unimpaired. He's in no condition yet for extensive tests."

"What about his nerve?" Loomis asked.

Wetherly said "Ah!" Chinn studied the tips of his fingers.

Loomis looked at the sleeping man's mouth. Always before it had been a hard line parallel with his forehead; now its corners turned down, almost into gentleness.

"You'd better get on with it," he said.

Wetherly said: "Simmons attacked his maleness in the most literal sense. Craig's mind appears to have converted that fact into metaphor."

"Never mind the codology," said Loomis automatically. "I have to know."

Wetherly tried again. "Craig was the most utterly masculine man I have ever known," he said. "He was hard, aggressive, ruthless. A tremendous fighter—and when he fought—completely without pity. Killing the right sort of enemy was part of being a man, to Craig.

"He was also very successful sexually. Women feared him, but in a way that gave them pleasure. This made them want him, and when he slept with them they enjoyed it intensely, sometimes with a degree of gratification they had never known before. This again Craig accepted as being a natural part of manhood. He was a strong, aggressive, even brutal lover, but in an odd sort of way he was also very polite in bed, even gentlemanly."

He broke off for a moment, as he and Chinn observed with pleasure that Loomis was blushing.

"His most recent conquest was Simmons's daughter, Jane," Wetherly said. "She is a healthy young woman, not a virgin almost certainly—" he looked at Chinn, who nodded. There was no appeal from that nod. "But she's young, to a certain degree innocent, and what Craig would call a lady. She appears to have gotten intense pleasure from Craig. Almost immediately afterwards she betrayed him to her father, who punished him by destroying his penis as a sexual organ, slowly and painfully."

"He's impotent?" asked Loomis.

"Not organically," Chinn said. "But impotence is in his mind."

"And with it the loss of his manhood," said Wetherly. "He couldn't possibly have withstood one more shock. And in his unconscious he knows this very clearly. He knows, too, that if he continues working for you he may suffer again. But he can only work for you while he is a man. That means a fighter and a lover. The two are absolutely intertwined for him. Take one away and the other must fail. You understand what I'm telling you?"

"Just tell it," said Loomis.

"His mind has decided that he can no longer make love. That way he won't have to fight either. Or risk the consequences of failure in a fight."

Loomis turned to Chinn.

"You agree with all this?"

Chinn nodded once more, and again there was no appeal.

Loomis said desperately: "He went for the nurse."

"He was afraid of her afterwards," said Chinn. "We had to send her away."

"You mean I've lost him?"

Chinn said: "He was almost played out anyway. I warned you at the nursing home—"

"You gave him three months—"

"Before he turned on you," said Chinn.

"I'd take care of that. But I need those three months."

"He would betray you at the first threat of pain," said Chinn.

Almost before their eyes the fat man crumbled as his aggressive optimism left him. He looked twenty pounds lighter, and twenty years older: a man with too much responsibility, too much power, and too little time. An old man.

"He had one more job to do," said Loomis. "He was made for it."

"To dispose of Simmons?" Chinn asked.

"And others," Loomis said. "Nut cases. Blokes who hate the Russians."

"He's the last man in the world to kill Simmons now," said Chinn.

"There's one way," Wetherly said suddenly. He turned to Chinn.

"I think not," said Chinn.

"But dammit man, it's got a good chance. For three months, anyway."

"How long would it take?" Loomis asked.

"Two weeks. Three at the most," said Wetherly, "and he needs that long to heal." He looked at the Napoleonic little man.

"A few days after that is all we need," he said.

Chinn said "No!" and for the first time he raised his voice.

"Can you do it?" Loomis asked, and Wetherly shook his head.

"It's Chinn's technique," he said. "There isn't anybody else."

Loomis swelled up in front of them like a combative bullfrog, growing lighter and more manic by the second, all his energies reaching out to Chinn, who speculated on how freely the adrenaline must be pumping into him.

"At least you can tell me about it," said Loomis, and his voice was soft and reasonable.

"You're being dishonest, Loomis," said Chinn, then surrendered. "Very well, I'll tell you about it. At least I'll tell you what I can do to Craig—then

I'll tell you why I won't do it."

"I'm listening," said Loomis.

"I can simplify him," said Chinn. "For a time, at any rate. I can seal off his fears about his sex life and canalize his energies into destruction. Turn him into a machine for killing people, or for hurting them."

"You're a very dangerous little feller," said Loomis.

"I've dealt with disordered personalities before," said Chinn. "Lots of them. Some of them have been the result of artificially induced stress—like Craig. It is possible to simplify such people up to a point—sometimes to the point where they can take their place in society at large. If I did what you want to Craig, that of course would not be possible."

"How d'you do it?"

"Drugs, hypnosis, certain Pavlovian techniques. Stimuli buried in the unconscious." He smiled a smile like midwinter. "That information is useless unless I were to be more specific. I shan't—any more than I shall do it to Craig."

"You said you would tell me why not," said Loomis.

Sir Matthew said at once: "Because it would contravene my conception of what one human being may morally do to another."

"All right," said Loomis. "And now I'll tell you why you will do it."

Chinn said: "Really, Loomis," but the fat man talked straight through it, his eyes bright with the certainty of what had to be done.

"Simmons is up to his ears with a group called

BC. They're a bunch of wealthy fanatics who hate Russia—and they'll do anything that hurts the Russians. Anything. Well we've had nuts before, and usually they're easy to cope with. But these particular nuts are good. They only do the big jobs —and they bring them off. And now they've ganged up with the Chinese."

"To attack the Russians?" said Chinn.

"The Chinese hate the Russians because they think they've betrayed communism," said Loomis. "The BC hates Russia just because it exists. But they both hate her, and they both want to hurt. They're pushing hard, trying to blame the West for the things they're doing. And the Russians don't push easy. They don't like it, d'you see? I met a feller in Paris recently—chap called Chelichev— head of the Executive Division of the KGB. He knows the things the BC's done. But his masters blame us. They'll go on blaming us until we can prove they're wrong—or get rid of who's doing it."

"And if we don't?" asked Wetherly, on cue.

"We'll lose all the gains we've made," said Loomis. "It'll be the cold war all over again. Or maybe the hot one."

"How could it possibly—" Chinn began.

"Suppose BC knocked off a few Russian politicians? The premier maybe, and a few members of the Presidium, and it looked like the Yanks had done it, or us? Because that's what they're after," Loomis said. "And that's what they'll do." He looked at the still figure in the coma. "Unless—"

"And there's really no one else you can use?" asked Chinn.

"How many like him have you ever treated?"

asked Loomis, and Chinn sighed. "Look, cocu, I want rid of him. He's dangerous. But I can't do without him. For what I want he's the best I've ever seen—or even heard of. Now try your moral conceptions on that one."

"There's no need," said Chinn. "If you are telling me the truth."

"Every word," said Loomis, and looked into the bright, unwinking eyes.

"I believe you," said Chinn, "and I'll do what you ask."

"Wetherly can help you," said Loomis.

"No," said Chinn. "Wetherly's concept of morality differs from mine. He might use the technique again for reasons that I would not approve." He turned to the bland, smooth man. "I'm sorry, Wetherly," he said, "but if Craig comes to my nursing home, and you attempt to observe the techniques I use on him I shall give him up." His glance flicked to Loomis. "I assure you I mean that," he said.

13

Chelichev poured vodka neatly and precisely. The woman tossed hers back at once, like a man, and still looked strong and female and beautiful.

"I have been through the English newspaper reports," she said. "Among the people in the café was a girl called Jane Simmons. Her father owns newspapers. I have read some. He does not like Russia."

Chelichev smiled at her, very proudly, yet with compassion. She had done so well.

"He also has a friend called Brodski who is going to Tangier," he said. "Simmons and his daughter will go there too. They are agents of BC." He smiled again. "No one in our department told me," he said. "You are the first. I congratulate you."

"Who then?"

"Department K," he said. "I told you. They are very good. You will go to Tangier, too, and meet Brodski. He is a Pole. If you are Polish too he will love you even more. Find out all you can. I want names." She nodded. "Simmons runs the organization. Brodski is liaison officer with people in Po-

land, East Germany, and Hungary. The Chinese
deal with Simmons direct. If necessary, you will
bring me Simmons or Brodski alive. We must have
the names of the people they hire in the next three
weeks. Is that understood?"

"Yes, comrade-general."

"I will send an executive to you. He will execute
the others."

"Yes, comrade-general."

"Craig will go with you also."

She looked surprised.

"Loomis insists on this. Anyway, the British are
very strong in Tangier and you may need help."

"Very good, comrade-general."

"You of course will be controller. There is also
the million pounds in Deutschmarks to be considered. You will steal it and destroy it."

"Destroy it?"

"It must not be used against us. By BC or anybody else."

"The British will want some."

"The British will get far more than money,"
Chelichev said.

"Very good, comrade-general. Will I have as-
sistance to steal this money?"

"You will," Chelichev said. "I am also sending
you a minor genius. He is emotionally unstable, as
genius often is, and the executive will get rid of him
after the mission. A pity in a way, his genius is un-
questionable. His métier is theft."

* * *

It took nine days. At the end of that time Sir Matthew Chinn had lost seven pounds, and was as familiar with Craig's unconscious as with the con-

tents of his own wardrobe. He had worried at first that Craig would resist the reintroduction of the urge to kill, but the resistance had been minimal. His craving was for orientation, a sense of purpose, and these Chinn gave him. The difficulty had been to erase the fixation that Craig developed for him almost from the beginning. But he had achieved it at last, as he had achieved an erasure of undue reliance on Hornsey. Under deep hypnosis, buried fathoms deep in the dark floor of his unconscious, Craig had acquired something else, too, something that Sir Matthew Chinn, to save his life, could not resist putting there, since to Sir Matthew the professional conscience was far more important than life. What Craig had acquired was the need to question Loomis's instructions, every time, but only to reveal that questioning when death was involved. Anybody's death, from Loomis's down.

On the tenth day Craig drove to the office and rang the bell. The porter looked at him, and even that phlegmatic man was awe-struck. From where he stood, Craig was completely unchanged. The porter remembered the soiled, naked mess under the blanket in the Lamborghini, looked at the man in the gray lightweight suit, silk shirt, Dior tie, and marveled. The Craig of that terrible night seemed never to have happened: the man was indestructible.

"Hallo, Mr. Craig," said the porter. "Feeling better?"

"I'm fine," said Craig.

He walked into the hallway and heard the porter shut the door, then suddenly his body swirled like a big fish in water, his arms came up behind the other man's back, pinning him, while his thumbs pressed into the nerves on either side of his jaw. The porter tried to kick back, but the thumbs pressed in, lifting him higher, forcing aggression out of him.

"Got a new one for you," said Craig.

Loomis appeared at the head of the vast staircase.

"Oh you're back, are you?" he said, and added pettishly: "Put him down, Craig. Go and look at your correspondence, then come and see me. There's a lot to do."

Craig let the porter go, and turned the man around. The gray eyes had never given warning but now they were flat as disks. Rage, love, anger, hate: they were all gone. Burned out.

"I'll see you in the gym," said Craig. "You're getting slow." He left him then, and the caretaker thought of how carefully he'd lifted him from the Lamborghini, and regretted it. There was just no point in being nice to Craig.

Mrs. McNab thought so too. She treated Craig as she always did when he came back from a job: bade him good morning, found him coffee, waited while he read through his papers. Neither of them referred to what had happened; neither of them wanted to. Craig worked steadily, making neat notes as he went, then drank his coffee, which had cooled, and dictated rapidly and precisely for twenty minutes. Mrs. McNab's pencil flew and her mind marveled. Craig hadn't missed a trick.

When he had done Craig said: "Book me a session on the range this afternoon." Mrs. McNab made a note. "And tell the caretaker and the other

chap to stand by. I'll see them in the gym at five."
He stood up and stretched, and his hands were
cruel.

"Tell them no beer or cigarettes until I see
them."

"Very good, sir," said Mrs. McNab. There was a
question in her voice.

Craig grinned. "I want them savage," he said,
and made for the door. "I'm off to see Loomis—
then lunch. I'll check that stuff I dictated before I
go down to the range."

Then the door closed behind him, and Mrs.
McNab wept softly, for perhaps five seconds, tears
of frustration. One never knew how to react with
Craig. He was a sort of Martian.

Loomis was as silent as Mrs. McNab about
Craig's sufferings. All he said was, "Pour the cof-
fee," then, as he sipped it, black and scalding,
"Make your report."

Craig took out a tiny notebook, and began to
talk, and Loomis heard of bulls and cowboys and
girls—two girls in particular. Tempest and Jane
made him blush; Craig talked of them as if they
were theorems in geometry. He talked of his attack, and Hornsey's rescue, and there he finished.
He said nothing about Sir Matthew Chinn, which
was what Loomis had hoped for.

"These cowboys," he said. "Who were they?"

"Chap called Ivo Clements—a banker," said
Craig. "Hamid Medani—rich young Moroccan.
Son of a Rif sheikh, I would think. And the Earl of
Airlie. He was the one I clobbered."

"You gave us most of that when you were de-
lirious. We've been checking. Simmons collects

men. He's had others," said Loomis. "Big men. All big. Barristers, BBC types, couple of Hungarian diplomats. A Rumanian. Greeks too."

"No Yugoslavs?"

"No," said Loomis. "Tito doesn't care for him."

Craig said: "Have you been to see him?"

"We sent Linton up there. Sort of thing a policeman can get on to. Said there'd been a report of gunfire. Policemen are always nosy about gunfire."

"Well?"

"Simmons had gone away on business—his daughter wouldn't say where—and taken his valet with him. That's Zelko."

"He must have taken him in a trunk," said Craig. "Hornsey shot him dead."

"We'll get to Hornsey in a minute. Jane did the talking. Said they'd had guests for the weekend and they'd fooled about with some old TV sets—backgrounds I mean. Not receivers. They'd played at cowboys for a bit. Fired blanks. The sets had gone back to Simmons's TV company when Linton got there. She said you'd only stayed one night. She didn't know where you'd gone after that. She said you'd asked her a lot of questions and she didn't like you. . .

"Linton had a word with Ivo Clements. He didn't like you either. You're not a gentleman, d'you see. But he remembered when you left in the Lamborghini. He also remembered Hornsey asking you where you were going. You said London—and he followed you." He held up his hand as Craig tried to speak.

"We can't reach Hamid, and the Earl of Airlie's in a private ward with a concussion. Nobody can speak to him. That leaves Ivo and Jane against you."

"What about Tempest?"

"She left the same day you did—a bit earlier. Jane Simmons knows nothing about her. Ivo Clements thought you were pretty well matched. Look, son—the whole idea was to make you look a liar and imply that if anybody had roughed you up it was Hornsey. I might even have had doubts myself, if—" he broke off then, and wheezed joyfully.

"Linton saw the bull himself," said Loomis. "It had a black eye."

Craig wasn't laughing.

"Hornsey didn't hurt me," he said. "He killed Zelko. Laid out Simmons."

"He tricked you though," said Loomis. "You thought he worked for me."

"You've done it before," Craig said. "Put someone on my tail without telling me. And he did turn up in Soho. But that's not the reason, is it? Simmons had just about broken me. I was past making any sense. I just believed what he said."

"What did you tell him?"

Craig said: "About the money and Fat Arthur—and the BC business."

"What about it?"

"How BC was trying to push Russia into war with us. And how China was helping. I think I told him that. Yes—I did, because he wanted to know about Soong."

"Did you talk about Jean-Luc Calvet?"

"I might have done," said Craig. "I can't remember." He paused, tried to think back, failed.

"He was good," he said. "Fast. Accurate. He killed Zelko and clobbered Simmons in about three seconds. Who's he with? The Russians? No. He couldn't be, could he?"

"Why not?" asked Loomis.

"He didn't kill Simmons—and he got me out."

"You're still thinking," said Loomis. The fact pleased him. "Whoever he is, you gave him our address. We've got to triple-check around the clock now. And we'll have to move—"

"I didn't give it to Simmons," said Craig. "He tried three times. If he'd tried four he would have got it."

"Some of you's human," said Loomis. "I've never denied it." His eyes flicked to Craig's, then away. "This Medani feller—he's Moroccan. From Talouet. He went back to Morocco the morning we found you. But he stayed in Tangier. Still there. Waiting for someone maybe."

"Simmons?"

"It's possible. Time BC did something big, d'you see. Something to make Russia look bad. In Morocco they got the money for it. In a bank called Crédit Labonne. They got a million there. I think they're going to take it out and use it—if you don't get it first."

"That's what you're doing for Chelichev?"

"That's it," said Loomis. "He's giving us a bit of help, too. Couple of experts."

"I'd sooner find my own," Craig said again.

"So would I," said Loomis. "But that's not in the deal. We're due to meet them tonight. Dress informal. No medals."

Craig said: "You think Simmons will be in Tangier?"

Loomis nodded. "And Brodski. And Hamid."

"They don't matter," said Craig. "Simmons does."

"You want to kill him?"

"I have to," said Craig.

"That's all right," Loomis said. "But do the bank job first."

* * *

The firing range was in what had been the cellars, and here Craig practiced till his arm ached and the crack of the gun hurt his eardrums like a blow. The ex-PSI who ran the range watched, and did not compete. This was something that Craig was working out alone. Over and over the gun flicked out, pointed, and bellowed its accusation, and over and over, if the targets had been real, a man would have died. The ex-PSI had carried a gun himself, quite illegally, in Youngstown, Ohio. He had been paid large sums for his skill with it, had known others as good as himself, a handful who were better. None of them could have taken Craig. At the end of the session Craig cleaned the two guns—a Smith and Wesson .38 and a Colt Woodsman—and himself, then walked into the room next door to the range. It was a gymnasium, and in one corner of it a dojo —a judo practice mat. Craig lay down on a bench and relaxed, and thought of what Loomis had said and not said. The BC must lose its money and Simmons could then die. Russians would be watching while it happened. And Hornsey might be there. Hornsey, who had saved his life. Craig hoped he wouldn't have to hurt him. Maybe the Russians might want to—Hornsey wasn't working for them. Craig wondered who he did work for.

At five o'clock the chauffeur and the caretaker came in. The chauffeur was also a bodyguard, who occasionally drove cars on jobs that required fast getaways. He was bigger than the caretaker, slower of temper, but fast on his feet and a fair judoka. Like the caretaker, he enjoyed cigarettes and a beer at lunchtime. They disliked Craig even more for stopping their treat, but they stayed wary of him.

Craig said: "No need to change. We'll fight as we are."

The two men removed their pistols and knives, then moved to the mat. Craig went to it, facing them. On the wall behind the chauffeur someone had stuck a pin-up picture of a girl. A girl both lovely and sensual, eminently worth fighting for. Craig's glance brushed past her as if she had been a "NO SMOKING" sign in a language he didn't understand.

"I want you to attack me together," he said. "One from each side. Stay as far apart as you like. And come at me—don't wait for me."

The two men whispered together, and Craig waited. They were not as good as Simmons and Zelko had been, but they would do. Somewhere there was a counter to the simultaneous attack that Simmons and Zelko had used, and he would find it. He had to. It might happen again.

Suddenly the two men erupted at him, and Craig's hand stopped only just in time from a karate strike at the chauffeur's neck, but as he did so the caretaker's fingers touched the nerves behind the ears. They tried it again, and this time the caretaker was open to the blow but the chauffeur survived. They came in again—and again, and at the ninth try, when the two were grinning at their success, for which they had waited so long, he saw the answer, and used it. The trick was to make your move a split second in advance of their signal, and take the attack to one of them before the other could get to you. Get in fast, with just one blow, and swerve as you struck it, spinning round to take the other man from the side, using the force of the spin to add momentum to the second blow, the killer blow, if you wanted it that way. They did it again, and it worked again, and a third time. After that they were ready for him. But Craig was satisfied. He had a new trick for Simmons now: one that Simmons knew nothing about. He went to shower and change his clothes. Soon it would be time to dine with Loomis and the experts from Russia.

There were two of them. They wore Italian suits, white shirts, discreet ties. They knew how to handle knives and forks and spoke excellent English. The shorter one, Boris, had almost no accent at all. He was about five feet eight, broad-shouldered, barrel-chested; his hands were like stones. The other, Istvan, was tall, slim, elegant, and his manners and accent had a bravura that were not Russian. His eyes, dark and slightly slanted, were limpid with dishonesty, but his charm was real enough. It was he who led the conversation, made the jokes, complimented the headwaiter on a remarkable wine. But he was afraid of Boris. Terrified. And his hands bothered Craig. They were coarse, broadened with hard work, the marks of old calluses and wounds still on them. Whenever possible he kept them in his pockets.

Loomis had chosen a private room in a restaurant. There was only one way in, and when the meal was over he had one of his own men at the door, while Boris and Istvan tested for bugging devices. There were none. Loomis was genial, and offered brandy and cigars. Boris drank brandy primly, but in enormous quantities. Istvan was more cautious, and more drunk.

"There isn't much time," Boris said. "We need to start in forty-eight hours."

He turned to Craig. "You have a plan here?" he asked.

Loomis said: "Yes. It's waiting for you to take away after dinner. You have to overcome some time locks, load up the money, and drive away. The rest is straightforward stuff."

"Straightforward?"

"Overpowering guards. Killing them perhaps. But the time locks are difficult."

"That is why we brought Istvan," said Boris.

Istvan looked modest and terrified at the same time.

Loomis said: "I've brought specifications of the kind of locks the bank uses."

"You're very good," said Istvan.

"We also have a safe for him to practice on."

"You're excellent," said Istvan.

"A lot will depend on how you show in practice tomorrow," said Loomis.

Neither Boris nor Istvan looked worried.

"How do we escape?" Boris asked.

"The easy way is to Gibraltar," said Loomis.

Boris said "No." He said it as every Russian at the United Nations has said it. There could be no argument.

"D'you fancy Algeria?" Loomis asked.

Boris said: "I do not."

"Where then?"

"Egypt," said Boris. "By airplane. That I can arrange. We will have friends waiting."

This time Loomis said "No." Egypt was unthinkable. The two men argued, gently, courteously, and Craig studied Istvan's hands. They had marks on them that were not calluses, but the scars of sores that must have been viciously deep. Frostbite perhaps? Beside him Loomis sweated at not losing his temper, and he and Boris agreed at last on a pickup by sea and two ships waiting, one Russian, one British, the money to be divided evenly; the Russians to keep all the Deutschmarks and pay the British the equivalent of their half in sterling. He was getting information too, but money always came in handy.

Loomis stopped sweating, and poured more brandy, and Boris turned to Craig.

"You say very little," he said.

"I've been thinking," said Craig. "I don't believe Istvan is a Russian name—"

"You're right," said Boris.

"And I don't like going into a job with a man I'm not sure of."

"You can be sure of Istvan," Boris said. "I guarantee him."

"You personally?" Boris nodded. "I wonder why," said Craig.

"Because I have very strict orders about him, and Istvan knows what they are."

Istvan put down his glass, and the brandy in it planed from side to side.

Craig turned to him. "How do I know you're such an expert?" he asked. Boris tried to speak and Craig cut in. "Let him tell it," he said.

Istvan looked at Boris, who nodded graciously in permission.

"I promise you, gentlemen, I have a great deal of experience," he said. "I am a Hungarian—born in Budapest, but I trained in France and the United States. Up to this point in my life I must have stolen about two hundred thousand pounds. It would have been more—after all I am forty-five years old —only. . ." He broke off and looked again at Boris, who again nodded consent. "I was foolish enough to go back to Hungary after the uprising. They picked me up. I had carried a gun you see— in the uprising—"

"You used it," said Boris.

"I'm afraid I did. At first of course I wanted only to escape to Austria—there was a job waiting for me in Switzerland, and Swiss francs are such a comfort—but I don't really know what happened. There was so much enthusiasm and so little technique. The tragedy of our poor country. I began to shoot out of sheer impatience with my countrymen. Then I found I was holding classes in weapon-training. Then I had to burgle a police barracks to get weapons for my students. It was a—" he looked at Boris, "a very busy time."

"Where have you spent your time since?" asked Craig.

"Until 1961 I robbed banks, then I went back to Budapest. Since then I have been in Siberia," said Istvan. "I saw you looking at my hands. One works hard there you know, and the weather is chilly. But I have been to a skin specialist. My fingertips are as good as new."

"Have you any further questions to ask him?" Boris asked.

"One more. How do I know I can trust you in this?" said Craig.

"Because if I do anything wrong Boris will kill me. And I know that he can. On the other hand, if I do my job, I get money—and freedom."

"A completely bourgeois mentality," said Boris. "The Soviet Republic does not need him."

He got up, and Istvan rose at once.

"A delightful evening," he said. "Where can we work on the safe tomorrow?"

Loomis told him, and the two men went to the door. Boris turned.

"I notice you don't ask where we are staying," he said. "No doubt we will be followed."

"My dear chap, we must look after you," said Loomis.

"No need," said Boris. "I shall look after both of us. But you'll do it anyway." He smiled. "I should perhaps mention that we are traveling with American passports. All quite in order. If we are molested, I shall complain to the United States embassy."

Then they left, and Craig saw how neatly Boris moved, for all his bulk. Istvan looked tired. Perhaps, after all those years in Siberia, he would always look tired.

"What do you think?" said Loomis.

"They'll be good," said Craig. "For this job they'll have to be."

"Chelichev says Istvan's a minor genius," Loomis said. "And he's got a hell of an incentive, too."

"Money," said Craig. "I gather we're due for half of it."

"We could do with it," said Loomis. "Power boats, ships, hotel bills, safes. It all adds up, you know. Then there's your bill to Matt Chinn."

"No," said Craig. "I'm going to pay that myself."

It was at that moment that Loomis first began to worry.

14

Department K had bought a shop in Pimlico. It had been an ironmonger's, a hatter's, a petshop, and lately had been owned by a philatelist with a persecution mania who had had it fortified like a bank vault. When the van finally came (he was being gassed by Arabs at the time, and had sealed all the keyholes with stamps) the place had had to be breached by direct assault. And even then it had taken an hour. His wife had been happy to sell the place. Department K's agent had made the only offer. It was a dead shop in a dying street.

Craig drove a van there: "MERRIDEW SHOP-FITTERS. HACKNEY AND SLOUGH." Inside the van were Boris and Istvan; like Craig, they wore overalls. Istvan also had a tool bag and a box filled with equipment worth five times the cost of the van. That morning he seemed far more relaxed, as if the promise of testing his skill had driven his fear of Boris far back into his mind. He chatted happily, and Boris smiled at him—an indulgent father enjoying his son's anticipation of a treat. The van pulled up and Craig got out. A wooden fence had already been erected in front of the shopwindow, and from the houses opposite curtains twitched in vain. When Istvan went to work, nobody would learn his secrets. Craig unlocked a door set in the fence, then went back to help Boris carry in the wooden box. Istvan followed, carrying the tool bag. When they were inside the fence Craig locked its door, and Istvan began studying the shop-window and doorway.

"It is better if you can see the whole frontage at once," he said. "Here we are too close. Even so I see the wisdom of the fence," he told Craig. "I do not like people to watch me when I work." He began to examine the window. At last he said "Ah!" in a voice of deep satisfaction.

"The glass is very thick," he went on. "Two centimeters perhaps. See at the corners where it joins the frame. And in it there is set fine, strong wire. If you smash the glass, the wire will hold. You must therefore cut the wire. But if you look at the shelf below the window you will see a junction box with cable going to the window. That means the wire is electrified. If you were to touch it with cutters you would find it very painful. Deadly even. I do not like electric shocks, Mr. Craig."

"Nor me," said Craig. His voice expressed polite agreement, no more.

"It would be necessary to cut off the electricity supplies from outside the shop," said Istvan. "That is a long and tedious business. We would have to dig up pavement—and even then we might encounter some surprises. Let us try the door." He walked to the door, and stared at it from perhaps a foot away from the frame. He then swore softly in Hungarian.

"Talk English," said Boris.

"I beg your pardon," Istvan said humbly. "This is a door of considerably ingenuity." Boris moved forward to it, and Istvan grabbed his arm, then gabbled as Boris looked down at the restraining hand: "You mustn't go inside the doorframe. See where it is guarded." His finger, carefully out of range, pointed to pairs of holes set in the sides of the doorframe, and at the top and bottom.

"Photoelectric cells," he said. "Each pair makes a circuit. Break the circuit and you set off an alarm. Perhaps you do more." He smiled. "This is very thorough. Sometimes with photoelectric cells it is possible to jump over them, or slide beneath them. Here there is no chance. The biggest gap is only ten centimeters square."

He brought his box carefully close to the door, stood on it, and peered at one of the cells, then another, then a third.

"How delightful," he said. "The wire is run into the woodwork. I have only a tiny piece to cut at." He got down to look at the cells that led into the door lintel. "And from beneath, no wire shows at all." He sighed. "It will take a long time, I'm afraid."

"We've got all day," Boris said.

Craig and Boris squatted, privileged pupils, and watched the master at work. With a long, thin chisel he cut into the wood near the wires to the photoelectric cells, and exposed them. One by one the rubber-sheathed pairs of copper strands came into view. Craig noticed that to each pair of wires that activated a cell another pair of wires was attached, running up vertically to a point above the door. Istvan saw them, too, and smiled.

"I was right," he said. From the tool kit he took a pair of pliers, and cut, first the vertical wires, then the horizontal ones. Then he attacked the lintel in the same way, exposing, cutting.

"It is as well to be certain," he said, and stood up. "We may now stand in the doorway," he said. "So useful if it should rain." He bent then to look at the lock, then more closely at the door itself. "Really, whoever did this was very thorough," he said. "Who did he fear? What did he have to protect?"

"He thought the United Arab Republic was after his penny blacks," said Craig. "There isn't an Arab in miles and he sold all his penny blacks to build this fort. He was mad."

"No doubt," said Istvan. "But so ingenious. Look at the lock."

Craig looked. It was a flat piece of dull, thick steel, with a tiny hole set in it.

"These are very difficult," said Istvan. "Make one false turn and the whole lock jams. And the key one tries must be exactly right."

"Why not cut round it?" said Craig. "Cut the lock out?"

"Excellent, excellent," Istvan said. "It is a way, of course, but a very difficult way. Look. I will show you."

He took the thin chisel again, and a mallet, and tapped into the wooden panels of the door. They gave easily for a quarter of an inch, then metal squeaked on metal.

"You see?" Istvan said. "The door is a sheet of

steel. This wood is decoration only. To drill would take time."

"Couldn't you blow it in?" Boris asked.

"It would take a lot of explosive, and make a lot of noise," said Istvan. "The only way would be to attack the hinges, and they as you see are inside the door. I can't get at them. Besides—there is another risk. Best, I think, to try with the lock."

He took a piece of fine wire from his tool bag, and probed the keyhole, listening intently as he worked. After a while, he inserted a pair of calipers in the hole, measured carefully, and put a slight bend in the wire. This went on for an hour, while Craig sat, watched, and wished it were time for a cigarette. Beside him Boris did much the same as Istvan probed, bending the wire, straightening it, bending it again. At last he was satisfied, and took a thin piece of steel from his kit. At one end of it was the hollow circle of an old-fashioned key. Next he produced a hacksaw, fine files, emery paper, and began to make a key from the wire template. When it was finished, he polished the steel key with emery paper, and oiled it.

"Forgive my vanity," he said. "But there are not three other men in the world who can do what I have just done."

"If it works," said Boris.

"It works, believe me," Istvan said. "Would you like to try?" He handed him the key. "One turn to the right, three to the left, two more to the right."

Boris inserted the key, and tried to turn it. Nothing happened.

"Forgive me," said Istvan. "It is new and stiff. Try this."

He handed Boris a short cylinder of bar steel. Boris pushed it across the rink of the key, and turned, his massive body stiff with strain. Slowly, reluctantly it grated to the right, then, with each twist, more easily to the left—once, twice, thrice. When he moved it the two final turns to the right there was no resistance at all.

Istvan pushed open the door, and had to use considerable strength to do it, then stepped inside. Boris and Craig followed, and he closed it again, looking up as he did so. Then he smiled, and his smile was quite beautiful. Craig thought that he would have a big future conning women in Vegas or Formentor. Then he too looked up.

"You see?" Istvan said. "How ingenious your stamp collector was."

Above the door was a massive steel shutter, rolled up, ready to slam down.

"If I had just cut the wires of the photoelectric cells this would have come down at once," said Istvan. "It was wired to them, too. Remember?"

Craig remembered the wires leading vertically to a place above the door. Istvan was good, all right, but there were still the time locks to face.

They looked round. The shelves empty now, dust settling, gentle as a requiem benediction on the kind of handy place round the corner the supermarkets had made obsolete. Istvan examined shelves and cupboards.

In one corner, by the stairs, stood a safe, massively squat. A heavy steel grille barred their approach to it.

"Difficult," said Boris.

"Not really," he said. "But that is not the one we want. Let us try the cellar."

Craig deliberately headed for the stairs, but Istvan forestalled him.

"I'll go first please," he said. "There may be more surprises."

He found another photoelectric cell at the head of the stairs, and yet another at the foot. As he worked on them, Craig and Boris sat and waited. They had no need of conversation, and Craig was grateful for it. While he sat he could think about what Simmons had done to that poor man he had once been, and feel sorry for him. Not that it wasn't the man's own fault in a way, he conceded. It was stupid to rely on women as much as that. And who needed them anyway? The only man who really mattered was the one who knew how to fight. And there he had nothing to worry about. Sir Matthew Chinn had said it, and it was true. . .

Istvan called to them, and they went down. The timelock safe was immediately visible. It had been taken into the cellar a section at a time, and re-constructed. Now the cellar was almost filled by it. Istvan patted its slate-gray side and grinned.

"This was the one they considered burglar-proof," he said. "It is a very remarkable construction. High-tension steel all over—back, sides, door, top and bottom. There is no question of attacking it from its weakest side. It has no weakest side. Nor is it possible to blow it. Look at that door, gentlemen—hinged from inside." Istvan, carried away by enthusiasm for a masterpiece, talked like a television art expert confronted by a Caravaggio. "To

insert a charge into that door would mean drilling
for days, and even then the charge would have to
be so great I doubt if we could survive the blast.
And if we did, the door would merely drop a little
and be jammed in grooves set in the base. If we
used an even bigger charge to blow it free, we
would of course destroy not only the safe but its
contents; 99.9 per cent of all burglars would simply
ignore a safe of this type. It is too much trouble."

"Safes like this have been robbed," said Boris.

"It is possible. One must break into the bank,
and wait for the time lock. If the lock has been set
so that the safe will not open for sixty hours, then
one must wait for sixty hours. If bank employees
arrive, one must kidnap them, keep them prisoner.
There is no other way. A safe with a time lock has
to wait for the time set."

"I doubt if we can do that," Craig said. "The
Tangier bank is too crowded."

"We will not have to," said Istvan. "There is another way. You see," he said, and his manner became more than ever that of the expert lecturer to
first-year students, "the trouble with time locks is
that they're too good. They even have the clock
inside the safe now, where people like me can't get
at it. But suppose something goes wrong, then the
bank has a problem. If the time lock developed a
fault you couldn't get in, not without boring holes
in the safe. And that could take days. So they put
a secret way in—almost always. There's one in the
bank in Tangier. There's one here."

"Where?" asked Boris.

"Through the safe upstairs," said Istvan. "First
you have to get through a grille with a key lock—

then there's the safe itself. That has a combination lock. Come up and I'll show you."

To open two sets of locks and work out two combinations took time, but there was no possibility of denying Istvan's certainty. They entered one safe at last. From there they could attack the other, now beneath them. This problem too he solved with massive certainty. As he prepared to open the trapdoor Boris said: "An hour to get in, an hour to open the safe. That's pretty good."

"It's brilliant," said Craig, and Istvan smiled. "And it'll take even less time to do the bank. The way-in's already been done. All we've got to do is the safe."

Boris lowered himself down into the time-lock safe, then a beam of light flicked at him, and he swore again in Hungarian.

Inside the safe sat Loomis, torch in hand, a flask of coffee by his side.

He beamed at Istvan.

"You're good, cock, d'you know that?" he said. "In fact you're better than good, you're bloody marvelous." He paused. "I knew you would be— or I wouldn't be here."

He beamed at Istvan once more. "You know a chap called Chelichev?"

"I do indeed," said Istvan, and Boris stiffened.

"I'll be writing to him soon. Tell him just how good you are."

15

They flew to Tangier in a Comet 4B, and Boris took advantage of the quaint local custom that allowed him to drink cheap liquor because he was on a plane. It didn't seem to affect him. Istvan tried it too, and it made him drunk, or at least talkative. Craig settled down to listen. So long as Istvan talked of the jobs he had done he was fascinating, and Craig, an expert himself, found no difficulty in tuning in to that part of his mind. The overwhelming need to solve the apparently insoluble was one he knew all about. It delighted him, and he was happy to hear it, and even as he grappled with the details of picklocks and tumblers found himself remembering his own pleasure at finding out how to defeat two men, two good men, who jump you simultaneously from opposite sides. But then Istvan began to talk of women, and Craig became first bored, then restless. It would be easy to shut him up, but Loomis had told him to be nice to him, so he went on listening. It was Boris who interrupted.

"You think too much of women," he said.

"But consider," said Istvan. "I am supposed to be an American."

Boris laughed. "That is a point, but even so, you mean it, Istvan."

"I was a very long time in Siberia," the Hungarian said.

"And were there no women there?"

"Not in the sense that I mean," Istvan said. "In that sense there were none at all."

Craig said: "Boris is right. Women get in the way—slow things up."

The Hungarian's eyes were both shrewd and pitying as they looked at him.

"That is the British way," he said. "It works, I suppose."

"It works very well," said Boris. It was his official voice; Istvan was silent.

"Our controller is a woman," he said. "She is quite young and very beautiful. It would be foolish of you to desire her, Istvan."

Istvan said at once: "Extremely foolish."

There was a pause: they both seemed to be waiting for Craig to speak.

At last he said: "I should have been told this earlier."

Boris said: "Don't worry. She is extremely good. Like a man is good. She thinks like a man, works like a man. Only the body belongs to a woman. That is very useful. And very dangerous."

"Will she meet us at the airport?" Craig asked.

"No, no," said Boris. "That will all be arranged in time." He pressed the bell above him. "I think we should all drink cheap brandy and stop talking about women. . ."

* * *

So much about Tangier had changed, Craig
thought. There was a modern airport now, and the
road linking it to the city was fast and new. Now,
too, the taxis were numerous, and the driver didn't
try to sell you a woman as soon as you opened the
door. The town looked cleaner, and more cared
for: the lights in the street came on first time. The
brothels had gone, and the shops where you could
buy anything, from a fountain pen to an automobile, below duty-free price, below cost price sometimes, so that you came out wondering if the ring
or the watch or the radio you had bought was
counterfeit, or merely stolen ... But the sea was
still there, the confluence of the Mediterranean and
the Atlantic, and the incredible view of it from the
headland: the water in solid bars of blue and green,
and behind it, softened by distance, the rocky
masses of Gibraltar and the mainland of Spain.
Craig thought briefly of George Allen, and
Dovzhenko, who preferred to be known as Jean-
Luc Calvet. Spain was a country he liked, and he'd
been there often enough in the old days, but here in
Tangier he was at home. He had no house any
more, and no doubt tourists now used the little bar
that had once belonged to the smugglers, but he
felt still as if he had roots here, the stability of language and customs perfectly learned and understood. Many of the people he had known would be
gone by now—particularly the Spaniards. When
Spain had abandoned Spanish Morocco a lot of
them had slipped back home across the water, but
a lot of them would be left. And Arabs and Jews,
and the Christians who were often so enchantingly
vague about their nationality. If they saw him they

would recognize him, but it didn't matter. The police couldn't touch him, didn't want to. After all, the arms he'd sold had all gone to the Algerians or the Moroccans themselves. Never to the French. That made him more of a local hero than a criminal. Nobody would mind if he brought over a couple of respectable business friends to look at the sights, though a few people might be disappointed to find that he was now respectable too.

The three of them dined in their hotel, a new one just off the Boulevard Pasteur, with a swimming pool and air-conditioned rooms, and an open patio that looked straight up at stars that seemed almost gentle in the black and tender sky. They ate well, and without preoccupation, and Craig sensed that the woman—their controller—was not in the hotel. Then they walked back to the Boulevard Pasteur, and sat outside a café, to watch the aimless meandering of a Mediterranean crowd that knows how to enjoy the cool of the evening by doing nothing but relaxing and gossiping at café tables.

That night, as every night in summer, the crowd was mostly foreigners, tourists with money who would stray inevitably into souvenir shops, cafés, and cabarets. But now and then there passed a man in a djibbah, or a veiled woman, shrouded from the bridge of her nose to her toes, walking behind her lord. And sometimes, Craig remembered, those toes were covered by shoes imported from Paris, and the scent on their bodies came from Cardin . . . He watched a donkey go by. An old countryman rode on it. Behind him walked his wife, bent double under a load of firewood. Between them they halted a line of American cars, and the policeman on duty let them. After all, they were citizens too.

Boris said: "There is a great deal of inefficiency here." Craig agreed. "And a smell, also. Have you noticed it?"

"Drains?" Craig asked.

"No," said Boris. "It is a strange smell—thin and bitter. A lot of the people here seem to carry it about on their clothes."

Istvan giggled.

"That's kef," said Craig. "A kind of marijuana. A lot of people use it here instead of alcohol. Alcohol's not approved of in a Muslim country."

"A lot of people seem to be drinking it," said Boris.

"They like it," said Craig. "So just for tonight they pretend they're Christians."

Boris said: "This is crazy. And we should not be here."

"Why not?" Craig asked.

"Suppose this man Brodski were to see you—and us?"

"Brodski hasn't left his villa since he got here," said Craig. "He's waiting for Simmons."

"You seem very well informed," said Boris.

"I didn't know about your controller being a woman," said Craig.

Then Boris sulked. If it had been a peace conference he would have walked out. Craig had never worked with an ally before and never wanted to again. He sighed and bought Boris a brandy. It was like a sweet for a naughty child.

Boris had almost finished his drink when Hornsey appeared. He wore a white lightweight

suit and a panama hat, and when he sat down at
the table next to theirs was at once besieged by
bootblacks. He tried to repulse them in painstaking
French and had no success at all. It was Craig who
drove them off, in a machine-gun burst of Arabic.
When they had gone he looked across at Craig.

"That was awfully kind of you," he said.

"Not at all," said Craig.

"You must let me buy you a drink."

"Some other time," Craig said. "We have an ap-
pointment."

"Ah," said Hornsey. "Well, thanks anyway."

He ordered mint tea, and when they left, merely
nodded.

The three men strolled on up the Boulevard
Pasteur to where a little formal garden looked
across at Europe. Below them the Casbah was
teaching tourists that every experience must be
paid for. Just across the road was the Crédit
Labonne.

"You were indiscreet," said Boris. "You made
that man curious about you."

"He looked so helpless," said Craig.

Boris began to lecture, and Craig thought about
Hornsey. It had been nice to help him, to spare him
embarrassment, and nice to know that they need
not recognize each other. It had seemed also as if
Boris and Istvan did not know him. It was difficult
to be sure about these things, but Craig was prepared to bet on it at reasonable odds. He didn't
want Hornsey to know Boris, but if he didn't, how
had he arrived in Tangier so opportunely? Perhaps
Simmons had told him to be there, before he had
messed up his chances by killing Zelko. *Or perhaps,*

thought Craig, *I told him myself about the raid on the bank, after he rescued me.* The thought saddened him. He didn't want to have to cope with Hornsey.

Boris went on talking, and Istvan filled in time by staring at the bank. *It will not be easy,* he thought. *The door is lit by streetlamps, and there are too many people. But stealing a million is never easy.* He switched the problem off his mind, like a radio changing stations. After all, finding a way in was Craig's problem. No doubt he had it in hand. It was better to concentrate one's mind on what to do when one had taken the million. Boris, for example, might prove an obstacle. So might his controller. Istvan's secret fear was that they would kill him when the deal was concluded. On the other hand, another Siberian winter would have killed him anyway.

Boris continued to lecture as they walked down the steps to the Casbah. The place was packed with conducted parties, independent parties, guides official and unofficial, pushing their way into tiny streets where the shops that lined them were the size of cupboards, and one could buy yataghans, camel saddles, brass-bound muskets or silver-filagree coffeepots, eat kebabs on skewers, drink mint tea, and watch the haggling. The haggling, Craig remembered, was half the fun, even when the stuff was good. They came to a tiny square, dominated by a pink-washed building that had once been an attractive cube. Now it was a mess of domes, turrets, and minarets, from one of which an endless tape broadcasted Arab music through a loudspeaker. A wooden board nailed between two

turrets had painted on it: "OASIS NITE CLUB.
FLOOR SHOW. FOOD. DRINK." Istvan looked at it.

"I should like to go there," he said.

Boris said: "What will they do there?"

"Dancing," said Craig. "And a bloke doing a
balancing act. They always do."

"Is this dancing sexual?" Boris asked.

"That's perhaps a little crude," said Craig. "I
think erotic would be a better word."

"Then I think we should go," said Boris. "We're
tourists after all. It would seem strange if we
showed no interest in sexuality."

Istvan risked looking pleased, and this time
Boris didn't look angry.

The interior of the club was of the standard pattern that Craig remembered: a marble floor and
walls of plaster and tile, fretted and carved into
graceful abstractions that at first were very beautiful. It was only their sameness that cloyed at last.
They sat on a padded banquette that was like a
divan and an Arab in a djibbah placed drinks in
front of them. All around European men and
women chattered and drank, and danced to taped
music—and Arabs in Western clothes sipped
Scotch and told each other they didn't like it, but
what could one do? When the dance ended, the
crowd settled down, and one by one musicians in
djibbah and fez squatted on the floor. Their instruments for the most part were European—violin,
clarinet, and flute—but the Negro drummer carried hand drums like bongos, and the music they
played was pure Arab. The crowd sighed its content; this was what they had paid for.

First it was just the music, then, as Craig had

predicted, a man came on and balanced impossible quantities of glasses, jugs, vases of flowers on a tray on his head, finishing up with a series of candles in glass shades, making them spin in a circle of flame as the houselights dimmed. Then it was a singer in an exquisite caftan of blue and silver thread, eyes sparkling with belladonna, face and hands delicately rouged, little feet hung with silver bells. The song was of love, as always, and gazelles and roses and moonlight: the dance that followed, demure, almost shy, yet with the erotic overtones that Boris considered so essential as the hips swayed softly and silver disks tinkled in the slender olive fingers. At the end the singer sank to the floor to a rather bewildered round of applause, though the Arabs shouted their tributes to beauty.

"I enjoyed that," said Boris. "It is not precisely what I expected, but I enjoyed it. The girl was very sexual, but she had a certain modesty also." He looked at Craig, who was smiling. "Don't you agree?"

"I do indeed," said Craig. "Except that it wasn't a girl. It was a boy."

Istvan found it necessary to take a drink.

Thereafter it was girls all the way, one after the other, small, shapely girls, tenderly fleshed, their skins every shade from walnut brown to palest olive. They each had a circlet to hold back their hair, a jeweled bra, and below it were naked to the hips, where a skirt cut to reveal their legs was held in place by a rhinestoned belt. Each one of them did a belly dance that was very erotic indeed, hips writhing, breasts shaking in a frenzy of sexuality. Kamar had danced like that, he remembered, and

she had been good to sleep with. As a teacher of
Arabic she had been unsurpassed. An American he
had worked with had described her beautifully.
"Look at that kid go," he had said. "Forty thousand moving parts." But all that was over. Done
with. Dead. He looked at Istvan's unwavering stare
as the golden bodies swayed, then at Boris's brick-
red blush: an even greater tribute to their beauty
and promise. And for him it meant nothing. Boris
had wanted to go in so they'd gone. He looked at
the girl dancing now. She was the third, taller than
the others, more rounded, with a pretty and mis-
chievous face. It was all very boring. Then she advanced into the audience, still swaying to the music, but looking round her, searching. Oh God—
he'd forgotten about this nonsense. The comedy-
sex routine. She came up to their banquette, and
stood there, and the drum beats marked the curv-
ing movement of her hips. She held out her hand to
Boris, who shrank away, then to Istvan, who
sweated hot and cold—lust and terror. At last she
grabbed at Craig, and tried to draw him on to the
floor, and all the time the drums beat, her belly
writhed to their rhythm. Somewhere in Craig's
mind a neat, angry man moved a pointer across a
dial. He looked into the girl's face, and spoke to
her, the guttural words snapping like whips. For
the only time she missed a beat, then her head came
up once more and she went to find another victim.

"I'm very grateful to you," said Boris. "That girl
is embarrassing."

"You're very welcome," said Craig.

The girl had found an American, had taken off
his coat and tie, and was now removing his shirt.

Then she tied the tie across his chest as a bra. The man was pelted like a monkey. She began to coax him into a belly dance, and the crowd was laughing to see what had been desirable made grotesque. Kamar had done that, too: it had given her great pleasure to degrade a man, any man. She had never liked Craig to praise her for it. . .

The American had been released, and was putting on his shirt while his wife told him how relieved she was that there was no one else there from Sandusky, Ohio. The girl accepted her applause almost casually; her body was already concentrating on the next part of her act. Slyly the music began again, and this time it was, Craig knew, the stuff the tourist doesn't see too often. He remembered a party in Fez, where he had been the guest of honor. He'd delivered a hundred Belgian rifles the day before, and this had been for him. It was the first time he had met Kamar . . . The girl's body moved as if tormented by the music, as if the wailing sounds were an aphrodisiac that drove her on and on, and the slow writhing of her body only intensified her need. One by one the instruments cut out, until the drum beats alone spoke to her and she responded exactly to their rhythm, kneeling in front of the drummer, answering each beat with a responsive and rhythmical shuddering, until at last her body arched backward, legs astride, her pretty belly rippled to the swift-flowing sounds. Then she shuddered, and the drums were still, the lights dimmed, then rose, and she was bowing as the audience roared.

"What an extraordinary thing," said Boris.

"Please, I should like to go home now," said

Istvan. "This is worse than Siberia."

They went back, and Craig marveled at Boris's docility. He had allowed Craig to take them all over Tangier, and be seen. That made him a fool. Craig didn't believe that Boris was a fool. This job was too important.

In the hotel a Negro porter in white robes handed over their keys and spoke to Craig in Arabic. His voice was low and rumbling, and he bowed as the three men went to the lift.

"What was all that about?" Boris asked.

"He hopes we enjoy our stay here," said Craig.

"He wants a tip," said Istvan.

Boris said, far too late: "You shouldn't speak Arabic, Craig. Tourists never do."

The three of them shared a suite. There was a living room and verandah, and opening off it, on either side, a double-bedded room for Boris and Istvan, a single-bedded room for Craig. It was Craig who now unlocked the door to the living room, and stood aside for Boris to enter. He didn't, but Istvan in some way he never understood found himself impelled by the sheer force of Craig's will into stepping over the threshold, and so Boris followed. Then came Craig, last of all. They had left a light burning in the room, and he stood outside its soft, golden pool, tense and ready, the snub-nosed Smith and Wesson no longer in his shoulder holster, but transferred to the waistband of his trousers as he followed Boris. He stood in the half darkness, his hand on his hip. The butt of the gun was only inches away from his fingers.

Inside the lamplight a woman sat. Her hair was very fair, almost white, and her eyes were green as a cold sea. She wore a white dress, and a mink lay at her feet like a trophy. Craig noticed at once her quality of repose. She sat completely at ease, not moving; the position of her body and the chair she sat in were sufficient to make sure that she could watch the door, and the men who came through it. In the silence they could hear the whisper of the air-conditioning, then her hand moved swiftly down to the chair. Craig jumped sideways, and the gun was in his hand as he leaped.

"No," he said.

The woman chuckled. It was a delightful sound, rich, deep, and lazy. The Smith and Wesson covered the small arc between her and Boris. Istvan began to think of Siberia almost with nostalgia, then the woman rose, and he gasped aloud. She was tall, full-bodied, and very graceful, with the grace of a hunting animal. From the corner of his eye Istvan saw the gun steady and point, its barrel a stubby, accusing finger, aimed an inch below her left breast. Istvan had no doubt that Craig would fire if he had to, nor had the woman.

"I think Boris had better introduce us," she said.

"This is my controller," said Boris. "She's known as Tania."

"I have a letter for you," Tania said. "In my handbag. Just a letter."

"Istvan," said Craig, "get it."

And Istvan obeyed at once. Boris might be responsible for his death, Tania might be responsible for Boris, but never had Istvan seen a man with a gun who looked as Craig did. He produced the letter and handed it over at arm's length.

"Put the lights on," Craig said, and again Istvan

obeyed. "Now up against the wall, all three of you.
Hands by your sides."

Again Istvan moved as if only his fear were real;
the other two followed more slowly. Even lowering
her arms in defeat, Tania's grace was deadly. Craig
read the letter. "You'd better pour the drinks,
Istvan," he said.

Istvan drank the first one himself, and didn't
even know he'd done so. By the time the others had
glasses in their hands, he was on his third.

"My chief says I'm to take instructions from
you," said Craig. "I don't like it."

She spoke in Russian to Boris, and he and Istvan
went at once to their bedroom. Istvan filled his
glass before he left.

"Craig," she said, and looked at him. It was a
long, comprehensive look, sexually arrogant, dom-
ineering. Its effect on men was usually remarkable.
Craig waited with a stolid patience that was obviously reluctant.

"We have a file on you," she said. "A very thick
file. You are a very successful agent. If you become
dangerous to us, all we can do is kill you. It will be
difficult, but it can be done, I promise you."

Craig yawned. "It's been a long day," he said.

She chuckled again, the same sound of purring
pleasure. "Please," she said. "I am not presuming
to frighten you. I just tell you a fact. Also, I am
trying to avoid wasting time in anger—as you are
so tired."

"Let's have it then," said Craig.

"Your orders were to stay somewhere discreet,
quiet. I find you in a big hotel. You use the bar and
the dining room. You go to cafés and nightclubs.

You are seen all over the town."

"I thought you'd have us followed," said Craig. "Didn't want Boris to have to keep making phone calls, I suppose. Embarrassing, pretending you have to go to the toilet all the time."

"Don't underestimate Boris. He did as he was told."

"I guessed he would," said Craig. "And if he didn't I'd have gone anyway."

"But why, Craig? You are known here. It could be awkward for you." Craig was silent. "You wish to be seen, don't you?" Again he didn't answer. "Loomis told you to cooperate," she said.

"We're taking a bank," said Craig. "All right. But our cover is we're tourists. And tourists tour."

"Brodski could have seen you," she said. "Or Simmons."

She made no mention of Hornsey, and Craig scarcely noticed.

"Simmons is here?" he asked.

"He and his daughter arrived tonight. They're staying at Brodski's villa. You have orders about Simmons."

"I'm to kill him," said Craig.

"After we have robbed the bank. You're in too much of a hurry." Again the long look, but angry this time. "I don't like that. It makes for carelessness." His impassiveness was absolute. "Why be so stupid, Craig?"

"You've got your orders, too. I bet they say he has to die."

She sighed. There was a fury in the man, an upsurge of personal rage that had nothing to do with the job. She sensed it at once, and was wary. Her only chance was to use it.

"We will take the money tomorrow," she said. "Your people have the escape route?" Craig nodded. "You will tell it to me, please."

He told her. There was a fast cruiser in the yacht club. Its owner was away, and to steal it at night was simple, particularly as the owner had orders that it should be stolen . . . She listened intently, and was pleased.

"That is your planning?" Craig nodded. "It is good. We wish this to look like a crime. And Istvan has a criminal record."

Craig grinned. "I didn't think Istvan was supposed to have a happy ending."

"He is a traitor," Tania said. "Traitors cannot expect to live—if they are caught." She hesitated. "Brodski also should die. The timing will be difficult. And it won't look like a robbery, either."

"We'll take them with us," said Craig. "Kill them at sea. That way it'll look as if they'd done a bunk with their own money."

She examined the idea, and found it flawless.

"Now you are thinking," she said. "That is really very good."

"You'll be coming with us?" Craig asked.

"I must," she said. "I am Brodski's fiancée." Craig started at that, and she laughed. "It was love at first sight. Very romantic—just what one would expect from a Pole. I was here when he arrived, you see. A Polish refugee, persecuted by the wicked Russians. How I escaped from them is a tremendous adventure. You would not like it very much, I think. You have no sensibility."

"None," said Craig.

"Also you do not like women."

"What makes you think so?"

"Because I am a woman." She hesitated. "No. That is the sort of stupidity I keep for Brodski. Because I have been trained to make men like me, and want me, and I cannot reach you though I have tried very hard."

"It's not important," said Craig. "I'll get you out and I'll kill Simmons for you."

"And Brodski?"

Craig shrugged.

"Maybe it is better if Boris killed Brodski—and Istvan," she said. "We cannot use Istvan as evidence if we use your idea, but he must still die."

"Just as you like," said Craig.

"There is one more thing," said Tania. "I wish you to stop speaking Arabic to servants. That is how they tell you what is happening, is it not?"

"That's how," said Craig. "The porter told me you had come in here."

"How unkind," said Tania. "After I had bribed him not to. He is one of yours then?"

"No," said Craig. "I just offered him more money." He paused. "I'll stop speaking Arabic if you'll stop having me followed."

"I agree," she said. "And you'll stay here tomorrow?"

"Most of the time," Craig said. "I've got to lay on the powerboat."

She nodded. "I'll call Boris tomorrow and arrange about the bank. You will be ready as soon as it is dark."

"All right," he said. "But tell me one thing. Why have you people bothered to work with us at all?

Why not just do it yourselves?"

"We needed you to take us to Simmons," she said, and watched for a reaction to the name, but his face stayed closed. "We knew he existed, of course, but not who he was. Also, if things go wrong, we shall need you to get us out." He said nothing. "You can do that?"

"After I've fixed Simmons," he said.

She came up to him and kissed him on the mouth, her lips and tongue a skillful torment. He made no move.

"No," she said. "You do not like women at all."

* * *

The nursing home was expensive. Its doctors were all consultants, its nurses not only qualified but pretty, its furniture of the kind that belongs to the newer luxury hotels. Loomis found it oppressive and said so. He didn't like mobiles, or Utrillo prints, or flowers arranged as if they were objects to be disliked, and he detested the receptionist in a mini skirt, no matter how flawless her legs. He began to indulge his anger, and three minutes later they were alone with Airlie, the nurse who had admitted them ruthlessly removed.

Airlie wore a black silk dressing gown like a kimono, white silk pajamas, white slippers. The bandage round his head looked like a turban. Wetherly salaamed.

"Who the hell are you?" Airlie asked.

"We're friends," said Loomis. "By God we must be to go to all this trouble."

His hand groped in his pocket and came out bearing a crumpled letter.

"Have a look at that," he said. "Credentials."

Airlie read it and looked at them, his face wary.

"Don't tell me you're—agents," he said.

"Nothing so grand," said Loomis. "I'm a civil servant. My friend here's a doctor."

He turned to Wetherly. "Go over him. Make it look official."

Wetherly went over him.

"It's a question of what the hell you think you're playing at, d'you see," said Loomis. "Mucking around with Simmons."

"I'm engaged to his daughter," Airlie said.

"You tried to beat up a feller," said Loomis.

The earl touched the bandage Wetherly was re-fastening.

"I ended up with this," he said.

"The other feller ended up with a bit more," said Loomis.

"I could do with a bit of good news. Tell me about it."

Loomis told him about it, and Airlie turned as white as his bandage.

"I don't believe it," he said at last.

"I do," said Wetherly. "I treated him."

"But-but why should Simmons—"

"Two reasons," said Loomis. "He's a sadist, and the other feller had information." He refrained, carefully, from any mention of Jane.

"One of yours?" asked Airlie.

"One of mine. You'd better tell it, son."

Airlie said: "Simmons called it a crusade. To stop communism. We pooled our resources—for me that was mostly brawn, I suppose, till your chap came along. But he had others—bankers, lawyers, those sorts of chaps. They had brains. Expert knowledge. The idea was to use that knowledge. Against Russia."

"How?" asked Loomis.

"Bits in his papers, on his TV station. The brains would work on information Simmons got from somewhere and use it to knock Russia. That was all."

"This somewhere," said Loomis. "Was it a chap called Brodski?"

Airlie looked stubborn.

"Look," Loomis said. "I know you think the secrets of the Black Hand Gang are sacred, but they're not. It's too bloody serious for that."

"I gave my word," said the earl.

Loomis turned to Wetherly.

"Well, good for him," he said savagely. "He gave his word. I suppose that means we better go." He scowled at Airlie. "Look, son, I'm doing you a favor. I could have sent the chap Simmons worked on to ask the questions. Or had you forgotten about him?"

"I don't understand that," Airlie said. "According to Simmons, Zelko and I just had to knock him out and search him."

"He wanted you in deep," said Loomis. "So deep you could never get out."

"But why?" Airlie asked.

"He wants a war," said Loomis. "Cold or hot, it's all the same, so long as it is war. The West on one side, Russia on the other. Tension and isolation—on and on for ever."

"But why on earth—"

"We think we know now," Wetherly said. "He was in Yugoslavia during the war. Had a girl there.

The Russians captured her village and raped her until she died. The village was anti-Communist, you see. Simmons found her after they'd finished."

"He wants revenge," said Loomis. "The whole of Russia for one girl. Just like Brodski wants revenge for Poland the way it used to be. Only they're not worried about who's innocent and who's guilty. They want the lot. They want arrests and trials and blockades and incidents. They want uprisings in Prague and Leipzig and Warsaw. They want us involved, and Western Europe and the United States. And at the end of it all they want war."

"But good God," said the earl, "Simmons never even hinted—it sounded like a good idea, you know. Keeping Russia in bounds. Showing her up. And anyway," he said, "what possible use could I be in a scheme like that?"

"How much money have you got?" asked Loomis.

"On me?" asked Airlie. "Do you need some?"

Loomis began to turn red, and Wetherly rushed in.

"How much are you worth?" he said.

"Oh," said the earl. "Oh, I see. Hard to say really. They reckon about four million." He frowned. "I wouldn't have let him have any, you know. Not for that."

"He'd allowed for that," said Loomis. "If he hadn't got you hooked on the crusade he could always blackmail you."

"Blackmail me?"

"You're like a bloody echo," said Loomis. "Of course blackmail. When you went to bed with the bird he found you he took pictures." Airlie turned scarlet. "And he would have involved you in the torture too. You keen on his daughter?" Airlie nodded. "He'd use that as well." He paused a moment. The earl had leaned back in his chair and Wetherly took his pulse, then nodded.

"I think you better tell us everything," said Loomis. "Make us all feel better."

Airlie swallowed hard, then began to talk.

16

The yacht club was smart, white-painted, chic, with silent-footed servants, tall, cool drinks, and a yacht basin full of the world's most expensive toys. Craig had a visitor's membership already made out for him, and walked into the bar easy and relaxed. He had half finished his Scotch before the man who was tailing him appeared. Craig wondered if he'd had to make a phone call. He was a chunky, relaxed little man, with a lot of friends at the bar. Craig had no doubt he enjoyed his drink. It was a hot day . . .Then suddenly he had a friend at the bar, too. Esteban. In the old days he had been a Spanish smuggler. Now he was a citizen of Morocco, a respected businessman who hired boats on charter. They bought each other drinks, and talked about old times. He looked at the yachts in the basin, staring out through the picture-frame windows.

"Lovely," he said. "Aren't they lovely? The stuff we could have run in them. Look at that one." He gestured to a beautiful twin-diesel painted white, with glittering brasswork. "Belongs to a man called Carter. He's in Meknes. Having it overhauled for a trip." *Indeed he is,* thought Craig. *A trip with a mil-*

235

lion. And as he looked at Esteban it was as though fifteen years had never been, and he was a much younger Craig, marveling how Esteban was always first with information and never able to use it properly.

"It looks like the fastest thing here," said Craig.

"Just about," said Esteban. "There's another that's almost as good. Belongs to an Arab called Medani."

Craig put down his glass. His hand was quite steady.

"Where is it?" he asked.

"Out I expect," Esteban said. "Medani's a poor sailor. Gets seasick. He lends it to a Pole called Brodski. Staying at the Villa Florida. He goes out with a woman—such a woman."

Craig endured a lovingly accurate description of Tania, then Esteban said: "I came here looking for you." Craig said nothing. "You are not surprised?"

"Nothing surprises me in Tangier," said Craig.

"Fuad is chief of police now. You remember Fuad?" Craig did indeed. "He said he'd heard you were here." Craig didn't waste time asking how Fuad had heard. "He gave me a message for you. Said you were welcome. But you weren't to start anything."

"I'm only here for a week," said Craig. "This is a holiday, Esteban. The old days are finished."

"That's true." Esteban sighed.

"Tell Fuad I said so," said Craig. "And now I have to go."

He turned from the bar and as he did so the chunky, relaxed little man bumped into him, clutched his lapel for support, apologized, and left.

"Who on earth was that?" asked Craig.

"I have no idea," said Esteban, who had begun life as a pimp, matured as a thief, and made his fortune as a smuggler. "Nowadays they let anybody in here."

Craig walked out of the bar. The relaxed little man was waiting, and fell in behind him at once. Craig walked along the short pier that led to the shore road, then took a taxi to the Casbah. The relaxed little man followed him there in a private car that contained two of his friends, and Craig lost all three of them in ten minutes. It is impossible to tail a man in the Casbah if he knows it and doesn't want to be tailed. Craig shouldered his way through a crowd that was watching a snake charmer who'd just been bitten by his star performer and was about to light straw with the venom; dodged a man with a rack holding perhaps a hundred sandals; old women selling eggs, tomatoes, live chickens; a man with a brass pot of lemonade. By then only the relaxed little man was left, and his relaxed air had left him. Craig lost him in a maze of side streets: tailors', silversmiths', potters'. He ducked back then, and came out of the Casbah near the Spanish cathedral, then found a garage that rented cars. For fifty pounds he was given an elderly Chevrolet for three days, and the tiresome formality of passports was waived. A policeman directed him to the Villa Florida. It was on the Asilah road, in a brand-new estate gratifyingly near the king's most northern palace. Craig drove there quickly, and with a growing respect for the Chevrolet. Its appearance might be deplorable, but its engine had plenty of stamina left.

The Villa Florida and its garden covered about a half a block of a wide, palm-shaded street. Craig drove past it, and parked under the shade of a palm. The villa had wrought-iron gates, and a ten-foot fence of iron stakes. There was a porter at the gate, armed with what looked like a walking stick; but often, Craig remembered, those sticks too were made of iron. He walked down the road, then round to the back of the gardens. The fence there was just as high, and behind it in the garden were dwarf palms, then flowering shrubs. Craig looked out for alarm wires. There were none, and he scaled the fence, moved past the palms, and into the shelter of the shrubs, moving as he had been taught, without a sound, until he came at last to a gap in the shrubs and looked down into the garden.

It was of the Arab kind that delighted in shaded walks, islands of flowers, and tiny fountains, and in its center was the swimming pool, which is now obligatory for every rich man in a warm climate. Jane Simmons in a yellow bikini lay at the pool's edge and watched as her father dived from a springboard, swam to her in a fast crawl, and hauled himself out beside her.

"Marvelous, darling," she said.

Craig stared at the man who had hurt him, studying every line, every muscle of his body, and there was greed in his stare, almost a kind of lust. He was about to leave when a man came out of the villa and walked over to Simmons. Craig saw the quick movement of Simmons's hand that sent Jane scurrying to shield her body from him in a yellow terrycloth robe. The new man was Chinese. His

glance ignored Jane as she walked past him toward
the villa. He was intent only on Simmons. Craig
wondered what Sir Matthew Chinn would make of
the fact that Jane wore yellow so often.

"We should not talk here," said the Chinese.

"I like the open air," said Simmons. "No one
can hear us."

"Someone could hide over there," said the Chinese, and pointed to where Craig lay hidden.

"There's a guard there," said Simmons, and
Craig froze. The Chinese looked satisfied and
began to talk, and Craig, guard or no guard, listened. This was big stuff indeed, the biggest he had
ever heard. After a moment he eased out, testing
every touch of hand and foot before he risked his
weight, until at last he could crouch, and look for
the guard. He saw a foot at last, protruding from a
dry ditch, and moved carefully to it, peering over
the edge of the ditch, ready to dive before the man
could yell. He was a big man, rather negroid, and
he was fast asleep. Craig slithered down the ditch
and looked at him. The man didn't move. There
was an empty food dish beside him, and a water
bottle. Craig spoke softly, then shook the man, but
still he slept. Drugged. Craig shook the water bottle. There was still some in it. He poured it on to
the ground and the thirsty earth received it avidly.
Soon it would disappear completely. Craig looked
back toward the bushes, and behind them the
murmur of voices, and wished he had been able to
carry a gun.

* * *

Boris and Istvan were by the hotel pool, in
swimsuits. Craig changed and joined them. They

sat beneath a beach umbrella, and talked with
Tania, who looked luscious and terrifying at the
same time in a green sundress exactly the color of
her eyes. She turned to Istvan at once and said:
"Go and swim."

Istvan seemed to go from his chair into the pool
in one movement; on his face was a look compounded of terror, bewilderment, and passion, like
a rabbit in love with a stoat.

"You went to the Villa Florida," she said. "After all I told you—"

Craig said: "Cut it out. You knew I would go.
You set it up for me. You knew it last night, when
you told me Simmons was here. You kept Brodski
out of the way this morning—and you slipped
some knock-out drops to the guard in the back of
the garden. Which was it—the food or the water?"

"The water," Tania said. "If they have it
analyzed—"

"They won't," said Craig. "I poured it away."
She looked pleased. "You also had one of your
tails check to see if I had a gun. I hadn't. If I had
I suppose you'd have stopped me."

"He can't die yet," said Tania. "First the money."

"I could have killed him anyway," said Craig.

Boris looked at him then, a careful speculation
in his eyes.

"Why did you let me go there?" said Craig.

"To learn the way in," she said. "You and Boris
must go back tonight."

Craig nodded. "You been there?"

"With Brodski. To the villa only. Not to the
garden."

"Meet the Chinaman?"

So far her manner had been easy, the movement of her hands pretty and flirtatious, a woman on holiday having a drink with two men. Now one hand came down on his forearm, pink nails nipped.

"What Chinaman?" she said.

Craig looked down at her hand, and she took it away at once.

"Simmons called him Chan," said Craig. "Little man. About fifty. Limped on his left foot."

"I know him," said Tania. "Go on."

Craig looked again at his arm. There was a hairline of blood where her nail had struck. "He doesn't like you," said Craig. "Any of you. You betrayed the revolution, and Lenin and Stalin, and Marx, too, for that matter. Worst of all—you betrayed Chairman Mao."

Boris said: "It isn't part of your agreement for you to mock my country."

Tania spat out Russian and he shrugged, but he stayed angry.

"Chan wishes you to look foolish," said Craig. "He knows a way."

"Go on," said Tania. "Go on."

"Next week Russia is sending a Sputnik to the moon," said Craig. "It will have men on it. It will land on the moon."

Tania and Boris sat frozen.

"You didn't know this?" asked Craig.

"Of course not," said Tania. "Go on."

"The thing is, it won't go to the moon at all. It'll land in New Mexico."

"But that's impossible," said Boris.

"Nothing's impossible if you pay a million

pounds," said Craig.

"But who will they bribe?" asked Tania.

"It's been done," said Craig. "And they didn't say. It'll look like a breakdown, I suppose. The computer will be programmed wrongly. General ball-up. Crash landing. And the astronauts come out in the U.S.A. Won't that be funny? Your president ringing up their president and saying, 'Please, can we have our Sputnik back?' "

"A Russian wouldn't do it," said Tania.

"Maybe," said Craig. "But are they all Russians on that project? No East Germans, no Poles, no Czechs? Or Mongolians, say—blokes in touch with China?" He paused. Boris was sweating now. "There's another thing," he said. "Suppose it isn't funny? Suppose your blokes think the Americans set it up? Would you go to war for a Sputnik, Boris?"

"Not just for that," said Boris. "But if there were other things—"

"There will be," said Craig.

"If there were, Simmons would die," said Tania.

"He'd be in China," said Craig. "He'd have a chance."

"But Brodski never told me—I mean, he didn't have this knowledge. Or I would have known."

"Brodski doesn't know," said Craig.

"I must tell my people at once," said Tania.

"I agree," said Craig. "But will they believe you?"

He got up then, and dived into the pool. Istvan swam up to him in a frenzied dog paddle.

"Mr. Craig, forgive me, but I have very little time," he said.

"Of course," said Craig.

"I think—after the job—that Boris will kill me."

"I think so too," said Craig.

They swam across the pool and sat on its side. Beneath the umbrella, Tania and Boris talked with furious concentration.

"In Siberia I didn't mind if I died," Istvan said. "But now I have seen women again—real women. Last night was too much. I refuse to die now, Mr. Craig."

"Good for you," Craig said. "How are you going to do it?"

"Best I should kill Boris," said Istvan.

"I'm afraid not," Craig said. "I'd have to stop you."

"But I'm working for you," Istvan wailed.

"You are, on Boris's strength," said Craig. "And Tania's of course. You'll have to take it up with them."

He dived back into the water, and swam across. At the table the whispered Russian words went on. Craig permitted himself a cigarette.

Tania said: "I must send this message." Craig nodded. "But it's so difficult. General Chelichev—there are people, important people, who do not like his idea that we should work with you."

"I bet there are," said Craig.

"These people will say that you lie."

"That seems inevitable."

"Craig, please. Is there any way at all to prove what you have said?"

"There's Chan," said Craig.

"There is also Simmons," said Boris.

"Simmons will die," said Craig.

"No," said Tania. "We must have Simmons alive."

"Chan's all you need, surely," said Craig.

"Chan is on a diplomatic mission here. He stays with the governor. He has immunity. It will be hard for us to get to him, just now at any rate. Simmons is much easier."

Craig rose. "It's time for my nap," he said.

"You will stay," said Boris. "You must."

"I'm sorry," said Craig. "My psychiatrist says I have to have a nap every now and then. This is one of the times. Too bad I can't help you with Simmons—but there it is. He really has to die." He started to go, then turned. "I suppose you'll be having the Villa Florida watched. As a matter of fact, we are too, now that we know where it is."

The ceiling was high, the room cool, and Craig lay on his back, hands by his sides, absorbed in the height, the coolness, letting his mind float above his problems in the tall, shuttered room. The great thing about Chan's scheme was that it didn't have to work. Even if the men to be bribed were blown the Russians would still be very angry indeed, and their anger would be directed against the United States. That was all China cared about. Simmons would want rather more for his millions; so if the thing was blown now—but that raised its own problems. Tania believed him when he said that Russian security would hardly be pleased about information from a British agent. Nothing could persuade the Russians that Department K—or any other department—didn't work for Washington, so the best that Craig could hope for was that the Russians would think he was a defector, in which case they would still suspect the United States. Chelichev had had a hard time establishing the existence of BC: there were plenty of men in the Kremlin who still denied its existence. The only safe thing was to take the money, and get rid of Simmons. Tania could try kidnapping Chan if she wanted to, but even in terms of expediency, it would be better if Simmons died. He stared again at the ceiling, but his mind refused to float any more. The checks Sir Matthew Chinn had built into his psyche took over. He knew he was lying. Tania needed Simmons. She had to have him. Brodski wouldn't do. He didn't know enough. Chan might be unobtainable. Simmons was the only one. Simmons alive. Craig began to sweat as he resisted what his reason told him. But there was no other answer. Simmons had to live. Once the fact was accepted, he began to think about Istvan, about the robbery, about Medani. His mind reviewed the coastline around Tangier, the place where the power launch would wait, the second line of retreat up the coast if anything went wrong. First the money, then Simmons. Brodski would be at the villa too, and Jane. It would be dangerous to take them all alive. And yet to kill them wouldn't be the answer. It wouldn't be the answer at all.

* * *

He slept until dinnertime, then rose, bathed, changed into a dark silk tussore suit and black crepe-soled shoes. Beneath his coat was the Smith and Wesson; in his leg was a sheathed knife, leaf-bladed, single-edged, needle-pointed. He spread his hands, then held them out. They were quite steady. He went into the living room.

Istvan and Boris were waiting. They too wore dark suits and, Craig had no doubt that Boris was armed. Neither of them was drinking. Food and drink would have to wait.

Boris said: "Istvan's being difficult."

"I'm not surprised," said Craig. "He knows you're going to kill him."

Boris began to deny it, fluently, passionately. It was obvious that Istvan was not impressed.

Craig said: "He knows it because it's logical. You're a nation of chess players, Boris. You always lose a pawn to take a king."

Istvan said: "Or even a king's ransom. You had better shoot me now."

Craig said: "Why not talk it over with Tania?"

"She's with Brodski," Boris said. "I can't reach her."

"Work him over then," said Craig. "We haven't much time."

Istvan said: "You do too good a job, Boris. If you hurt me, I couldn't work for you afterwards."

Craig said: "I'll do it then."

He moved in on Istvan, one fist clinched, the other hand out flat, like an ax.

"No," said Boris. "No karate."

Craig stood still.

"You're right," he said. "All he'd do is agree, then rat on us when we got to the bank. Right?"

Istvan managed to smile. It was a kind of courage.

"Absolutely," he said.

"It's a stand-off," said Craig. "Unless—" Boris looked at him. "Give him to me when it's over," Craig said. "He knows a few tricks that would interest my chief. So long as he's useful, he'll live. And I promise you he won't chat."

Boris said: "All right with me," and looked at Istvan.

"London," said Istvan. "Swinging London. Birds. Mini skirts. Le topless." He stuck out a hand to Craig. "Okay," he said.

Boris said: "We pick up Tania at eleven. Until then we should go over your plan."

They sat round the table, and Craig began to talk. The Russian and the Hungarian were very patient listeners.

* * *

At ten forty-five the three men left their room. In the lobby the night porter handed Craig a package that had been left for him. They went out of the hotel to where a rented car waited, a Mercedes 300 SE. The chauffeur was Tania, in black slacks and sweater and a short black coat. They got in and Craig opened the package. It contained two keys.

Tania said: "Brodski stays at the villa. So does Simmons—and Jane. Chan is with the governor."

Craig said: "It'll have to be Simmons then. Can you get in?"

"You have decided not to kill him?" she asked.

"It looks as if I have to," Craig said. "Can you get in?"

"He thinks I'm dining with a girl friend," said Tania. "I said I'd try to get back for a drink about one o'clock. He told me he's working late tonight."

"He's going to get his orders from Simmons," said Craig.

A beggar came up to the car, and Craig wound down his window, handed over a dirham. They talked softly together in Arabic, then the beggar salaamed as the big car moved away.

"Listen carefully," said Craig. "I want you to know where the launch will be—just in case one of us doesn't make it."

He began to talk, and the others listened with the same furious patience. At last Craig said: "If anything goes wrong with the boat we make for Ceuta. I've got a friend there with a fishing boat. But if it comes to that, the only chance we've got is Gibraltar."

Tania said: "Very well," and drove into the town, waited patiently for a left turn into the Boulevard Pasteur, then turned into a side street. The street was dimly lit after the boulevard, and there were cars parked on both sides. As they turned in, a Fiat van pulled out, and Craig congratulated Tania on her efficiency as the Mercedes slid into the space the Fiat had left.

They got out then, and Craig looked down toward the lights of the boulevard. The Crédit Labonne building was on the corner, dark and shuttered as a fortress. Beside it were houses with a narrow frontage and heavy doors, their tiny windows latticed. Craig waited as Boris opened the Merc's boot, then he and Istvan took out the two neat leather cases that contained Istvan's equipment—*Brought in, no doubt, by diplomatic pouch,* thought Craig. He walked down the street to the house next to the bank and went in. The others followed, lagging, giving him time to open the door. For this he needed the key with the string tied to it. The lock worked easily, and in he went. The others followed, and the door swung to. Craig

led the way down the flight of steps that led to a
basement room, and from there down older steps,
carved into rock, that brought him to the cellar beneath the house. Once grain had been stored there,
or oil. A ring set in the wall hinted that it might
have been a private prison, a place where slaves
were taken for discipline. Before the liberation,
Craig remembered, it might have contained weapons, waiting for transport south to the Sahara, then
over the border to Algeria. Now all it held was an
old bicycle and the remains of a pram. An un-
shaded bulb gave off a grudging light, and Craig
moved to the wall adjoining the bank. Patiently
someone had chipped away the stone, just enough
to admit a man of Boris's size, or Craig's. Behind
the stone was a sheet of steel, and someone had cut
a hole in that, too, just enough. The steel plate and
broken rock were piled neatly by the hole. There
was no sign of tools, or a blow torch.

"Your people are thorough, too," said Tania.

"We rented the basement for a month," said
Craig. "The rock was easy, but we had to wait until
the bank closed tonight to cut through the steel."
He turned to Istvan. "In you go," he said.

Istvan disappeared as naturally as a rabbit into a
burrow, and Boris followed.

Craig turned to the woman.

"You'll keep watch?" She nodded. "If we're
blown and there's time, come into the bank. We'll
set up an escape straight through to the front door.
If there's any excitement, there'll be a car waiting.
A green Buick taxi."

"It's a pleasure to work with you," said Tania.

He went through the hole, and Tania sat, her

back against the wall. It was cold in the cellar, and for that reason only she shivered, then took from her pocket a Makarov 9mm. semi-automatic pistol. It was made in the USSR and was very, very accurate.

One corner of the bank cellar was filled with the massive outline of the time-lock safe. Istvan examined it by the light of a pencil torch, then grinned with the affection reserved for an ancient enemy, as Craig led the way up the stairs to the door that led to the mezzanine. He moved aside for Istvan to join him, then held the torch as the Hungarian used his picklock with slow, careful skill. On the mezzanine floor an armed guard was posted, and above him on the ground floor was another. Until they were silenced they could risk no noise at all. As Craig watched, the picklock engaged, and Istvan's gloved hand reached out, the door handle turned. Slowly, a fraction at a time, he opened the door. Craig watched through the widening crack, then his hand touched Istvan's arm. The door stayed still. The room was lit, and Craig could see the guard sitting in a chair, his back to the door. He looked over to the windows. They were completely shuttered. He watched as Istvan took an oil can from his case and oiled the door hinges, then pulled the door open wider. Craig went through like a cat, moving up to the guard. The man sat still until Craig almost reached him, then suddenly became aware of the other's presence. He started to rise as Craig's hand struck out, moving into the blow, then fell back into the seat; that would have fallen too if Craig had not held it steady. No cry, no crash, no sound at all. Craig looked down at the guard as the other two came in. He was an Arab in a uniform that looked vaguely military, blue battledress with the initials C.L.—Crédit Labonne—on the shoulders. Behind his ear a bruise darkened to purple on the olive skin. Istvan took wire and tape from his bag and tied him to the chair, then gagged him. When he had done, Craig felt the guard's pulse. He had not thought the guard would move. That increased the force of the blow, and he hadn't meant the guard to die. The pulse was thin and ragged, but it was there. Only Sir Matthew Chinn knew why Craig was relieved.

Istvan oiled the hinges of the mezzanine door, then looked at the grille in the room, and the safe behind it. He pointed at his watch. Time was running short. He listened, then opened the door to a half flight of steps and a third door above them. Behind it was the second guard. Again Istvan worked with the picklock, oiled the door hinges, eased the door ajar. This time the guard was sitting half facing the door. Boris began an elaborate pantomime, and Craig nodded. Istvan closed the door and began to lock it. Boris shook his head, and Craig and Istvan moved back to the mezzanine. Boris took out a Makarov, then a ten-dirham coin about the size and weight of a shilling. He let the coin fall on the stone steps. From behind the door he heard in the room the creak of a chair, footsteps, the grating of a key in a lock. Then the door opened, and as it did so Boris pushed it from his side. It slammed into the man behind it and Boris swerved through and struck with the butt of the Makarov as the guard opened his mouth to yell. From the mezzanine they heard the thud of his body hitting the floor. Istvan looked down at Craig's right hand. It held the Smith and Wesson, and it was rock-steady. He began to feel better.

Boris called to them softly, and again Istvan wired and taped the guard, then threaded his way past the caisse to inspect the main door, unlocking it, leaving only one heavy bolt in place. Then they went back to the mezzanine, and the fiendishly complex lock that protected the combination of the grille. Craig held the torch as Istvan examined it.

"The same as before," he said. "Good. This will not take long."

Once again he probed and tested, then took out the key he had made for the safe Loomis had set up for him. He tried it, and it didn't work. Delicately, with extreme care, he filed two of the wards. Again it failed. Istvan swore, then filed a third ward, oiled the key and eased it into the lock. It clicked as it engaged, then he again put a bar of metal into the ring end and twisted—one to the right, three to the left, two more to the right. The lock opened and Istvan pushed across the shutter that screened the combination. His hand reached out to turn it, then froze into stillness. Inside the combination panel were two tiny photoelectric cells. Boris shuffled with impatience as Istvan searched for their wires. To reach them he had to dig into the plaster walls. He cut them and went back to the combination.

"No nation thinks so highly of money as the French," he said. "They revere it as they do God. Even the West Germans don't treat the Deutschmark like that." His hand turned the dial, and the tumblers clicked.

"I would prefer you not to talk," said Boris.

"It soothes me," Istvan said, and turned the dial again. "To the West German, the Deutschmark is a symbol, no more."

"The swastika was a symbol," said Boris. But the tumblers clicked again, and Istvan was listening. He took a stethoscope from his bag and listened even more intently, and Craig wondered why the conversation should seem so important to him. They had come to steal money—but there was more to it than that. What Istvan had said was important. Loomis had said it too, weeks ago. The Deutschmark was a sacred symbol. They would do anything to protect it. The tumblers clicked, and Istvan sighed, and Craig put the problem from his mind.

"That's it," said Istvan.

He pressed a button on the wall and there was a whirring hum as the shutter folded upward. Behind it was the door of the safe, and two more cells.

Istvan said: "These electronic eyes are a nuisance. But I dare not switch off the electricity. The bank must show some light on to the street."

Again he found and cut the wires, then worked at the lock protecting the combination of the safe. When it gave at last there were more photoelectric-cell wires to cut before he could begin on that. The stethoscope swung from his neck. In his dark suit he looked like a doctor called from a dinner party to an urgent case, and he moved with a doctor's jaunty professionalism.

"Last lap," he said.

Craig looked at his watch. Eleven fifty. They had been in the bank for forty minutes. It seemed like forty hours.

The combination to the safe was more difficult than the grille's, and Istvan played it like an angler with a twenty-pound salmon. Again and again he spun the dials and listened, isolating the possible permutations of numbers until he gave the sigh that Craig had been waiting for. The dials spun for the last time, and Istvan's lips moved as he repeated the numbers, then the lock clicked loud in the stillness, and Istvan began to twist the wheel that opened the massive door. As he did so, there came a muffled thud from above them. Craig motioned them to be still, then went back upstairs. The guard there had slouched forward and his chair had fallen. He was still unconscious. Craig picked him up and jammed the chair with its back against the clerks' desk that ran the length of the bank. The man was breathing in great snoring gasps, probably concussion. Boris, he thought, was no sadist, but he had a damned heavy hand. He turned to go back down and the phone rang. Craig cursed. There wasn't time to ignore the phone. If they let it ring they would have to leave now, and there could be no second chance. No one had told him about phone calls, either. This might be a new spot-check, or a policeman might have spotted them going into the house next door . . . It had to be answered. Even if his bluff failed, they still had time to run. He moved to the switchboard behind the tellers' desk, and picked up the operator's phone, then grunted: "Who's this?" in Arabic, trying to sound sleepy and irritable, and not at all like Craig.

The voice at the other end said in English: "I'm terribly sorry. I seem to have the wrong number."

Craig spoke in Arabic again, and the voice at the other end apologized and hung up, then Craig replaced his own receiver.

He went back to the mezzanine. Istvan was inside the safe now, working on the lock of the trapdoor that led to the time-lock safe below. He was working with a furious but carefully controlled speed that Craig found admirable. He had understood the significance of the phone call without waiting to be told.

Boris said: "What happened?"

"The guard's chair fell over," said Craig, "then some fool dialed the wrong number." But it hadn't been a fool, Craig was sure. It had been Hornsey.

When the trapdoor opened, Istvan swung down, as sure as a cat. Craig followed; Boris stayed on guard on the floor above. They were now inside the time-lock safe. Istvan switched on the lamp he had brought with them, and they looked about them. The safe was a vast cupboard, lined with shelves, and each shelf was divided up into enormous pigeonholes, each with its own safe door.

"Number three on the right," said Craig.

Istvan nodded, but went first to the main door of the safe. He carefully cracked the glass panel that covered its four clocks, took it out, then unscrewed the metal panel that covered the mechanism. They could hear the clock ticking quite clearly. Delicately then he detached the springs from the balance wheels and the ticking stopped. He went over to each of the four large steel bars that secured the door in turn, and swung them into a vertical position, then turned the wheel by the door, making it swing open. Carefully he measured the gap. When it got to a foot he stopped.

"Another electronic eye," he said, then grinned. "It's lucky they have a wheel on both sides of this door. I'd hate to try to push it open."

Craig said: "All right. We've got an escape route. Get on with it."

He watched once more as Istvan tackled the lock. Before he had thought of a fisherman playing a salmon, but that was wrong. Istvan would never do anything so energetic. The analogy, he thought, should be different. Hungarians were often musicians, and that was what Istvan made him think of. The capable fingers working with such loving skill; it was like watching a pianist resolve a difficult cadenza. He looked at his watch. 12:30. Tania would be late at the Villa Florida. Then, for the last time, Istvan sighed, and the small safe door swung open.

He hadn't known what to expect. Bundle after bundle of notes probably; hard, useful currencies in sets of a hundred. Instead there were suitcases, six of them, a matched set in black leather with hand-forged brass locks and the initials BC in gold. Istvan hefted one from the shelf, then swore as it slipped in his fingers.

"I'd forgotten how much good paper weighs," he said.

"Get them all out," said Craig. "I'll go for Boris."

Craig scrambled into the safe above, then heard the soft click of a picklock on metal. He grinned and counted to a hundred before he fetched Boris. That was all the start Istvan could have.

The guards were still unconscious as Craig and

Boris scrambled down into the safe. Istvan had the cases drawn up in a neat row, but Craig made Istvan open one. They seemed almost too heavy to contain paper, but they did. A hundred and ten bundles of one-thousand-Deutschmark bills, a hundred bills to the bundle. Eleven million Deutschmarks, crisp and clean from the printer.

"It is almost too beautiful," said Istvan. "Really, people should take better care of their property."

17

She was waiting by the hole in the wall. As Craig
came through the Makarov disappeared into her
pocket and she helped drag out the suitcases, then
went up to bring the Mercedes nearer. The men
carried them up into the hall, waiting. They heard
the sound of a key searching for a lock, and moved
into the shadow as a fat and very drunken man
staggered in and went toward the stairs. Boris's
hand moved toward his coat, and Craig shook his
head. The fat man lunged at the banister, caught it
at last and began ponderously to climb. They
waited until he turned the corner of the stairs, then
heard a thud, followed by a woman's voice
spraying Spanish like bursts from a machine gun.

"Let's go," said Craig.

Outside the Merc waited, and they loaded it with
the cases, and Istvan's tools.

"What now?" Boris asked.

Tania said: "Simmons. I have worked out a
plan. It should be possible, I think."

She began to talk as she drove, and Craig agreed
with her. It should be possible. Only Istvan was
excluded, and that made him very happy. To wait

in the car was the height of his ambition.

They drove to where Craig had left the rented car, then Craig took its wheel and Tania sat in the back. Behind them Boris and Istvan followed in the Merc. She said nothing until they reached the street where the villa was, and when she did speak at last, her voice was worried.

"Remember, Craig, I must have Simmons alive."

"I remember," said Craig. She looked back out of the window. The Merc was still following.

"You're really leaving Istvan behind?" Craig asked.

"He can't steal that car," Tania said. "Nobody can—not without tools. And his are in the boot, with the money. Istvan won't go without money."

Then he pulled up outside the villa, and honked the horn. A watchman came up out of the darkness as Tania fumbled in a purse, handing Craig money.

Craig said in Arabic: "This lady is expected."

The watchman stared at her, then began to open the gate. As he did so, Craig began to explain in English why he could not wait for her. The gate opened, and Tania walked in, the Craig called: "You've forgotten this," and moved forward. The watchman turned too late, half lifting his iron club. Craig's blow was already on the way. He fell at once and Craig caught him, dragged him into the shadows, then put his hands behind his back and took piano wire from his pocket. From further down the street he could hear Boris's hurrying footsteps. He finished tying up the watchman as Boris joined him in the shadows. Tania walked down the path, and the two men moved alongside her, in cover, then sped to the steps that led to the villa's door, and stood waiting, one on each side. Tania looked quickly from one to the other, then pressed the bell. A burly Arab in a djibbah opened the door and said at once: "Good evening, madame."

Tania said: "There has been an accident, I think. Your watchman—"

"Yes, madame?"

"He seems to have been attacked." She turned and pointed. "Just over there."

The burly Arab called out, then he and another Arab came out through the door. The sound of flesh meeting flesh was very small in the darkness, and both Craig and Boris caught their victims before they could fall, tied them with piano wire, took away the pistol each man carried as Tania walked into the hallway. They followed, their shoes noiseless on the floor's inevitable marble, then moved to the door behind which was the sound of voices to stand again one on each side, guns in their hands. Craig noticed the swell of Tania's splendid breast as she breathed in—she gave no other sign of fear. Then she opened the door and walked in, leaving the door open behind her. There was a split second for her to choose the words that would tell them how to act. "Forgive me," meant go ahead; "Excuse me" meant get out quick.

"Forgive me," said Tania. "I know it's late—"

Craig went in fast, pushing Tania clear as he leaped to one side. There were three men in the room: Simmons, Brodski, and Medani. Their look of surprise at the sight of Craig was perfectly genuine. For a moment it seemed almost a scene of farce, so intense it was.

"Tania," said Brodski. "What on earth—" He looked at Craig. "The man who fought with Jennifer," he said.

"Is that all you know about me?" Craig asked. Simmons moved at last, and the gun followed him hungrily. He stayed very still. From where he stood Craig could see Boris in the doorway.

He said: "I don't have to tell anybody not to move." Their stillness was no longer comic; it was full of terror.

"Keep your hands where I can see them," said Craig, and they obeyed him.

Brodski said: "I don't understand why you should be with him. You—a Pole—"

Tania said: "I'm a Russian."

Brodski had lived all his life on instant decisions. As a fencing champion in Cracow, as a fighter pilot, as a club owner, learning when to fight and when to bribe, and as a spy, buying information in London; always it had been the moment of absolute certainty that counted. He made a decision now. This woman whom he adored had him marked for death. He would not die alone.

He dropped suddenly to one side, and his hand moved to his pocket. Craig and Boris fired together, and Brodski died, with a Smith and Wesson bullet in his right shoulder and a Makarov bullet in the heart. He fell very close to Tania. She did not look at him. Her eyes were on Simmons. When he saw Craig's gun swing to Brodski, Simmons had risen, but the barrel was pointing at him again, and he was still.

"Your daughter in bed?" asked Craig.

"Yes," said Simmons.

"Anybody else here?"

Simmons shook his head.

"Watch the door," Craig said to Boris. "Keep the girl out of here."

Boris looked at Tania, and she nodded. He left.

Medani said: "Are we all to die?"

"It's possible," said Craig.

"Because if so I should like time to pray," said Medani.

"Pray then," said Craig, and Medani did so, his lips moving. Tania looked at him in wonder, then began to go through a desk in the room, turning out papers.

"May one ask what you're looking for?" Simmons asked.

"Not your money," said Craig. "We've got that already. All of it. Out of Crédit Labonne."

The news shook Simmons. He rocked back on his heels, then came in again.

"In exchange for your manhood?" he asked.

Craig chuckled, pushed his gun into the waistband of his trousers. "I wonder what you hope to get by making me mad. A quick death?"

There was the sound of Jane's voice outside the door, calling out to her father.

"You'd better answer her," said Craig.

Simmons took a step forward.

"Everything's all right," he shouted. "Go up to your room."

"But there's a man here with a gun. And I heard a shot."

"Thieves," said Simmons, moving closer to the door. "They ran away. Go to your room."

He was now very close to Craig. Medani stopped
praying. Behind them Tania still searched through
the bureau. Deliberately Craig half turned away
from Medani. It was the chance they had been
waiting for, the system that Zelko and Simmons
had used when they—when they—Craig closed his
mind to what had happened and concentrated on
the practice session in the cellar. That was how it
would be. Medani slumped forward in his chair,
crouched like a runner, feet tensed for a spring.
Craig looked again at Tania, and Simmons moved.

His fist curled up from his side, aimed at Craig's
neck, but Craig was already leaping away from
him, hands grabbing for Medani as he came out of
the chair, clutching his arm, pulling him into the
three-fingered strike that slammed into his stomach, spinning him round to spoil Simmons's attack, the young Arab clutching at Simmons for
support before Craig's final blow cracked to the
back of his neck and he fell. Simmons leaped over
him, and Craig swung his head aside just in time
from a punch aimed at the throat, then his own
return blow was countered and Simmons threw
him, then leaped after. Craig rolled away from a
kick that would have killed him, then flicked a
blow at Simmons's outstretched foot, making him
stumble as Craig scrambled up again. They faced
each other, and Craig could see no fear in
Simmons's eyes, only the boiling hate that can take
a man to a lightning victory, or betray him into
disaster. Simmons's hand, held flat, swept at his
shoulder, seeking the collarbone, and Craig
swerved, wary for the second blow that would follow the feint. It was a fist strike, the one he wanted,

and Craig grabbed the fist, his hands locking round it in a clean smack, using Simmons's own momentum, pulling him into the bar of his outstretched leg so that he dived at the wall. Even then the man's reflexes were fantastic, as he hit the wall spinning, his head tucked in, arms in front of him to take the blow, cushioning the shock so that he could leap straight back. But this time Craig too had moved, and it was his foot that shot out, leg rigid from thigh to ankle, slamming into Simmons's body even as he leaped. A terrible blow, its force carefully controlled, worked out in exact accord with the vengeance Craig had to have. It took Simmons in the groin, and the fight was over. Simmons lay on the floor and screamed until Craig went to him, hauled him up, and struck again. Then he was silent.

Tania said: "That is all, Craig. You will not touch him again."

Craig looked at her. The Makarov was back in her hand. From the doorway he could hear Boris's voice as he stood and looked down on Simmons.

"We have been kind to you," Boris said. "Be satisfied."

"Do you know what he did to me?" asked Craig.

Tania looked down at Simmons. Even unconscious, he was in agony.

"We don't know," she said. "We don't want to know. But whatever it was, you have paid him."

Craig turned to Medani, now struggling to his feet, his hands pressed to his stomach.

"What about him?" he said. "And the girl?"

"The girl's locked in her room," Boris said. "We don't need this one." He smiled and raised the

Makarov. "And he has said his prayers."

Craig said: "We'll have him."

"Alive?" asked Tania.

"His father is important," said Craig. "No doubt he'll do a lot to get his son back unharmed."

Tania's head came up and he added quickly: "You've got Simmons after all. That just leaves the girl."

"We don't need her," said Tania. "But we can't leave her here."

Craig said: "I'll take her, too."

"Such chivalry," Tania said. Craig shrugged.

"She might be useful," he said. "She's her father's heir." He turned to Medani. "We will speak in English," he said.

Medani groaned, and rubbed his stomach.

"I feel as if I had been stabbed," he said. "What did you hit me with?"

"This," said Craig, and held up his three fingers. "You're lucky. I used my foot on Simmons."

Medani looked down at the man on the floor. His face showed the fatalism of a race that knew defeat inevitably meant death at best; at worst torture, mutilation, not only for the loser but for everyone connected with him. It had always been so; it could be no different now.

"You won," he said. "We lost." He looked at Boris. "Why do you not let this man kill me?"

"You fool," Craig said. "You stupid bloody fool." The proud head came up to the whip of his voice, arrogant even in defeat.

"Don't you understand yet?" said Craig. "Why did you join Simmons?"

"He and Brodski were going to save us from the

Russians," Medani said. "We do not want communism here. Simmons would keep it out."

"By letting the Chinese in?"

The arrogance turned to a childish bewilderment.

"He would not—" Medani began.

"A man called Chan was here yesterday," said Craig.

"He's staying with the governor. My father would not meet him," said Medani.

"Simmons did. I saw him. I heard him. He'll give Chan anything he wants—for help against Russia."

"You lie," said Medani.

Tania said: "No. It's all here. Among his papers. May he see?"

Craig nodded, and watched the birth of disillusion as the young man read. At last he raised his face, and there was no hope in it at all.

"He told us it was to be a crusade," said Medani. "We were fighting for Islam, he said. Our way of life. Our history." He turned to the unconscious figure and spat. "We fought only for him."

"We'd better let your father know," said Craig, and turned to Tania. "I'll have to stay," he said. "This is important."

"You may be caught," she said.

Craig's hand weighed down on Medani's shoulder.

"I am this man's guest," he said.

* * *

He went up to the bedroom. She lay on the bed, seeing nothing, feeling nothing, the little bottle still clasped in her hands. Craig strode over to her, twitched it from her fingers. The bottle was almost full. He sighed his relief and hauled her upright, then his hand cracked against her cheeks, left and right, till she whimpered and her eyes opened.

"I couldn't," she said. "I wanted to, but I couldn't." Her fingers moved up to her cheeks as the pain came to her. "Did you kill Daddy?"

"No," said Craig. "He's going on a trip."

"A long one?"

"He's never coming back."

She said: "I know what he did to you . . . Will I see him?"

"No," said Craig.

She began to cry then, and he left her. It was time to talk to Istvan. He took the Merc's keys with him.

He was still in the car, and beside him sat an earnest young man in a crumpled lightweight suit. The two of them were talking furiously in German.

"Mr. Hornsey," said Craig. "How nice to see you."

"Nice to see you," said Hornsey. "At least I hope so. The trouble is—it's the money, you see. Simmons's money, I mean."

"Our money," said Craig.

"Well, our money really," said Hornsey. "At least not even ours. Not really. Oh, I better explain. My name's not Hornsey by the way. It's Heinze. I'm a German, Mr. Craig. At least my father was— my mother's British. I work for the Defense of the Constitution. I was controller for Driver. We hired him to work for us too."

"To find forged twenty-dollar bills?"

"No," said Hornsey, "to find forged Deutschmarks. The dollars were just bait. Unfortunately they made poor Driver greedy. You have the Deutschmarks, Mr. Craig. A million pounds' worth."

"Oh my God," said Craig, and began to laugh.

"It gets better," said Istvan bitterly. "Guess who made the plates."

"They made two actually," said Hornsey. "A twenty-dollar bill and a hundred-Deutschmark note."

"Who did?" said Craig.

"The Russians," said Hornsey, and Craig began to laugh once more.

"It was done during the cold war," Hornsey said. "They got the idea from a scheme of Hitler's during the war—forged five-pound notes to wreck the British economy, you remember?" Craig nodded. "The Russians were going to do the same —against us and the Americans. For some reason or other they didn't use it, but Brodski's agents found the man who had the plates. He defected, and they bought them from him, made the money and stored it here. The twenty-dollar bill was poor —Simmons only made a few and got rid of them."

"Calvet got hold of one," said Craig.

"So did we," said Hornsey. "Driver used it to reach Brodski. It was very foolish of him. But the Deutschmark was excellent. We cannot allow it to be used, Mr. Craig. It would make West Germany look foolish."

The sacred symbol, Craig thought. *The god who must not be mocked.*

"What do you want us to do?" he asked.

"Destroy them," said Craig.

"Destroy a million?" said Istvan. There was hor-ror in his voice.

"I'll see," said Craig.

* * *

He told them what Hornsey had said, and at first they hadn't believed him, but when at last they did, Tania had laughed, Boris had drunk brandy, and Medani had continued to brood on the wickedness that Craig had only just prevented him from com-mitting. Compared with that, a mere million was of no interest. Tania and Boris looked at the spec-imens he had bought, compared them with the gen-uine article Hornsey had given him. The differ-ences were minute, but they existed. Tania rolled up a forged note, flicked a table lighter to it, lit a cigarette, and watched the note crumple into ash in her fingers, then dropped it into the ashtray.

"In a way I'm glad," she said. "After all, we're not criminals, Craig."

He looked at the dead Brodski, at Simmons writhing in a coma.

"No," said Craig. "What criminal would behave as we do?"

He sent Medani for Jane then, gave him the keys of the Chevrolet, and told him to take the girl to his father's house in Tangier. Then he went back to the Mercedes, drove it to the villa gates, and waited as Boris loaded Simmons into the car.

"We've given him a shot," Tania said. "He won't be any trouble." She smiled at Hornsey. "Nor will we, young man, not if you destroy that money. Our government might find it embarrass-ing."

"It will be destroyed, I promise," Hornsey said.

"Let's go then."

Craig drove them out of the town, and along the road that led to Ceuta. The launch was waiting offshore, and in the Atlantic, off Gibraltar, the inevitable Russian trawler waited for it. They would be home in a week, Tania promised, and Comrade-General Chelichev would be delighted to see them, and Simmons. With his evidence the next space shot would be a success.

"We are grateful to you," she said. "The comrade-general will tell your chief so."

"Thanks," said Craig.

"It will be easy for you to get out?" Tania asked.

"Medani will fix it," said Craig. "He'll alibi Istvan and me for the night. Then we'll go to visit his father. We'll be okay with him."

He pulled up on the roadside. The sea was a black line against a smudge of sand which in daylight was a blinding white. There was a dinghy with an outboard beached, and behind it, out to sea, port and starboard lights glowing like jewels, a power boat waited.

"We must go," said Tania, and left the car. Boris followed, carrying Simmons like a parcel.

"Good-bye, Craig," he said. *"Do svidanye,"* and trudged off down the beach.

Tania kissed him on the mouth, demanding a response. There was none.

"Good-bye, Craig," she said. "I wish I had known you when you liked women."

Then she too went off to the dinghy.

They watched as the outboard sputtered, saw the faint silver wake cut its way to the power boat, then listened to the deep, muted roar of her engines as her mast lights dwindled and died.

"This is a very deserted road," said Hornsey.

"You want to do it now?" Istvan asked, anguish in his voice.

Craig said: "The longer we put it off the harder it'll be."

"Wait," said Istvan, and turned to Hornsey. "I have people I can contact," he said. "Businessmen. They would pay perhaps ten thousand pounds for this money."

"No," said Hornsey.

"Twenty thousand," said Istvan.

"No."

"They would be very discreet. They would not distribute more than a hundred thousand pounds' worth in one year." Hornsey was silent. "Twenty-five thousand," said Istvan. "It's the top price to pay for hot money."

"You can't buy this money," Hornsey said. "You couldn't buy it for a million. It has to burn."

"At least let me keep the cases," Istvan said. They let him.

They dug a hole on the beach, filled it with crumpled notes, soaked them with petrol siphoned from the car, lit it with a wad of notes lit like a torch. One by one they dropped the sheafs of stiff, elegant paper into the flames, watched them writhe into glowing ash eager for the next consignment.

Istvan held his hands to the flames.

"I used to dream of being warm in Siberia," he said. "It was a lovely dream. This is a nightmare." He scowled as Hornsey went to the car for the last consignment.

"They promised me I would be rich," he said.

"They lied, for they were going to kill me, but they promised—and a Hungarian lives on promises. Now I have nothing."

"You're lying," said Craig. "You took some when I left you in the safe. I heard you."

"A trifle," said Istvan.

"You've still got your tools."

"How can I use them again? I stole a million. There are no more worlds for me to conquer.

Hornsey came back, and the last of the money soared up in golden heat.

"You'll drive me back to Tangier?" Hornsey asked.

"Of course," said Craig. "I'm very grateful to you." Istvan sniffed.

"That night—I should have killed Simmons," Hornsey said.

"He hadn't led you to this," said Craig, and pointed to the heap of glowing ash.

"No. You did that," said Hornsey.

"When I thought you were one of us? After he—" Hornsey nodded. "I had to do it, Craig. That money had to burn."

"That's why you phoned the bank? To make sure we were getting on with it?"

"That's why," Hornsey said. "You did my job for me. We've won, Craig." He paused. "I thought you'd have killed Simmons."

"I thought so too. But he had to live."

"And Brodski?"

"Boris killed him." He hesitated. "I could have liked Brodski."

His hand flashed to his chest, came out with the Smith and Wesson, spun it by the trigger guard, then replaced it under his coat in a blur of speed.

"Killing's all I know," he said. "It's time I learned something else."

They went back to the car, and Craig backed and turned away from a million pounds of ash.

Istvan said: "This Medani's father we visit. Will he have women with him?"

"I suppose so," said Craig. "Chaps like him used to have two or three hundred in the old days."

"Belly dancers?" asked Istvan.

"I dare say he could find you one. After all, he'll be grateful to you."

"I find such gratitude very consoling," Istvan said. "Only a woman can give me rest now."

Craig thought of Kamar.

"I don't think you'll find Berber women restful," he said. "But by God they make you feel like a man."

CHARTER BOOKS

Edgar Award Winner Donald E. Westlake
King of the Caper

WHO STOLE SASSI MANOON?   88592-6   **$1.95**
Poor Sassi's been kidnapped at the film festival — and it's the most fun she's had in years.

THE FUGITIVE PIGEON   25800-X   **$1.95**
Charlie Poole had it made — until his Uncle's mob associates decided Charlie was a stool pigeon. See Charlie fly!

GOD SAVE THE MARK   29515-0   **$1.95**
Fred Fitch has just inherited a fortune — and attracted the attention of every con man in the city.

THE SPY IN THE OINTMENT   77860-7   **$1.95**
A comedy spy novel that will have you on the edge of your seat — and rolling in the aisles!

KILLING TIME   44390-7   **$1.95**
A small New York town: corruption, investigators, and Tim Smith, private investigator.

The Mitch Tobin Mysteries
by Tucker Coe

THE WAX APPLE	87397-9	**$1.95**
A JADE IN ARIES	38075-1	**$1.95**
DON'T LIE TO ME	15835-8	**$1.95**

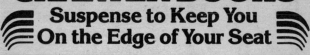

HEALTH AND BEAUTY—ADVICE FROM THE EXPERTS